Also by A M Gatw.

THE TEA ELF & OTHER STORIES

Thread

A M Gatward was born in Coventry and educated at Oxford and The University of Chicago. He is the author of *The Tea Elf & Other Stories*. He lives in Bristol.

For Lucinda

Adam G

Thread

A M GATWARD

JELLICLE

First published in Great Britain by Jellicle 2013

The right of A M Gatward to be identified as the Author of Work has been asserted by him in accordance with the Copyright, Designs, and Patents Act 1988.

This is a work of fiction. Names, characters, places, and incidents either are products of the author's imagination or are used fictitiously. Any resemblance to actual persons, living or dead, events, or locales is entirely coincidental.

Cover design by Teabag 2013

Set in Garamond
Printed in the United Kingdom by Lulu

First Printing: July 2013

ISBN 10 149054223X
ISBN 13 9781490542232

Jellicle Books

Bristol

To my family

Acknowledgements

I would like to thank the following comrades for their help, comments, and generosity: Kathleen McCully, David Svolba, Kate Gatward, Isabella Pereira, Karen Pagani, Barbara Rusbridge, Monica and Michael Gatward. Thanks also to all the unknown people lurking behind sockpuppets with whom I have bickered, bitched and learned from in forum wars over the years. We passed like ships in the night.

Endaf Kerfoot let me ring him up and rant down the phone, and gave me a place to stay in London; Tom Davies and Liza Whitney put me up in Oxford. Anna Strudwick and Keith Bailey read my manuscript, fed me, and went well beyond what could be reasonably asked of one's neighbours.

Most especially, I would like to thank Alan Wall for painstaking attention to detail, solidarity, and too much perspicuity and good advice than could possibly be fitted on one white page.

The final shape of this book owes something to all of these people – peace be upon them.

When all candles be out, all cats be grey.

JOHN HEYWOOD, *Proverbs* (1538)

Part One

Above The Line

Editor's Note

A newspaper article under the following title appeared in the review pages of *The Correspondent* earlier this year. It was also posted to their web pages on January 29th.

We are unable to print this content for reasons of copyright; we would have been even more unwilling to print it because it was quite boring.

The content can be gathered or surmised from the thread which followed the article online; and it is this thread, which is included here – *below the line.*

(spellings and other infelicities have been corrected)

Books and the Internets

The Correspondent, Friday January 29th 6.15pm

Peter Piper

Comments

BifidusRegularis

 31 2

January 29th 6.19pm

> **PeterPiper** says:
> We live in a time when the book itself is under threat, very possibly from the threat of piracy which proceeds from the digitisation of texts.

Then there are enhanced eBooks where you can get the sound of bullets, rain and thunderclaps as Philip Marlowe trudges his way down the mean streets. Information technology is changing the way we read as well as the way we think.

JesterJinglyJones

5 0

January 29th 6.23pm

laJester approves of this topic very much. The end of the book, if it is nigh, must be lamented. laJester has little time for many things outside of her act since the revolution waits for no-one. I will provide you with the time and location of my next act of terror aimed at the very heart of a corrupt and uncultured establishment. The event will be enough to sear her into your hearts and minds more than any love affair can do d:-o)

ThomPayne

 18   2

January 29th 6.25pm

@PeterPiper

The bejewelled narrative intricacies of Nabokov's Pale Fire, the wry sad voice of Saul Bellow's wonderful Moses Herzog, the extremes of a Houellebecq or the arch satire of Will Self's vividly imagined man-ape inversions, all point to a thing that is common to all serious writing.

There are two kinds of people in this world, my friend. Those who are interested in similarities and those who are not.

If I know you as I think I do, you are someone of the latter variety. Then there are people like me Peter, who are interested in both (alright there aren't strictly two kinds of people...I like to make up rules that don't apply to myself).

What it all points to with writing, I would say, is something like a process of distillation, or an ability to boil down and extract from an ungodly mixture the most valuable constituents, to provide a reader with nutritional value.

This thread is like a field strewn with plums and carrots.

@JesterJinglyJones

laJester has little time for many things outside of her act since the revolution waits for no-one

I have often wondered whether the word jester is gender specific. Are you not a jestress?

BlindBoyGrunt

 11   0

January 29th 7.05pm

@BifidusRegularis

Information technology is changing the way we read as well as the way we think.

Bif, who's to say whether it's good or bad; when you need some piece of information, you don't need to rely on your memory. You look it up on your phone. Maybe a big memory isn't big or clever – merely a redundancy of evolution. Being clever might be knowing how to use technology to generate results.

I have spoken.

Gaunt

 9   4

January 29th 7.25pm

> Further, in the language of Shakespeare and Milton, one that can so effortlessly conjure the human need to express things in terms of something different.

Effortless isn't the word I would use.

> The *sterile promontory* which signifies the loss of Hamlet's mirth, the hiss of the snake in the sibilant opening lines of *Paradise Lost.*

What's the reason for it all, officer.

ComradeJenny

 9   4

January 29th 7.28pm

ThomPayne, Jester is not a gender-specific word. A female jester would be called a jester rather than a jestress. In medieval days buffoonery was one of the few professions open to women.

Weathereye

 15   1

January 29th 8.04pm

> **BifidusRegularis** said:

Information technology is changing the way we read as well as the way we think.

Certainly. It's like this: when you watch a movie on digital as opposed to film. Digital gives me headaches, and it's to do with the medium. Watching film at 24 frames per second has an entirely different effect on alpha waves from watching digital. With books, it's probably just that. You relate differently to the page. Then again, when you move house, schlepping a shitload of hardbacks around in crates is a fucking pain in the ass, if I'm honest.

FarmersBreakfast

January 29th 8.29pm

couldn't help chuckling when my friend got her tablet thingummy wet and lost her entire book collection.

AMGatward

January 29th 8.32pm

This comment has been removed. Click here for FAQs regarding moderation

MopDog

14 1

January 29th 8.45pm

Stories emerge in the strangest places.

Where were her back-ups? Why couldn't she just download them all over again?

If your neighbours leave the bath running, it's a fuck sight harder to replace a shelf full of paperback.

PeterPiper says:
The trick of course is always with the voice, why and where it emerges.

Couldn't agree more.

Consider the characters we come to recognise, the spontaneous eruptions of counterpoint that emerge in the dark-web wreckage of our threads and bulletin-boards.

Easy, Augustine.

with their manic cast of maniacs and clowns, the self-made philosophers and savants who

Hang on, are you talking about us?

JesterJinglyJones

January 30th 3.01am

Hang on, are you talking about us?

Clown is a strange pejorative indeed. Clowns and jesters are not primarily there to be laughed at but to be feared and worshipped. To be a jester is to be frivolous only in the eyes of the frivolous and those men who scoff that laJester is for the babies. Those who throw around this pejorative willy-nilly, like that of Muppet and Fraggle perhaps, live in mortal fear of the potential within the clown for disruption and terror d:-O)

ThomPayne

January 30th 5.08am

Gaunt, possibly you have an offspring named Jonty…and who knows; maybe you are one of those people with a tick-like 'partner'… one of those club-footed earth mothers who haul the child around in a papoose-like sling. You're not seeing the bigger picture. The thing with books: we're looking at the destruction of a medium, and which can only lead to the mutilation of our minds. I can go to Bit Torrent and download 50,000 volumes if I want to, all the classics there are and I can put them onto a thumb drive and share them with my friends. Will I ever read them properly? What we may see happening within even a few years or less because of piracy is the same thing that happened with music, where you can only get a record out on a label if you're willing to pay money for the studio time. This is precisely why you only get trustafarians releasing albums any more, enough to make you wish that they'd slit their girlish wrists in real life. AM Radio – Anodyne Music. Atrocious Music. Audible Muck. Do you want to live in a world where a trip to the bookshop results in a horrifying confrontation with a table full of ghost-written celebrity bios or my God, the autobiography of a fictional talking meerkat? Plus books are sexy. Bring a girl home to a shelf full of literature versus telling her what you have on your Kindling…who could fail to spot the difference…who could fail to level up? I'm drinking at the moment and faintly addled, but there were times in my life when the only way I could afford to read was by sitting in book-shops until they dragged me outside. But Christ, a pile of good books is so……so……sexy ☺

I hate fucking films and books that revolve around the internet, they're always antiquated by the time they come out. Look at films like *Hackers* or *The Net* from the '90s. They're all but unwatchable now. Frozen in time.

@Peter Piper
As TS Eliot puts it:

The wounded surgeon plies the steel
that questions the distempered part.

Peter, I feel apocalyptic.

You omit a line from Eliot, further down the thread of the *East Coker* you quoted…the part about the curse.

The part where he says:

And that, to be restored… our sickness must grow worse.

.

THIS THREAD IS NOW CLOSED

1

THE DEWEY DECIMAL SYSTEM for books and publications is an attempt to organise all knowledge into ten main categories. These ten classes, it has been decided, comprise in the following order the fields of Computer Science, of Philosophy and Psychology, of Religion, of Social science, of Languages, of Science and Mathematics, of Technology, of Arts and recreation, of Literature and rhetoric. The tenth and final class is the one that includes History, Geography and Biography, which is to say that there is a certain sense, as there always is when we try to carve the world at the joints, that however useful this system may be in a practical sense, the divisions have nonetheless been arrived at somewhat arbitrarily. Each of these ten classes that we listed is further apportioned into ten divisions, and each division is subdivided into ten sections, thereby dividing all books and publications into ten main classes, 100 divisions and 1000 sections. For example: the class known as *Science* is divided into such sub-divisions as Astronomy, Animals, Plants and so on.

The division containing works on Animals, let us say, is then further cleaved into sections concerning Invertebrates, Mammals, Birds and so forth, all of which may then be subdivided into yet more precise taxonomic categories, presumably in whatever fashion or arrangement as experts in the fields of librarianship and zoology consider helpful. This system of divisions and sub-divisions, of which we have provided only a single example, is applied to all ten of the main classes of scholarship, with one or two exceptions, and we ought to pause and be grateful for the invention of a system which divides such diverse areas of human enquiry as causation, medicine and railroad transportation, or folklore, diplomacy, snakes and grammar, into discrete and accessible parcels, for the reason that without such a system, a thing like a library, not to mention the sum of all human knowledge and the learning process, might easily turn into the most chaotic and head-destroying jumble imaginable.

The principal advantage and innovation of this particular system of classifying books and knowledge, not the only one they have invented, lies in the use of decimals to demarcate all the categories, which is a feature that allows the system to be purely numerical. The system is obviously also infinitely hierarchical, thereby allowing for an infinite number of additional categories and sub-divisions to be added at such a time as is appropriate to the subject material, which – we might add – may also be as inevitable an outcome as can be imagined, given what we know about the pattern-seeking nature of human curiosity and the continual way in which information is expanded, refined and thus in need of more sophisticated methods of codification. Aside from fiction and so-called *generalities*, books and publications are classified principally by subject, with extensions for subject relationships, place, time or type of material, a system which produces classification numbers of at least three digits but otherwise of indeterminate length, with a decimal point before the fourth digit, where present. For example, 330 for economics + .9 for geographic treatment + .04 for Europe generates the number 330.94, thereby yielding according to the rules we are describing the fascinating and mysterious discipline of *European Economy*. To take another example, all of this can be proved to be true by consulting *Wikipedia*, 973 for United States + .05 forms a division for periodicals, so 973.05 yields the equally fascinating subject area of *periodicals concerning the United States, generally*. Books are replaced on the shelf in increasing numerical order, left to right, for example 060, 285, 301.75, 330.93, 331 and so forth. The attentive reader may have already thought of an additional complication faced by the bookworm and by designers of library coding systems, which reveals itself when we realise that more than one book may share the same number. After all, if there were only one book on the biology of fishes or on Enlightenment epistemology or the history of Slavic languages or any other line of enquiry, we would surely be constraining ourselves unacceptably by presuming that one volume would be sufficient to contain all the different arguments, or diagrams, or facts, or interpretations of texts that are pertinent to those noble and sapiential disciplines. A solution to this new conundrum lies in the use of a cutter number, which is added to the Dewey place-holder, and which consists usually of the first letter of the author's name followed by a series of yet more numbers. And given the additional truth that some authors are more prolific than others, which is to say that some authors write more than one book, a *work mark* or work letter can also be used to distinguish the various creations of a single person.

Another interesting thing to point out is that in the case of some authors, they are considered so important that they have other writing by yet more authors devoted entirely to them, and so it has been proposed that in order to keep books of criticism or comment upon an author and his or her works shelved together, a capital Z is to be placed at the end of the first cutter line, to ensure that all criticisms and commentaries are shelved after the original author's work in such a way that it is clear which works of secondary literature are related. A second cutter line will then begin with the first letter of the name of the person who has authored the criticism, and so on. This system too is infinitely hierarchical, and could accommodate an infinite number of critiques of critiques – an absurd and nightmarish eventuality to be sure, but nevertheless a state of affairs that could yet one day quite easily come to pass, if it hasn't happened already.

*

The National Library of Books and Publications stands in the centre of our city, and is merely one of the hundreds upon thousands of libraries worldwide that utilise the system we have been sketching, for the categorisation of books and their content. The striking thing about the library in which our narrative unfolds is the fact that along with the Bodleian Library in England and the Library of Congress in the United States, it is a library that catalogues and holds a copy of every single book yet published; moreover in the case of the National Library in our city, it has done so ever since records began. This is to say, although it by no means follows as a matter of logic, that the National Library of Books and Publications has itself existed since records began, and that it was dreamed up at precisely the point that someone first had the idea of the need to retain records of all writing in a central location and thereby keep a record of all mankind's attempts to explain its sorry predicament by the express and admirable medium of the written word. As a consequence of this, as a consequence of the voluminous world of literature and the vast quantities of writing that we have generated for ourselves, the National Library of Books and Publications is extremely large, its vastness and cavernous interiors dwarfing even the very largest of all other libraries. It is therefore to be expected that such an institution is even more reliant perhaps than usual on so fortunate and ingenious an invention as the Dewey Decimal System, to keep everything organised or at least in some semblance of working order.

Every day, more books and journals on a bewildering variety of subjects are delivered to the library's Post Room, books concerning themselves with electronic circuitry, fisheries policy, atomic science, ethnomusicology, animal husbandry, the weather, weaving techniques, the lives of saints, the structure of plastics, depression. The Post Room sits adjacent to the main library and is connected by a short corridor to the Classification Room, where workers pick up each new volume that has been sent from the Post Room and inspect it for signs of the content and subject matter; once they have decided upon this between themselves, because sometimes and as everyone knows, it is not always clear in this life of ours what is what, these workers then proceed to generate for each book a catalogue number, according to the precise logic we described, the system of which is methodically collated in a series of old-fashioned ring-binders which are kept on a table in the central aisle. These ring-binders, which happen to be the kind with three rings, understandably see a lot of use and it was found a long time ago that some of these pages had become torn or weakened at one or other of the left-hand holes, as is continually the case with pieces of paper stored in three-ring-binders in offices or homes the entire world over.

As a consequence, it used to be common in this curious place of work for the pages in the ring-binders to become detached and continually fall to the floor, so in order to prevent the horrifying possibility of this bible of our library's cataloguing system becoming jumbled and thereby useless in the classification process for which it was invented, it was decided that all the pages should be laminated in plastic, or placed in transparent document wallets with a view to preventing their further deterioration, and that meanwhile a team should be employed on the laborious task of transferring the contents of these files onto a computer system for faster and more durable ease of use.

To return to the daily activities of the Classification Room which we were describing before pausing to observe the inevitable and disheartening nature of ring-binders, once a decision has been reached as to the proper part of the library that the book should be sent, a record of the book is inscribed by hand in brown ink onto an index card and entered at the same time via a terminal, into the library's computerised database. This electronic system, which all staff members must master, enables one at the touch of a button to activate a machine, which generates a barcode and a small violet sticker; upon the violet sticker is printed the book's new and priceless identification number, and one or other of the librarians will then lovingly place it onto the spine of each new volume. Quite naturally the Post Room, and by extension the Classification Room, is always amongst the busiest of the many busy rooms in the library, thanks to the sheer number of new folios and monographs, tomes and treatises which are sent to the library each day, from publishers, from vanity authors, from the warehouses of massive media corporations, and quite often from all kinds of similar and dissimilar places abroad.

Each morning there is a fresh delivery, and the Post Room workers must rip open hundreds of packages and envelopes and make pile after pile of books and journals concerning all the conceivable subjects that exist, not to mention newspapers, compendiums and almanacs. These piles are then carried to the Classification Room, which is connected by yet more corridors both to the vermicular book stacks that run for miles in gloomy, crepuscular tunnels beneath our city, and also to the upper level reading rooms of the Main Library itself. Once the violet sticker has been placed on the book's spine and the appropriate records of its arrival and category made, the books are placed onto metal trolleys, which are marked according to whichever region of the library those books belong. Throughout the rest of the working day, workers will merrily wheel these trolleys along the long corridors of the stacks, or along the balconies of the reading rooms or along the levels of the central rotunda; and in an orderly fashion, they will place the books into whichever space on the shelves the classification system insists they belong. There the books and manuscripts will sit with their colleagues and bedfellows until such times as it becomes necessary for the book to be retrieved, either by a patron if the book is in one of the reading rooms, or by a stacker if it lives in the stacks, where it may be taken to a table to be opened and read, the purpose after all for which books are designed, and the only process we know of by which a book might reveal its secrets or its knowledge or its lies and falsehoods, to the mind and brain of a beholder.

The index cards inscribed in the Classification Room, which bear the handwritten names of authors, the title of the book and its number, are collected at the end of each day and taken to the central rotunda of the library, which also serves as one of the library's main reading rooms, and through which members of the public may enter via the ancient and beautiful Gothic entrance. Facing the entrance are electronic barriers, and a reception desk which serves as a point of enquiry or reference where one may speak to a member of staff, or if one so chooses, ask for directions to a garage or return a book or request a volume to be retrieved from somewhere down in the labyrinth. At the back of this giant rotunda, facing the entrance, there is a flat wall against which are stacked identical units of wooden drawers reaching almost up to the first level gallery, and it is the front of these little drawers, with their tarnished brass handles, in which are slotted cards with faded letters on them, A, De, Mc, Sa etc., to indicate which books are by whom, and their whereabouts. These units are arranged around a door that leads to other collections and reading rooms, the drawers are organised alphabetically, and as one might expect, the cards within them are alphabetised according to the surname of the author, and then subdivided in ascending numerical order. At the end of each day, one or other of the librarians will file the new index cards away in the appropriate drawer, ascending an old wooden ladder if necessary to reach the top units which are some nine feet or so from the ground. Not all of the drawers are filled for the reason that, every so often, and in order to preserve the high level of precision which must be maintained in such a system of record keeping, the index cards must be re-organised and new drawers inserted here or there into the units, or shifted around, and if things get extremely confusing, the Chief Librarian may instruct one or other of his underlings that a section here or a section there has to be completely consolidated, according to the logic of our alphabet and the system we have been describing. This time-consuming task, strictly speaking, is an unnecessary one these days, given the more recent introduction of computerised record systems, but it is a task which is nevertheless carried out lovingly by the librarians; after all it doesn't take that long. Under the influence of the Chief Librarian's fondly remembered predecessor, the library employees still regard this manual system of brown ink, wooden drawers, index cards as more or less symbolising the finest traditions of the institution in which they are privileged to find themselves working.

To request a book from the National Library, one must either take note of the number given on its index card or, if one is so inclined, attempt to look up the item on one of the computer terminals installed at various points in the reading rooms, and then one must consult a map of the library to see where that book is located. If this fails, given the difficulties of trying to find a particular book by good fortune or happenstance in such an enormous place, one may also ask a librarian, for example Bartleby Flynn, who will of course desist from whatever it is they are doing, and then attempt to discover the location of the anticipated volume by one or other of the methods described. Of course not everybody necessarily visits a library with a specific book in mind, or with the decision already made as to which one they will pull from the shelves, run their hands over and choose to borrow or read. We do not always choose the books and texts that end up haunting us and illuminating our world, any more than we choose the voices or the other people who haunt us or who make life bearable or unbearable as the case may be, the evidence for which lies in the observation that sometimes we may make a new and wondrous acquaintance quite by chance in a doorway, or a book may fall mysteriously from a high shelf and open itself or display its cover in precisely a way that makes it seem suddenly that the book itself has made the decision for us, so to speak, that it must have chosen us to receive whatever treasures or secrets are buried within it, just as others choose whether or not to reveal themselves, or keep their true faces hidden.

2

I T IS WITH THIS SETTING and these abstruse musings in mind that we introduce the solitary person of Bartleby Flynn, a lower-level librarian employed by the National Library to do such things as stacking books, retrieving books, placing them back on the shelves later, organising the index cards; he is also someone who makes himself useful in a variety of back office duties that include cataloguing, processing invoices, ordering the newest publications and renewing the library's annual subscriptions to the journals, newspapers, almanacs and magazines that it houses within its walls. Flynn, as we shall call him, has worked in the library for twenty-three years, and began his career in the Post Room at the age of seventeen, opening, packaging and placing books on the trolley bound for the Classification Room and sorting the invoices, the delivery schedules, the bills of lading and all the other categories of post there are into appropriate piles, ready for distribution to the offices or desks of the people who deal with them.

At a certain point, it was decided that his understanding of the inner workings of the library had become sufficient for him to be promoted to the Classification Room, where he spent several years categorising and sorting the new arrivals sent from the Post Room, and so undertaking the more complicated process of cataloguing them in preparation for despatch into the vast ocean of texts in the open library. Although he does not have any higher academic qualifications, having started work at the library immediately after leaving school, he began during this period to attend night classes at the University, taking vocational courses in such things as Library and Information Management, Word Processing, and Basic Book-keeping, thereby attaining the various certifications necessary for the advance of his career, and which he had assumed, in turn, would improve his chances in the sphere of social relations. This strategy has worked well for Flynn, because soon enough he found himself promoted yet again to became one of the clerks entrusted with the responsibility of placing the books in their correct location on the shelves; soon after he was elevated to the position of Chief Clerk, a supervisory role which required not just an advanced knowledge of all the fields of enquiry, but also a sense of the physical location of the relevant sections in the building. Most recently, Flynn has been promoted to a Full Librarian, albeit of the lower level, and he has been enjoying the modest increase in salary which comes with this attainment, hopeful that if he keeps up his hard work and loyalty to the place in which he is employed, there ought to be no reason on earth why this upward trajectory should end at his current level within the hierarchy.

Flynn lives alone in a modest flat at the top of one of the terraces in the square opposite the library, thereby directly overlooking the wide flight of steps which leads up to the main entrance, and he can see the massive stone colonnades which divide a hexastyle portico from the walkway and atrium that run before the main door, and where in summer there is a coffee stand. From his window, on the days he does not work and if he is so inclined, he can watch the people who come and go from the library, the patrons, the other librarians, the delivery men, the panhandlers, the tourists, and if he arises early for some reason, perhaps because of a bad dream or even if he has something planned for his day off which requires an early start, he is able to see the Chief Librarian who arrives early each day in his enormous black car and who unlocks the wooden doors of the main entrance, switches off the alarm and puts on the lights in readiness for the first of the staff. Flynn, owing to the longevity of his service, has for a long time been one of four secondary keyholders and if for some reason the Chief Librarian is late, or ill, or on holiday, or in some other way prevented from opening the door himself, or if the Deputy Chief Librarian is otherwise occupied in a similar fashion, Flynn may be called upon to carry out this little ceremony himself. Given the proximity of Flynn's home to the library, he is generally the first person called upon to perform this task when the Chief or

Deputy Chief Librarians are otherwise occupied, because he can simply nip down, in his slippers or with his clothes pulled over his pyjamas if necessary, to unlock everything and deactivate the alarm system, so that the library can open on time, just as it has done every working day for as long as anybody can remember.

Bartleby Flynn is an unassuming and quiet man, not much prone to socialising or any form of excitement and impulsive behaviour. He has never married, and since leaving home at eighteen, has always lived modestly by himself and surrounded by the things that he loves, things such as books, the music of Schumann, strange wooden *objets d'art*, Pre-Raphaelite paintings. His world, as may be gathered from the yarn we have started spinning, is precisely ordered, and his life consists of strict routines, all based around his work at the library and his personal interests, and to which we must shortly turn. We do not know for sure if a woman or a girl has ever intruded into this solicitously arranged universe, for he has never as far as we know spoken of anybody who has, so to speak, set his socks on fire or otherwise made him sweat, and the private conclusion of his workmates and friends is quite possibly that he is a very shy man, a man of possibly private phobias or neuroses, very likely a little repressed in the sexual arena, a conclusion we might also reach for ourselves since it so happens we are taken with observing him. Flynn's gentle disposition is such however that nobody would dream of ever mentioning to him that he might think of finding for himself a life companion or maybe a mistress, or that he should even perhaps take a casual tumble in the hay for the sake of some warmth on a cold night and to come into more intimate contact with another human soul and body, for the reason that it is immediately patent to anybody in whom this idea takes flight, that Flynn would almost certainly be embarrassed and possibly mortified at the suggestion, and would feel compelled to hide his face for some time in a form of shame he would only partly know how to articulate. Flynn does not know, and we do not know either, whether he once unwittingly caught the eye of some flower girl, or one of the elderly cleaners, or a classmate, or a neighbour, or a complete stranger, or the girl with the big eyes who works in the café where he has recently been going out of his way to buy his coffee each morning. He does not know this because, wherever he goes, Bartleby Flynn looks straight ahead or at the ground, he moves through the threads of people he encounters, through the people whose voices make up the subjects and countersubjects in the fugue of this world, with an air of introversion and obliviousness, a sort of indifference which is possibly a little cultivated, but one nonetheless which may indeed have been cultivated, if that is the right word, because deep down he is afraid and possibly terrified of what things he may find. And who knows, whether after a day in the library, on a particularly bleak winter night, shall we say, maybe it is the case that he arrives home wearily to his rooms, takes off his winter coat and hangs it neatly on the peg, puts on the little lamp and draws his curtains, before standing forlorn and solemnly for a moment in front of his bed, deep in contemplation over some long-lost connection or the name of a new and untouchable secret hope, perhaps muttering inaudible words and putting his hand to his brow in a gesture of operatic extravagance that he would never make in anybody else's company, more or less flinging himself forward onto the soft bedding in the most melodramatic way imaginable, pulling the covers towards his face and then weeping into them bitterly.

If Flynn suffers in this way he does not show it openly or speak of it to anybody he knows, although to the trained eye of a fellow sufferer, or even simply a keen observer of this circus of human relations, the deep-seated distresses and turmoils of which we speak are sometimes, and maybe all too often, written like words all over the white countenances and comportments, and embedded or wired like electrical circuitry into the nervous systems and behaviours and decisions of their bearers. And sometimes, as it is written, our choices and actions are, so to speak, circumscribed by such neural circuitry, just as they are circumscribed by the geometries and curfews, the bric-à-bracs and furnishings of the bone structure which surrounds our brains, and as a logical consequence of this suggestion, our choices are sometimes made for us, either by luck or by some combination of experience, and whatever nature we happen to find ourselves stuck with. This observation, which perhaps sounds slightly trite a thing to be harping on about with such prolixity, is worth making nevertheless, not just because it is true for a great many, but also because it describes precisely the combination of circumstance and nature which is tangled in the thread of the narrative that we seem, in our capacity as guide, to be writing down.

*

To return once more to the subject of Bartleby Flynn, to attempt to give as rounded an account as we can of his days and ways, we should note that he is one of those people for whom newspapers function almost as a form of sustenance or nutrition. He scours the pages of his preferred national newspaper *The Correspondent* each day, a newspaper whose political affiliations are pinned roughly in the middle as opposed to the party of the left, although, as Flynn knows, such a spectrum as the political one is not so easily indicated by a compass or on the Cartesian framework of an x-y axis as perhaps some politicians and theoreticians would have you believe. Flynn has for many years quite privately thought of *The Correspondent*, which is published right here in our city, as *his* newspaper, and he is intimately familiar with the copperplate of the paper's title banner and with the correspondents themselves, not to mention the names of the green-ink brigade who inhabit the letter pages, or the crossword devisers, the bridge and poker column writers – who on earth can understand the language in those? – (players of bridge and poker and other bridge and poker columnists, quite naturally), or the obituary writers, or the writing styles of the famous op-ed journalists and their miserable ghost-writers, just as he is familiar with the index cards and the shelves and subject categorisations and the rules he follows during his work at the library. He thinks of his newspaper as fair-minded, unlike say *The Reporter* which affiliates itself far more closely with the party of the right and which therefore contains all kinds of insane and bigoted ideas about religion, or sexuality, or harrowing types of punishment, or indeed any number of the smaller papers and tabloids that are tossed from the backs of the newspaper vans in bundles, come rain and shine, at the news-stands and corner shops at the dusky hours of the day.

Each day before work, he stops at the shop on the square, and he hears the little truckle of the metal bell which sounds so much to him like the sound of a mountain stream moving over pebbles, and he picks up his daily newspaper after the briefest of pleasantries, or expression of familiarity with the obsessive-compulsive proprietor, who each day arranges the chocolate bars, fruit, canned goods, animal food, sandwiches, beverage containers, biscuits and so on in the most precise and ordered way imaginable. How beautiful and fresh and pristine the newspaper looks in the morning before the ink has hardly had time to dry, Flynn thinks, how creamily smooth to the touch, how essentially wet, and the prospect of reading and informing himself of the latest updates to the parlous economic situation, or the foreign wars, or the social divisions, or the violence, or the newest films, or the egregious levels of corruption which exist and have always existed at almost every level of society and so-called government, is a genuinely exciting one to him and he inhales these new developments and perhaps some of the ideas and stories depicted by the columnists he enjoys as though his very breathing depends on it. Flynn's colleagues, some of whom are of a more conservative political persuasion, and why shouldn't they be, after all that's democracy, regard Flynn as something of a bleeding-heart, a pinko, a liberal; but it is widely acknowledged in the circles within which Flynn occasionally floats that he is very well-informed about all manner of current affairs and events, very much on top of his brief, not only with the details and names of the protagonists of these dramas, but also the background and the ideological and economic foundations which gloss why certain events come to pass. Flynn is not by nature argumentative or contrarian, and he regards, as we do, the co-existence of multiple viewpoints and voices as more or less essential for the healthy functioning of a human society or organism, and he therefore tolerates with equanimity and a sense of irony the more strident views he sometimes has occasion to encounter.

It should be apparent by now that although there may be some enigmatic features to this man Flynn about whom we have been speaking, and although he is not in any sense an educated man by the standards and preconceptions of the professors and the university graduates whom he sometimes serves, he is a person nevertheless who in-ternalises what he encounters and polishes it to a gleam, so to speak, a man who is capable of speaking honestly and maybe even eloquently about the few corners of the world with which he happens to have become acquainted and who in his work at the library actively seeks new corners of human endeavour with which to apprise himself of novel developments. This observation applies also to the manner in which he carries out his work, for as one might expect of someone who has laboured in the same place for so very long a time, he knows his job inside out and the other way around. He knows where each section of the library is, and how it is sub-divided by the methods we tried to outline earlier. On reflection, Chapter One was a very poor way to begin a novel, anyway, it goes without saying that Flynn has developed a working proficiency in many of these systems and fields of enquiry simply by being exposed to them, in the sense that he can remember and reel off long lists of authors and books, including obscure ones, that relate to some field or object of study. For this reason, he has always been considered by the Chief Librarian, who knows so much more than we do, more or less a prize asset to the healthy functioning of the institution, and we have lost count of the times that the people who work at reception have referred hesitant patrons or visiting scholars to Flynn for a quick answer about where some book or other may be hiding, or why a book is not where it is supposed to be, and he is only too happy to point them in the right direction and even, upon occasion, with a quiet recommendation as to which other books they may care to dip into while they are at it, books that may prove to be relevant to the course of their investigations.

The National Library in its entirety is now far larger than had originally been imagined in the initial conception, and as a consequence has been continually extended over the centuries in every direction, in order to house the ever-increasing aggregate of books that it acquires each day and which it is expected, in a moral sense, to house and preserve for posterity. The subterranean levels of book-stacks which can be moved left or right by levers and wheels along a pulley system, likewise, are stretched in all directions of the compass from the nerve-centre of the rotunda and its adjacent wings of reading rooms and offices. We noted earlier in our digression about the ring-binders that the library has attempted to keep pace with this technocratic age by installing a computer system to house an electronic catalogue or database of the collections the library owns. This process of cataloguing, which is not much more than two-thirds complete even today, is a laborious one, and involves one or other of the workers taking a drawer-full of the index cards we described, and carrying it gingerly to a computer terminal before entering the information through the self-same interface that is used to document the new arrivals. Likewise, the records of the existing library members have been computerised and the old hand-written system used to document withdrawals and returns entirely abolished in favour of the more convenient, not to say accurate, system afforded by electronic machines.

Each week, the computer system produces a list of those members who have failed to return their books on time, it generates reminder letters which are printed automatically and sent out in admonishment, to remind these lackadaisical characters of their obligations to the strict rules of the noble institution to which they subscribe. This is not the only part of the daily operation of the library which has been entrusted to mechanisation. Likewise, the purchase ledger which used to be amended by hand and with red ink in a large leather book, has itself been replaced with advanced accountancy software which automatically calculates the various dates by which accounts and debts need to be settled, an electronic system which is maintained by an apocalyptically inclined computer technician known as The Socialist, a system upon which is input the vendor's name, the invoice number, bank account details, cost centre and ledger codes and so forth, each and every time the library is sent a fresh invoice or statement. Likewise, hardware has been installed which is capable of interpreting the digital information that is stored in barcodes, which are nowadays placed as a matter of course on the inside front of any new arrival, and which are also added to any older books that do not already have such a sign, by the people who work at the front desk, whenever they come into contact with such an item that happens to be borrowed. A method such as this is rather hit and miss in the grander scheme of things, for the simple reason that some books are far more popular than others, but over the two decades or so that such technology has been in use at the National Library, it has been estimated by the ventripotent Chief Librarian, who is so extremely clever, that roughly half of the books have been tagged in such a fashion, to the extent that the mammoth task confronting those who originally thought to implement the system now seems a great deal more manageable and achievable than it did at the outset, and all this despite the fact that the library's collections are considerably larger than they were and that they get bigger and bigger by the day.

Likewise, in the case of a book which cannot be found in the electronic catalogue, and which must therefore be requested through an index card, there exists a system of pneumatic tubes into which a cylindrical container is placed and which mechanically relays handwritten requests to the stackers who work in the labyrinth of rooms below, rooms to which the public has always, and for reasons of health and safety, been denied personal access. Upon receipt of a request from the bright world above, these stackers then retrieve the relevant item and send it up to the surface in a central elevator, with a note that duly mentions the request number and the name of the person for whom it is intended, and (for some strange reason) the time. Likewise, at a trade show, the Chief Librarian reported back to the staff his impression of the prototype of a robotic system he had been shown, which with the aid of a digital camera and electronic scanning intelligence was capable of moving up and down the relevant corridor of shelving and automatically recognising the catalogue numbers which are placed on the spine of every book, and thereby retrieving them by means of a delicately designed artificial arm, with sensors that speak to the book, as it were, through a specially invented shelf.

The consequence of this, which is the matter to which we shall next be turning, is that for quite some time now Bartleby Flynn and his colleagues have been aware of a variety of ways in which their own jobs at the National Library might conceivably be replaced by a more efficient and cost-effective system than the time-worn and overburdened one of the human mind, and although the Chief Librarian has given repeated assurances until now that there is no way that a library of this scale and importance could ever be genuinely automated, it has not escaped anybody's attention, least of all that of Flynn himself, that staff who leave the place through such forms of natural attrition as retirement, finding a job somewhere else, long-term illness, death, are not for the moment being replaced by any freshly scrubbed and eager new faces. It was with this in mind, furthermore, that Bartleby Flynn decided to take an urgent interest in the possibilities of computers and information technology, no doubt in the belief that if he could learn how such new systems work, and display a willingness to adapt to such new working methods and equipment as might one day be demanded by his industry, this would undoubtedly curry some favour with his superiors, not least the Chief and Deputy Chief Librarians, further, it might even render him all the more irreplaceable if he became proficient in them, in the dreadful eventuality that the excellent managers of this Library should look at a list of figures one day, and suddenly decide that a cull of the human staff might just prove economical.

3

I**N THE LIFELONG ABSENCE** of a lover or close companion upon whom to direct his attention, and from whom he might in return expect to receive some degree of human intimacy and affection, in the absence of siblings or other close family relationships, in the absence of a well-defined and immediately available network of social contacts or comrades or beer-buddies, Bartleby Flynn often works late into the night at the National Library, long after the rest of the staff have left and long after the doors have been closed to the egregious public. It could be pointed out that this life choice of his, if he cared to reflect upon the matter, constitutes a final cause for his lack of success in those other areas as well as being an effect of them, or if failure is the wrong twist, it explains in both directions why he has never established the typical kind of personal relationships which for most people assuage anxiety, and which provide entirely welcome and natural consolation, succour even, to their existences.

Since this extra time in the library is freely given and in no way demanded, what Bartleby Flynn does in there during those hours is largely up to him, unless there is some pressing matter which needs attending to before the next morning, some bibliographic crisis in need of an expert trouble-shooter to rectify, someone with his knowledge and experience perhaps; or unless there is some need to transfer the contents of a book via electronic scanning to the ever-increasing digital archives of published material available to the general enquirer. Sometimes during these extended shifts, he goes to the Classification Room and wheels any new books that have not yet been housed along to their correct places, sometimes he sits in the Accounting Office and creates purchase orders for new publications and puts the order slips in envelopes ready for postage, or he works his way through logging and processing piles of outstanding invoices to prepare them for payment; sometimes he works at consolidating the wooden drawers in which the index cards are kept, sometimes he picks up an armful of books which have been newly returned, and he takes them to whichever obscure part of the library the cataloguing system demands they be returned.

Sometimes he finds a desk in one of those places, and he switches on a reading lamp by its tiny brass thread, and beneath its shade of forest green, he will sit reading his beloved *Correspondent* illuminated by nothing but a yellowy-green puddle of light while the chestnut trees rustle darkly outside, reading about the previous day's news events, the murders, the scandals, the political commentary, the miraculous escapes, the matters of policy, the diplomatic questions, the obituaries, the literary reviews, the inevitable; and sometimes he takes down a precious volume from a shelf about whatever subject it is he happens to be currently interested in; and he will idly thumb through it, allowing it to release its distinctive and fusty odour, damp patchouli or sandalwood perhaps, absorbing anything in the pages that his gaze alights upon, or which he happens to find interesting. At times, such forays into the books result in some new inkling or other crepitating through his head, and this then sets off an additional chain-reaction of ideas, which sometimes reach a critical mass of thoughts inside his skull. This in turn will cause wholly fresh – and unheard of – lines of enquiry to bloom like roses or kaleidoscopic patterns – which in all their shifting shapes and tessellations then spark his interest yet further. Essentially, we hope you find, this is more or less how curiosity, at least of the human kind, seems to work – at least for some of the time and when at its most beautifully free and desultory. Sometimes, he spontaneously tears off his clothes somewhere deep in the underground corridors of the old library, and leaps wildly or runs up and down the aisles like a madman, running his finger-tips along the spines of the books, or through the dust that gathers on the metal shelving of the stacks; now this is a piece of inexplicable behaviour which would be considered quite possibly a sign of lunacy or derangement should any of his colleagues happen to discover him locked into this very private act at such an awkward moment, or get to know of it through a private email, or whispered rumour, or security camera footage, or if indeed the books themselves were to conspire with each other and somehow put it in writing. Sometimes he will walk to the empty kitchen of the cafeteria and inspect the sparkling steel surfaces, the heavy pots and pans that hang neatly over the ovens, or he will lift the handle of the industrial-dimensioned dishwasher in order to sniff the miasma of citrus hygiene, or simply to see what is inside. Sometimes he will go to the Function Room, which can be booked for a fee during the day and in which there is a grand piano that is often used for chamber concerts and musical examinations; sometimes he will sit at the piano, an old Hamburg Steinway with ivory keys. He lifts the lid and softly plays a note or a bar or two, and then listens to how the sound of the instrument hangs and reverberates in the stillness, vibrations moving across the soundboard until they collide with the maple rim, before travelling back again to produce that light and resonant sound for which German pianos are so justly revered. Sometimes he will lift the lid of the instrument, lean his head right over the soundboard to smell the sweet and heavy dampness which emanates from the felts and hammers of all older pianos, and which seems to him so perfectly in harmony with the smells of paper and leather and the controlled humidity which characterise his olfactory comprehension of the library.

It should at this point be emphasised that these habits of Bartleby Flynn, although perhaps eccentric, in no way mark him out as a particularly lazy sort of man, whack job or basket case. Indeed, for the most part, these extra hours he spends in the library at night are generally put to productive use, and are entirely consistent with a strong work ethic, otherwise we could be sure that the Chief Librarian, in his wisdom, would almost certainly withdraw the keyholder privilege. Following his most recent weekly class at night-school, a school which is affiliated with the University and which itself has a history that is intimately tangled with that of the library, Flynn has of late taken something of a new interest in computer technology; in particular he has become more acutely aware of the world-wide-web itself, an invention which, strange as it may seem, had for many years rather passed him by. Aside from the electronic mail which he sends and receives, messages that surround work-related questions, for example the status of an order or confirmation of the receipt of a package or invoice, the world-wide-web never struck him as especially useful, given the way he has lived his life up until the point that we are blushingly, sluggishly moving towards. After all, what use does a lower-level librarian have for the internet to look for books and information, when all the knowledge and tidings he could possibly hope for are housed in the volumes and catalogues of the place where he works, as they should be, and not four hundred feet from where he sleeps? This is all the more striking of course, given that he has been granted access to the whole demesne owing to his status as a keyholder, and potentially at least, at any time of the day or night. Why sit peering into the internet for hours, when one could just as easily be rummaging in the book stacks and catalogues to look for things, with the attendant unexpected delights that follow; and what use does he have for social networks or chat forums when nobody pays him the slightest attention, or has ever displayed much interest in what he has to say? Why, furthermore, should it occur to him to pay a bill, or book a holiday, or order some music, or do anything of that sort via the internet, when people have always managed to do those things until recently *without* such a system? With the completion of his computer course however, for which he was awarded a shiny certificate, and bearing in mind his concerns about the inevitable impacts that such technology may have on his future prospects as a curator of knowledge, he has of late begun to take a much greater interest in the powers of the internet than he ever had before. For this reason, he has latterly acquired the habit of using the library systems to access the web from time to time, to read the articles or to follow the comments and interactions of the unknown people who stalk the comment threads of forums and message boards, behind the disguises of their hysterical invented personae. And of course, it has already occurred to him that what he has discovered here are vast archives of writing of all varieties, and which have never been classified or properly codified, or subjected to very much in the way of indexing or verification. He has never been tempted nor is he ready to begin writing anything himself, nor has he ever attempted to strike up temporary allegiances or start flame-wars or feuds with strangers; there is no reason in particular why a humble librarian would think he had anything constructive or witty to add to a thread he is reading if he has never before been bitten by the bug which compels people to do so. Furthermore, he only tends to be able to do his browsing at one of the public access terminals which are available during working hours; and he is careful to ensure that he only does this in his spare time, in order that he not be seen to be abusing the internet freedoms which his status as a librarian confers upon him. What has been striking him with increasingly poignant resonance however, the more time he spends hearing the voices of these unknown characters, is the sense he also has when observing the people who file in and out of the library each day; what he is left with is the sense of a dreadful cacophony, of random collisions, which at the same time, and at the most unexpected moments possible, conspire to harmonise suddenly with one another, to establish dialectics with themselves, producing in the most peculiar contexts supposable something that suddenly and inexorably strikes him as music.

*

It is on just one of these evenings then, that we pick up the thread once again, and find Flynn alone in the library, or alone apart from the sound of a distant hum from the machine operated by a cleaner who as we speak is stoically and miserably pushing it up and down one of the corridors in order to polish its wooden floor, or alone apart from the vermin which scurry about in the nooks, crannies and crevices of the old building, or alone apart from the deafening silence of the hundreds upon thousands of books and millions upon billions of words which comprise them, as they sit in solemn judgment over anybody who passes through these hallowed aisles, these sacred chambers; and here he is wheeling a trolley of books, both old and new, towards the section of the library that holds the old maps, one of the library's most valuable collections, so valuable in fact that the ancient volumes have been chained to the wall with enormous padlocks to prevent their removal or theft. It is not a part of the library that Flynn frequents terribly often, partly because it is rather remote, and partly because he does not have a great deal of interest in the books and manuscripts which are stored there. As he walks along quietly, the regular squeals of the wheels of his trolley are the only sounds he can hear, and at this moment he is thinking of little more than the task he has set himself, along with the matter of what he might choose to prepare for his supper, perhaps a tin of beans and some boiled potatoes, he thinks, or something indistinguishable out of a frozen packet. The wooden roof of this reading room is extremely high and particularly grand, because it was long ago built as a chapel, and when it was eventually and inevitably absorbed by the Library next door to it, they saw fit to keep the large stained-glass windows on the North and West walls instead of bricking them up or covering them with dry-wall or building balconies lined with shelves that would occlude the images. The windows, depicting the usual baffling biblical scenes and illegible writing, nonetheless let in the most wondrous kind of light, photons, quanta of visible radiation which glance through the little individually coloured segments and point in myriad directions and angles, and which at the right moment can make the wooden tables of the reading area appear as if they were shimmering under rainbow-coloured water. The sepia light which fills the place in late afternoon, furthermore, makes it in our opinion one of the loveliest of any of the library's many reading rooms, a place where one can simply lose track of time at that particular hour of day and forget entirely why one had gone in.

There is a balcony along the east wall which used to be an organ loft, and which is accessible by a spiral metal staircase that has been fixed with bolts directly under the balcony floor, a declivitous and cochlear coil between the cantilevers which emerges through a trap-door into a small divinity library; and it is for this reason that this gilded helix is sometimes referred to ironically between library staff as the stairway to heaven, such is the difficulty of ascending it with your hands full. Flynn climbs the steps carefully, a pile of books precariously balanced between his hands and chin, and he wearily puts them down atop the little reading desk which is up there. His attention is caught momentarily by a book which has been left in the middle of the old wooden table, and he picks the volume up and looks at it, in order to ascertain whether it belongs up here on the divinity balcony where we are currently floating, or whether it belongs elsewhere and has been left there carelessly and inconsiderately, during the day. Upon examining the book, he is surprised to note that it has no barcode, nor any identifying mark whatsoever on its spine, and so he quite naturally assumes that it is a book which does not belong to the library, and which somebody has left there quite fortuitously, by mistake. There is no name written on the inside cover, no sticker bearing the words *ex libris* Jane Doe or Sam Smith, which might signify whose personal collection the book might have come from; and Flynn is then struck by the absence of any lettering on the front cover at all. He puts the book back on the desk, and turns back to the task in hand, methodically reinstating the other volumes he has carried up with him to their correct places on the shelves. He ascends a wooden ladder, to put back on the very topmost shelf an extraordinarily thick volume of intractable German Theology, a thicker and possibly even more intractable text than one might ever expect to encounter in such a collection if that is possible, anyway, he realises that it is getting late, probably time for him to close up the library and go home to make himself that meal, to drink a glass of Calvados perhaps or some coffee, to bunker down for the night and try to welcome the dreams which will come.

This reading room, he notices as he descends the ladder, has become rather plain now that the sun has fully set, altogether more sombre and tenebrous a place than earlier in the day, when the magical optical effects of the stained glass we previously mentioned prettify and bathe it in shades of apricot sunlight. He pauses at the top of the spiral staircase, and once again notices the unmarked book sitting on the table, a book which is not strictly unmarked since the cover displays an oil painting of a library, and which upon closer inspection also bears the letters 'N.O.' in a tiny serif typeface, near the bottom left of the cover. Flynn picks the book up, intending to put it at Reception, along with a note, in case the unknown owner should be murmuring at this very moment, perhaps to themselves, perhaps to a friend or lover:

Oh, I left my book at the library.

That's ironic.

It's always in the little things.

How right you are.

I often am.

You'll have to go back there tomorrow and get it though, won't you?

Flynn makes his way down from the balcony in the old chapel, along the corridors, back towards the break-room that stands just off the central rotunda, and where his coat and hat will be hanging. As he walks, he idly looks at the book again, curious as to who wrote it, wondering what it might be about. The book, he now realises, is really rather singular, in the sense that it does not bear the names of a publisher or an author either, nor does its cover display any of the blurb or sound-bites or artful photos we typically associate with the backs of books, and which are intended to make them more marketable and accessible to readers. It occurs to Flynn then that the absence of these identifying characteristics is of course the very thing that makes the book so readily and immediately distinctive, although he cannot for the life of him think how such a book should be categorised or how one might archive its existence in the catalogue. Since the book has no name, either on the cover or within its pages, since the letters 'N.O.' seem to form either an acronym of some kind, or perhaps the initials of the writer, he finds that he is feeling a little sorry for the volume, to have been created and brought into the world and not been designated by a sign or a soubriquet, he thinks, is surely an intolerable state of affairs, something that needs to be corrected or at the very least settled with some kind of answer; and as a consequence of this thought, for his own benefit as much as anything, he decides that he will simply have to name this book himself. This business of naming is no easy thing, despite its fundamental necessity in all sorts of ways, and it strikes Flynn that to call the book *'No'* would be the simplest option, 'No' in the sense of negation, refusal or denial, yet this seems to him rather too blunt and indecorous a title to choose. To be sure, there are the volumes of *Either/Or* by Kierkegaard, he thinks, the *Yes* of Thomas Bernhard, as well as the beloved film *If*, which proves that the deployment of the concepts used by logicians is not without precedent when it comes to giving things titles. Nevertheless, Flynn decides to pay no heed to the maxim that one should never judge a book by its cover in this instance, because it seems to him that the title *No* would be wholly at odds with the image on the front, depicting a library as it does; and he suddenly remembers the words of one of his teachers, *always reduce a problem to its simplest terms*, wise words if we may be so bold, words which we would do well to remember in such circumstances, and perhaps even in our general lives, such is their universal applicability. It is with this apophthegm echoing and resonating within him, as the words of the best teachers often do, that he decides upon *The Book of the Unknown Author* as the title he will choose for himself, and we shall follow him in this appellation from now on, we can learn as much from him as the other way around, nobody likes a plagiarist but nor do we like to be accused of putting words into somebody else's mouth either. Upon closer inspection, Flynn also finds that this is a book that has been quite exquisitely produced, printed on paper of the highest quality, the back of the book is glossy and jet-black, and as we noted, the front cover bears a picture of a library which Flynn now realises must be a depiction of the famed library of Alexandria, in which are painted the bowed and hunched figures of men carrying scrolls to and from the high shelves, as well as a depiction of some learned-looking characters, seated at a rudimentary table, and discussing whatever it is they have been reading.

Flynn stands at the reception desk in the central rotunda, and before he places the book in the lost property container beneath, he runs his thumb over the pages and rifles through them, perhaps to see if there is any indication within the text as to who has written it or perhaps who was responsible for publishing such a finely made object; but after a few blank pages at the beginning, the text simply opens, and he realises with surprise that the entire book comprises one long paragraph, a single monstrous looking paragraph of possibly three hundred pages or more, judging by the thickness and lateral dimensions, for there are no numbers on any of the leaves either. It may be gathered at this stage that Flynn is becoming increasingly puzzled by this nameless book which has shown up in so peculiar a spot in the library and at so incommodious a time, a volume which possesses so many distinctive features yet is so hard to categorise, or perhaps more accurately, we should say, a book which lacks most of the usual features which one expects to find on the books we sometimes find lying around. The cleaner has long gone and let himself out through a side entrance, the main lights have now been switched off, and because only the faintest splinter of moonlight comes through the small windows that line the top levels of the central rotunda, Flynn stands with just the green glow of the little computer monitor at reception to light his world. This computer, mainly used for the purpose of scanning the books that people either borrow or return, can also be used as a reference tool for determining where a given volume is in the electronic catalogue, and if so, the wherefores of its location and how it might be retrieved. We noted earlier that the electronic catalogue is not yet complete, but given the newness of the book that Bartleby Flynn has found and its pristine condition, it ought to be certain that it is recorded somewhere, because the library copy would have been entered into the electronic archive immediately, as a matter of course and protocol, on the day that it arrived.

Unable to resist looking a little more deeply into the enigmatic *Book of the Unknown Author*, he places his hand on the mouse and moves the pointer to the box on the screen which enables the user to search for books by title or author. In the box marked title, he types 'No', followed by a function key from the top row of the keyboard, which by the wonders of the digital signals interpreted by semi-conductors somewhere in the bowels of the library information system, then tells the machine to search for the input string of words, in the tables and files of the database. The machine clicks and whirs and an egg-timer appears as it always does – on such occasions why did they choose an egg-timer to indicate that a computer is thinking, when the whole purpose of egg-timers is that they are supposed to measure precise periods of time and not the frustratingly unpredictable time periods we spend waiting at computers for the magic to happen? Anyway, as we were saying, the system has done its work and produces a list of books with 'no' in the title, *No Country for Old Men, Trust No One, Things You Can't Say No To, 1997 Wiring Regulations, incorporating Amendment No. 15:2013, Dr No*, and so forth, but nothing strikes him as relevant to what he is holding. Flynn performs the search once more, this time with 'N.O.', but search results for this acronym produce only the heart-sinking and ironic answer, *<no results found>*. He immediately expands the search via the internet, to include all known published books available, on the off-chance that there has perhaps been an oversight on someone's part and that the book was simply never ordered or maybe was lost in the post or never correctly recorded, but once again the computer clicks and whirs and generates the same output, *<no results found>*.

This is most irregular, thinks Flynn, perhaps not in the whole history of his time at the National Library of Books and Publications has there ever been a case of such a book, especially one produced so delightfully and with such transparent affection and attention to the material quality, to the tactile and aesthetic aspects of bookbinding, a volume that for all intents and purposes and in so far as all records and technology are concerned, simply ought not to exist, since there is no trace of its production ever having been documented. Flynn suddenly finds that he is beginning to feel somewhat irritated by the existence of this book and its rude intrusion into his evening routines, a book whose appearance in the library, whose owner, whose author, whose publisher are so entirely confounding. After all, there is scarcely any need to point out that the book must have been written by someone and printed somewhere, and that somebody must have, in whatever sense, given birth to the thing, and also that someone must have brought it into the library and then left it behind, either by mistake or on purpose. These observations are common sense, given what we all know about the regularities and mechanisms of the world, and at this juncture it is worth saying, as a word to the wise, that any observer who has presently taken to imagining that our preceding considerations have any religious or metaphysical implications, or which are somehow meant to form a childish analogy with the authorship of the world itself and the usual ridiculous mythologies, would do well to banish any such thought, for they would be so utterly mistaken in this presumption as to be almost unwelcome participants in the forthcoming narrative we intend to relate.

Flynn muses for a moment that the person who left it behind must have known full well of the lack of distinguishing features to this book, and if this person were malicious or even just a little mischievous, they may have left it there specifically in order to annoy one such as Flynn, and if they knew anything at all about the way books and manuscripts are classified by professionals, such a malicious demon would also know that nobody would quite know what to do with it once it arrived in their hands. To continue with the Cartesian thread of our musings, it might follow that someone may have left it on the theology balcony intending its provenance to appear to us as a sign or miracle or an Act of God, or maybe, Flynn then thinks, maybe a more likely story is that *The Book of the Unknown Author* was simply written by the very person who left it there, who had it printed and so tastefully bound but chose not to publish it properly for the entire world to see, an explanation which would answer the question we raised earlier about why the book does not appear under that title in any known electronic library catalogue. Flynn looks again at the wilful refusal of the unknown author to submit to the tacitly recognised convention amongst writers of dividing text into paragraphs, and it seems to him that the very prospect of such a book, with its tiny print, is a rather daunting one to the casual reader, as though the breathless torrent of writing were perhaps one long exhalation or cry of loneliness that somebody simply had to expel, onto paper, into words that we can follow across a page, lexical shapes which remind us of tiny dancers etched against a horizon, or long lines of the dark and enigmatic footprints we sometimes see embedded in snow. This peculiar object, this manifesto of the unacceptable, this statement of sorts which in its very form and mysterious origin is suggestive of someone wishing to say exactly how they feel about this world of ours, with its brutalities, its sorrows, its extinctions, its incomprehensible systems, its indifference, its irrational rules, its absurdities, its moments of astonishing tenderness, its forbidden music and its sublime moments where the whole world is aflame around us, in the crash of thunder or the howling of animals or the cracking of whips, or when we find ourselves, perhaps fancifully, atop a cliff in the middle of a raging tempest and bolts of lightning split rocks and trees asunder, we all of a sudden find that it is we ourselves who are burning because we are bearing witness to something mysterious and which possesses an extraordinary might and beauty that holds us in suspension. Flynn, who has been reading extracts to himself quietly, during the time we were rattling through the presumptions and hyperbolic extravagance of the preceding sentences, has become even more struck by the mysterious book once he reads the first page.

> There is more to the life of an
> office clerk than simply putting
> things in metal drawers and taking
> them out again, copying and pasting
> chunks of meaningless data between
> software applications, opening envel-
> opes, inserting things, closing en-
> velopes, then sealing the envelopes,
> borrowing a stapler, answering the
> telephone, or grimly forcing large
> numbers of documents he doesn't know
> what to do with into the jaws of an
> enormous shredding machine. He needs
> to learn the solecisms, the pleo-
> nasms, the stupid phrases, *the
> bullshit*, the faces and names of the
> stupid people he works with; and he
> needs to endure the frozen hours of
> tedium, punctuated with streams and
> threads of interminable, mindless
> drivel. An office clerk, if he really
> knows what he is doing, must learn
> how to look busy, how to look dili-
> gent, *how to look sharp*, how to
> maintain an air of impregnability
> from the sea of faces in the people
> who are like cows and sheep and
> amongst whom he finds himself, as he
> walks through the electronically

controlled turnstile each morning. He must learn how to disguise the fact that instead of working carefully at the tasks with which he has been entrusted, he really does them as quickly and as carelessly as pos- sible, without paying the slightest attention to any of the details, and he must also disguise the fact that he is forever writing – writing comments on the website of *The Cor- respondent*, stories, letters, writing the book he fears he may never finish – continually writing to try to capture something of the world in which he finds himself, in a net of words and to craft it into the best sentences he can and with whatever meagre talent he has at his disposal. In order to facilitate this disguised process of continual writing, he must also learn to disguise the fact that he is continually reading, but not the training manuals or the new pol- icy statements or the financial forecasts or the share prices or the company newsletters which are sent pointlessly around on ludicrous and expensive headed paper. Rather he must disguise the fact that he is continually reading stories or poems, or reading news articles or opinion

threads on websites, or weblogs or
Wikipedia entries on taxonomy, types
of medical procedure, chemistry, and
distant periods of history, or philosophy or logic or types of animals
and nutrition. It takes a form of
feral cunning to disguise the fact
that one is not really doing the work
the company is paying you to do,
although writing which for me is
living and which because life is work
must therefore logically also count
as working, and it is this state of
continual hyper-vigilance and mental
activity which is why the life of an
office clerk is a totally exhausting
one, and it explains why he is always
so tired at the end of the working
day. This total disdain for the idea
of working, this complete lack of
productivity, also explains why the
life of an office clerk is a lonely
one, for the simple reason that he
appears ill-favoured in the opinion
of the others, maybe because of some
flicker of his eyes when he sits down
in the morning or a careless remark
he makes at some new outrage, or his
*ideological detachment from extran-
eousness*, because people are more or
less like little dogs sniffing at
each other all the time, sniff sniff,

> and they conclude that the troubles
> in life of a lowly person who is con-
> tinually reading, writing and ignor-
> ing his responsibilities on purpose
> boil down to the fact that *he quite*
> *simply doesn't smell wholesome.*

Thus read the first few pages of *The Book of the Unknown Author*, the mysterious book which Flynn unexpectedly happened upon earlier, and over which he has been standing open-mouthed for a good ten minutes at the reception desk of the library. Upon yet more scrutiny of the text he is holding in his hands, if such a thing might even count as a tale or story, it appears to continue onwards and upwards in a similar vein of high and exultant misanthropy, an apocalyptic way of thought quite alien to Flynn's persuasion or way of seeing things, yet also slightly thrilling to him, for we have to remember that he is neither as worldly nor as cynical as we are, and nor is there any reason why we should even expect him to be. How interested I will be, he thinks, how fascinating if I ever get to meet the owner of this mysterious book, the owner who for all we know is also the writer of those incendiary words, and glancing over a few more choice irruptions within the text, he places the book under the reception desk, and walks out of the library for the evening, he sets the alarm system and we can just about still see him walking across the square to his building, which he will soon enter, with a view to proceeding directly to his bed.

4

THE LIBRARIAN BARTLEBY FLYNN arrived early to work this morning, and thought immediately of the mysterious book he found last night. He also finds that during the night, who knows the processes by which these things arrive in us, he has sleepfully formed in his head an idea of the character of the unknown author, finding himself more or less assuming, quite without justification, that the owner of the book is one and the same person as the individual who wrote it. Why Flynn's intuition is telling him this, he cannot quite say, his face is pale because he has lain awake almost until dawn and there are bags under his eyes thanks to the expressions from the unknown author's manuscript that kept turning uncontrollably over and over in the theatre of his thoughts. In a single page of this enormous paragraph, not the one we quoted, Flynn read of how:

```
'the only thing to say about
work is that it is a big
```

```
building full of either
boredom, base stupidity, or
continual despair.'
```

He read of the unknown author's doomed mésalliance with a:

```
'duplicitous and spiteful
wretch,'
```

whose

```
'mendacity and idiotic
ramblings were matched only by
breath-taking ignorance about
simply everything of value.'
```

This was the person, according to the unknown author, who:

```
'cost me for a time my sanity
and my most private hope, that
of an ideal woman of rarefied
wit and the greatest
conceivable physical beauty and
grace that I lost, and whom I
am constantly doomed to
remember.'
```

The unknown author had then experienced,

```
'a darkness at noon moment,'
```

(and also,

>   'a Damascene revelation of
>   horror and dread,')

that left him drinking:

>   'wine without limit',

and a heart that felt:

>   '**crushed;** squeezed in my chest,
>   like a foot jammed in a wrong or
>   opposite shoe.'

Over and over these impotent descriptions of rage had tumbled through Flynn's head during the night, as he lay in bed and wondering, wide-eyed and wakeful, about the nature of who it could be that had written these sentiments and then had them all so carefully printed.

Throughout the day, Flynn does his best to stay within the central rotunda so that he can keep an eye on who is coming and going from the reception desk, in the eventuality that the owner of the book, perhaps the unknown author himself, might arrive. Not suspecting he is being watched from a distance by an eagle-eyed and timid librarian, perhaps he will ask quietly whether somebody has handed in a book that was left on the theology balcony yesterday by mistake. Perhaps his face will express a mixture of nervousness and gratitude as whoever is standing behind the desk bends down and hands the book over with a brief exchange of words that, because we are not lip-readers, can only be guessed at. Flynn is unsure what he would do once he had caught a glimpse of this stranger, after all the owner of the book would hardly need to give his name and address or library card when asking for something so simple as the return of some property, nor would he be likely to imagine that the contents of the book could have so impinged upon the imagination of so lowly a stranger; so if the scenario described were to obtain it would be quite impossible to make any determination as to the true name or true story of this person merely from the fact of their showing up in the way we have imagined. In turn, Flynn begins to worry that should this turn of events come to pass, he would never be able to read more of that demented single paragraph or discover more about the voice and observations of the writer, for the reason that once retrieved, there would be no way that another copy of such a singular item could ever be easily located. For all I know, thinks Flynn, this copy is an *editio princeps*, the only copy that exists, and it is therefore imperative that if I want to know more, I must find out who the owner is, if only to ask where it came from, who wrote it, and whether I might be permitted to slip one more time between the book's covers and soak myself with the writing. On the other hand, thinks Flynn, maybe this person will ring ahead and ask over the telephone whether a book has been found, suspecting it might have been left in a café, or on a bus, or in a taxi, and not at the National Library at all, in which case it would be a bother to come all the way here to look for something, only to find that it was not there to begin with. Flynn therefore decides that in addition to remaining in the central rotunda to watch the reception desk for signs of intrigue, thereby ignoring his duties in other regions of the library, he also needs to position himself close to a telephone so that he might be the first to answer it, in case the owner of the book should call to ask whether the book is there, and whether they might stop by and retrieve it. There is no guaranteeing of course, as we have already pointed out, that the owner and the writer are one and the same, for all we know the book may have been left by a woman, and this thought initiates in Flynn *a most atypical feeling*, for it hits him that if a woman owned such a thing, she would in all likelihood be a highly unusual and interesting person; given his repressive tendencies however, this is a thought he immediately drops for fear of thinking too transgressive or inappropriate a thing, not a point that in any sense should be made lightly.

Although we know that Flynn is preoccupied with other things which are more important to him than his work, and which are certainly far more alive and interesting, his colleagues of course have absolutely no idea of the strange state of nervous excitement which he is currently experiencing; and as a consequence these colleagues begin to get annoyed at Flynn's inexplicably distracted behaviour, standing all morning as if rooted to the spot next to the telephone at the reception, without lifting a finger to be helpful or courteous to people in the way that he usually is. These professional associates naturally have worries or suspicions that he is making a point, perhaps has an axe to grind, some peculiar grievance against them which they cannot yet fathom; and they exchange quizzical glances with one another on the matter, when they think he is not paying their whispers any attention. They are baffled yet further that on the few occasions he reluctantly has to move away from the reception area, he is constantly looking back towards it, past the face of whoever it is he is talking to, thereby giving the impression to all and sundry that he is really rather uninterested, distracted, and not concentrating at all on whatever it is which is at hand. They were even more baffled when, during one such field excursion to give hurried and inaccurate directions to a library guest as to the location of the dictionaries or the pornography or the engineering sections, the telephone started to ring; and with a wild cry Flynn had leapt into the air, flinging himself towards the handset, snatching it from under the outstretched hand of a colleague who was looking in the other direction and who appeared most surprised to see a sweating, hysterical-looking Flynn leaning over the counter, with the handset clasped the wrong way round and insanely pressed to his ear, mumbling: 'Hello? Thanks for calling the National Library of Books and Publications, no we do not do that, *Goodbye.*'

The day passes in this fashion, and it seems that today Flynn too would *prefer not to* when it comes to doing work that someone else has asked him to do; more than once the Chief Librarian asks for some minor thing to be done, but whenever such tasks are delegated to Flynn, he simply prefers not to do them, with the result that at the end of the day the Chief Librarian gives the staff a little lecture to express his displeasure at, as he put it, the 'slovenliness and lackadaisy', and his disappointment at the *'unmistakeable signs of lassitude'* that are creeping into a team of colleagues who seem to think it acceptable to leave so many important tasks left undone at the end of a working day. In his little peroration, the Chief Librarian also refers to a platitude that is well known in workplaces across our planet, that when lots of little things are left to the four breezes, it almost always follows that the entire structure will soon come crashing disastrously about one's ears when least expected, and before anybody has a chance to put any of the wrong things right. Flynn immediately offers to stay late once again in order to remedy these oversights, which everybody knows were all down to his own negligence and stubborn refusals in the first place, and it is to the consternation of his colleagues that the Chief Librarian, who is aware of everything that goes on in this kingdom, the Chief Librarian who lives in the most wonderful country home, then goes out of his way to praise Flynn in front of all of them, in the most embarrassingly effusive way possible, describing him as the very model of a team player and a shining example to the rest, a *bright star in the constellation of librarians,* as the Chief Librarian puts it, and as he adds, who on earth knows how high such a person might go in the hierarchy of things whilst displaying such exemplary attitudes? Flynn's colleagues leave, muttering between their teeth to one another about this fresh outrage; and Flynn, whose heart has been fluttering all day for other reasons, even begins to feel an extra level of nervous disturbance and shock, as he witnesses for the first time how quickly a team of co-workers who can be as nice as pecan-pie to you whilst you are in their good books yet who can also turn unbelievably quickly into a conspiratorial army of seemingly mortal enemies, a crowd whose safety in numbers could quite easily and if it saw fit turn a person's working life into, according to the unknown author,

```
            'day after nightmarish day of
            Unbearable shamelessness.
            Interpersonal mayhem.
            Unbridled ignorance.
            Social torture.
            Recklessness.
            Insolence.
            Hell.'
```

As a consequence, Flynn busies himself this evening and works extremely diligently at putting right all the things mentioned by the Chief Librarian in his little pep-talk to the troops, and Flynn resolves to bring in perhaps some cakes or peach pastries for his colleagues tomorrow, as a form of tacit apology, to win them back as it were, *I need these people on my side*, he thinks, if it comes to the point that he should have to ask them to help him discover the identity of the person who left the mysterious book, and who may or may not be its strange progenitor. Weary from the spinning, fractal spirals of thought that characterise mental exertion of this sort, and we should know, Flynn again stands alone at the reception desk, illuminated by the green light of the monitor, and he looks once more at the mysterious book he found yesterday evening, and again he picks it up to read from that huge and remorseless paragraph, a text that veers wildly from moments of raging bitterness to moments of whimsy, fragility and even tenderness, and which, as is becoming increasingly clear the more he looks into it, also contains a striking breadth of allusion to different subject matters, of literature, cinema, the history of anarchist movements, drug taking, classical music, hieroglyphs, philosophy, pornography, foreign affairs, ephemera, and pop culture references that go quite above Flynn's head – a single paragraph moreover crafted in short sentences that often begin illogically or wilfully, as though written down by a person frantically scribbling things immediately and as he thinks them or as soon as the ideas and forms of words pop magically into his or her head. We have already noted some of the punchy expressions of the unknown author that haunted Flynn during his previous sleepless night, and he is struck by the writer's fondness for *italics*, an expressive and musical typographical gesture which is almost certainly underused, just as writing in block capitals can give the impression of SHOUTING, he reflects how judicious italicisation of a phrase or part of a sentence can add a humorous and ironic tone to an otherwise bleak proposition, a technique of which the unknown author of this manuscript appears to be fully aware and at which he is even artfully proficient.

Flynn is struck in particular by a German proverb which crops up numerous times in the manuscript and always without translation – *in der Nacht sind alle Katzen grau* – and although he does not yet know what this sentence means because he does not know German, he is starting to have an inkling that this expression may prove to have a significance that at the moment is still opaque to him. Nonetheless, the regularity of its appearances in the text, and the contexts in which it is used only make the matter of the unknown author and his manuscript all the more impossible to ignore or forget.

As a consequence of noticing this repeated reference in the book to the proverb *in der Nacht sind alle Katzen grau,* which is always mentioned after the bitterest denunciations of some aspect of the world or the received wisdom of others, Bartleby Flynn writes the words down on a slip of paper at the reception desk, and knowing that he will not be able to sleep again tonight without discovering the meaning of this foreign expression, he decides that instead of going home immediately to rest his weary bones, he will go to the computer in the office, fire the machine up, and see if he can find a quick means to translate this sentence, perhaps using the famous search-engine which we once heard mispronounced as *Gargoyle*, or on the kind of automated translation software which renders foreign idioms into forms of amusingly broken English. Flynn moves to the office, still wearing his coat, and sits back in the chair in wait for the computer to wake itself up, and he slumps back holding his finger-tips together to form the geometries of a pagoda, which he absent-mindedly pushes against his chin whilst a leg jerks up and down, a behavioural signal we can take as signifying that inside himself, he is feeling rather agitated. He enters his username and his password in order to log into the library computer network, pausing before he opens the web browser as he thinks of the library's strict policy on the recreational use of the internet by the staff, and he immediately wonders whether the Chief Librarian, unbeknownst to everybody, secretly monitors the ways in which his staff use the technology, whether the Chief Librarian sits recumbent behind the desk in his eyrie, with the door shut, perhaps twirling a tiny spinning top on the desk with one hand and watching its gyroscopic convulsions shine as it wobbles about, whilst with the other hand casually outstretched to his computer mouse, idly clicking through and reviewing the computer logs of the library servers, data collated for him by the Socialist perhaps, though we do not know ourselves whether such protocols exist. Perhaps the Chief Librarian examines these computer records in order to see what the unique staff identities on the computer systems have been doing on the firm's time, perhaps to monitor their personal emails or to check what they have been writing on the comment threads of social media websites, message boards and discussion forums; for a second, Flynn pictures what might happen the moment that the Chief Librarian's eye is caught by what he, Flynn, has been doing at night on the world-wide-web and when nobody is watching. The Chief Librarian will doubtlessly want to know why Bartleby Flynn has been performing a peculiar search for translations of the German proverb *in der Nacht sind alle Katzen grau*, all on his own and at a time of day when by rights he should have been out making love, or in a cinema, or repeatedly crying '*hit me!*' whilst playing blackjack at a casino table, or even simply tucked up safely in bed with a hot-water bottle and an enormous hardback spy novel, or the crossword page of *The Correspondent*.

Flynn suddenly thinks to himself that he regrets the fact that he does not himself own a computer, not because they are prohibitively expensive for his salary, but for the kinds of reasons we spoke of earlier, that up until today he would not have had sufficient use for one in his tiny flat to make the purchase worth his while, his modest home which in any case is probably not even wired up with the fibre-optic cables and equipment necessary for the establishment of an internet connection. He thinks about this for a while, and decides to proceed with his search for the translation, despite his lingering reservations about what the Chief Librarian might do; Flynn does not have to answer for himself or to anybody else this evening. The meaning of the proverb that lingers so tantalisingly behind the words *In der Nacht sind alle Katzen grau* is eating into his imagination like a parasite, a proverb known of course in many languages:

En la nuit tous les chats sont gris, according to the French.

Ночью все кошки серы, according to the Russians.

En la nit, tots els gats són grisos, according to the Catalans.

And on we go.

This proverb, of course, is itself a locution dreamed up by another unknown author, we do not know for the life of us who came up with it initially or how these things get started. And now it seems to him, that even if the Chief Librarian does find out that he, Bartleby Flynn, has used the library's computer system to make a quick search for the meaning of a proverb, moreover after the working day was over and all jobs complete, for some kind of inscrutable dark purpose of his own, that this nevertheless is not the kind of transgression which should lead a Chief Librarian to dismiss or punish for misconduct someone who has always been a model employee and who, as far as the Chief Librarian is concerned, is one of the best workers he has ever managed. Resolved therefore, despite reservations, and despite his usually timid and, as we are now beginning to realise, somewhat neurotic nature and way of thinking, Flynn types the words of the proverb *in der Nacht sind alle Katzen grau* into the little box of the search engine, and much to his delight and further curiosity he discovers the answer he is looking for. *In der Nacht sind alle Katzen grau*, a German proverb and seemingly the favourite

German proverb of the unknown author, if his continual use of it is anything to go by, means, and we reproduce a translation here because we cannot expect everybody to be conversant in the orchestral complexities of the wordramming German language (sic), anyway the proverb means something like *all cats are grey by night* or perhaps more figuratively, *all cats are grey in the dark,* and Flynn sees immediately that not only is this a rather wonderful and mysterious metaphor on a number of different levels, it might also be considered to give birth to the additional suggestion that all cats *seem* grey by night – a further level of meaning to these translated words which renders such a proverb not only true in a far greater number of factual cases but also (we hope you concur) lends to the expression a certain and unmistakeable air of menace.

Flynn needs to look at the translation for only a second to register all this, and sharply closes the browser window again, perhaps his earlier worries and questions about the Chief Librarian's attitude to staff internet-usage are once more beginning to scream like express trains through his nervous system, and once more he leans back in the chair, his fingers formed into the pagoda, pondering this new piece of knowledge with which he has become acquainted. He says to himself almost inaudibly, but just loudly enough for us to catch wind of the words he utters in the stillness of the old library, *the unknown author is alone,* and naturally begins to ponder what the next move ought to be, in this brave new world which is unfurling before him. We should pause to reflect at this stage that the librarian Bartleby Flynn has never much been prone to obsessions, or suffered from the horripilations that accompany compulsive thoughts; from this we can take it that he probably has no idea what obsessions even are, or what having continually obsessive thoughts, about things such as varieties of pasta, different colours, types of fabric, making lists, makes of detergent, categories of plants, capital cities, watching people (because how can't you?), might feel like. He is simply, and without any additional level of self-knowledge, pondering a problem with which chance or destiny, who knows which of those things rules our lives, has spontaneously presented to him, a mystery which he now suddenly feels motivated to look into further, in order to see what things may lie buried and waiting, under the surface. The empathetic reader may also feel, even ought to feel, that it is completely natural for a man of such precise habits as Flynn to encounter at some point in his life an enigma which diverts him from the humdrum regularity of his usual routines; this for the very reason that his quietude and deferential nature form, so to speak, the perfect vessel in which such an interest might form and then take flight, an interest which of course leaves behind its own thread of coincidences that slowly but surely, inch by inch, seem to lead him onwards, downwards or inwards towards some kind of new catharsis or source of illumination. Much has been written about destiny over the centuries by the eminent and esteemed, they know far more than we do, humble torchbearer as we are, entire books have been devoted to the subjects of determinism, causation, spontaneity. A deterministic fate is said to be implied by a world subject to strict laws of causality, and so the precise status of any freedom of the will that lies or does not lie therein is a thorny issue, one that sets the humanists against the Catholics, the Catholics against the other Christians, the philosophers against each other, and more or less everybody against the Jewish people; the only thing left to say about it, at least as far as we can fathom, is to suggest that destiny might be most profitably thought of as something that belongs to wherever it is that we happen to find ourselves, or perhaps, a feeling that is found sometimes, in whatever it is we find ourselves doing.

Flynn gets up suddenly from the chair, returns to the reception desk and once more picks up *The Book of the Unknown Author* and starts to read, of the:

> 'voluptuousness of the solitude one feels where everybody else is talking.'

a scenario which:

> 'makes one feel like an alien life-form in a hostile and inhospitable environment.'

And he reads of how:

> `'continual miseries and`
> `penury in the face of such`
> `insolences,'`

turn, of their own volition,

> `'into butterflies.'`

(And also:

> `'shattering and hilariously`
> `brutal confirmations,'`

of the:

> `'dreadfulness of`
> `freedom.')`

And now Flynn reads how:

> `'The briefest thoughts of`
> `those terrible craters on`
> `our bombarded moon, of the`
> `murderousness of oceans,`
> `make me shiver with all the`
> `terror of a man stepping`
> `forward to his execution.'`

Flynn is sorely tempted now to take the book home with him, to prop himself up in bed with a pillow and a hot milky drink, to stay up late into the night reading the entire paragraph, which is to say to read the entire book, cover to cover. Yet he is so tired from the day's hysteria that his nerves feel exposed like cold air passing over raw skin, and he wants to arrive at work rested and sharp tomorrow, lest he fall victim to further resentment from his colleagues, and so he resolves he will take the book home with him tomorrow if the mysterious one fails to appear, because tomorrow is Friday and he will be able to stay up for as long as he wants, since the following day is Saturday, which is his day off.

Flynn then becomes worried again because it occurs to him that if the curious owner were to stop by tomorrow and ask to retrieve the thing which is rightfully his, this would more or less throw an enormous and inconvenient spanner into the works, a big greasy spanner at that, because this would prevent him from carrying out the plan he has just been concocting, thereby thwarting his intention to study at greater leisure and in more detail the text of which he has chanced to become aware and which is currently occupying every aspect of his thinking. With that in mind, he now has the thought that he might hide the book somewhere in the library for the time being, for the reason that if he happens to be nowhere near the reception desk tomorrow, should the owner arrive, the thing he fears will simply not happen, because the librarian on reception detail, blissfully unaware of what has been going on in the fevered mind of Flynn, would not be able to hand the book back because it wouldn't be there; rather they would look and see that the book was missing from beneath the desk and utter some locution such as, 'Hold on a moment, let me just ask where it is', at which point Flynn could assert a far greater level of control over the situation and either choose to hand the book back to its owner personally with a searching and inquisitive look perhaps, or simply ask for the owner's name and even address, with a view to contacting them and returning it whenever he felt ready.

It is with these kinds of thoughts in his head then, that Bartleby Flynn walks briskly and purposefully towards the exit of the National Library, having locked *The Book of the Unknown Author* into the back of a desk drawer in the break-room; and then he arms the security alarm system and locks the great door of the library behind him with its antique and heavy iron key. He steps out into the square, into the murmur of a palpitating city, and makes his way back towards the building in which he lives.

*

It is raining a little, and having been inside the stuffy library for so long and with such unfamiliar thought patterns, the wind which whips up piles of dead leaves lying around in the square and then sends them skitting and spinning in circles around one another, suddenly feels a little more abrasive to Flynn than perhaps would be usual; and it is hard to say whether it is this or the words of the unknown author, or whether it is the uncharacteristically devious thoughts that have been gathering in his mind which cause him to look suddenly upwards at the sky. He peers into the darkness, and for a moment he feels more alone than he ever has before, trudging as he is through a deserted and windy square towards his empty dwelling and carrying a secret which nobody on earth save we observers can know anything about. And so we ask you to think of yourself as Flynn for a moment, as an idea in his brain begins to present itself with the adamantine indestructibility of the lattice structures in diamonds, an overwhelming sense of a world flogged raw of hope and providential significance, filled with nothing but ghosts and ruins, clouds of poisonous dust, everything stumbling or being blown towards a final, terrible dispersal of lingering warmth.

It is with these maudlin thoughts beating in his skull that he ascends the four flights of stairs to his flat and takes a scalding shower. Drying his hair with one hand, his shoulders red and steaming, he is unable to shake off the bleakness that descended over him during this brief walk across the square, and he stands at the window a while, listening to the rhythmic pattering of the rain against it, watching as tear-shaped droplets gather and trace their paths down the glass in little rivulets, shifting, pausing and hesitating, tiny threads looking for one another so far from the ground, beads of silvery light like miniature creatures with a sentience of their own. This city, which will always for us remain an empty, De Chirico city, with its streets below the window that appear oily under the sodium haloes of the lamps, this city now seems to him a monstrous and unmappable maze, something directionless and bottomless, unfathomable and chillingly proximate, a city that contains him and his perceptions yet which is entirely indifferent to their content and presence. If only he could recognise, we might interrupt, if only he could realise that in this lonely and captive hour, in his capacity as an observer and participant, he too is more than a worthy and interesting subject for observation and compassion, as our text is proving, even though in our present capacity we are unable to do anything to alert him to this idea or show him somehow that this is what we are feeling. The only things Flynn sees at present are diagonal slants of wind-flecked rain flashing in the burnt-orange nimbuses of the street lights, fizzing in and out of existence against the darkening sky like trails of the elementary particles that in his imagination blaze in and out of measurability in the horrendous magnetic forces of high-energy accelerators. The lights shine in the cocktail bar on the far side of the square and he sees people scurrying about below the dripping awning, half-disguised by umbrellas, a sight which reminds him of wounded birds, an entire flock of these neglected creatures hobbling along the turnpike shielding themselves from the elements with broken wings. He sees overcoat collars turned up to the throat and hat-covered heads, shoes that step over and into the puddles that are gathering in the drains and gutters. He catches a glimpse of a thumb hailing a taxi and of crooked figures dodging through an urgent stream of traffic in order to clamber onto the rammed and humid night buses which seem to boil and steam from within. He stares across this pulsating and wheeling world from his vantage point, and feels suddenly comforted by the idea that he, Bartleby Flynn, is warm, safe, protected for the time being against the threats, insults and complexities of our ineffective carapace, and now, finally, he begins to savour the insistent and inevitable melancholy of his moment. Then he thinks again of the idea of voice, and not just that of the unknown author, but the vast array of these voices gathering themselves into choruses and dissonances as they proceed in their myriad directions, gathering together in crescendo waves under the soaking, velvet rinse of what we sometimes call the heavens. Presently, he closes his curtains decisively against such a backdrop, no doubt with a resolution to end ruminations and morbid thinking of this sort and possibly for all time, thinking now more positively of the plan he has constructed for tomorrow, with respect to the mysterious book and its author. And so he gets into his single bed, the fact of its singleness tells a story entire and of itself, a bed whose springs creak and groan in pantomime protest at his ambivalences and ambiguities, and he turns off the reading lamp and lies for a while in the darkness as the clock ticks, staring upwards at the ceiling with his eyes wide, listening to the gentle, insistent rhythm of the rain on glass and the diminishing complaints of the traffic. Then, as if by magic, and as happens to all of us in the manner to which we are happily and reassuringly accustomed, all thought suddenly leaves his body, and he turns on one side and falls asleep.

5

FEELING ALERT AFTER AN unbroken night, and wonderfully rested by the healing power that good sleep can have over the epiphanies and dolorous episodes of brooding which gather in us sometimes at gloaming or witching hours, Flynn hurls himself energetically into his morning routine. He crosses the square to the coffee shop as he usually does, and today he picks out a selection of pastries and treats with which he will attempt to placate his colleagues following the previous day's workplace aberrations. He is anxious that they shouldn't think anything is awry, he has shaved meticulously and is dressed in his smartest clothing in an attempt to make himself look and smell as fresh as a daisy and as good as his modest appearance might allow. With this extra attention, he hopes that his colleagues will conclude that his uncharacteristic behaviour yesterday was down to no more than a poor night's sleep or a disappointment of some kind, perhaps some private or embarrassing medical matter which has now been quickly and unproblematically resolved.

He enters the library with a renewed sense of vim and purpose, and proceeds directly to the desk in the break-room where the book of the unknown author is hidden. He opens the drawer to reassure himself that the text is still there, just to be reminded that it is safely buried, in such a way that there is little-to-no likelihood that anyone rummaging around, perhaps for a stapler or a highlighter pen, or some post-it notes or painkillers, might happen upon it lying under a pile of envelopes; if somebody finds it, after all, they might begin to wonder, in suitably fateful fashion, for what earthly reason it is there. Should they then proceed to examine it for the relevant signs and markings known to library professionals, they might either take it away to a new location from which it might be swept anywhere, or maybe they will start to become as fixated as Flynn has become regarding the nature of its content, cause and origin, to begin an obsessive investigation of their own. And that would never do! This sudden thought of his alarms Flynn to such an extent that he fails to acknowledge the salutation of another librarian walking past the door, that's a mistake, all because he is picturing himself locked in mortal struggle with this imagined Moriarty on the highest of cliffs, trying to prise the book from their grasp, thinking of new ways in which he would have to outwit such a nemesis in order to regain possession of the manuscript and restore justice to the universe, *and by whatever dark and devious methods necessary.*

Flynn realises there and then that he would have no reservation or compunction at all, should the need arise, about going into somebody's handbag, or their coat, or personal locker or briefcase if such a scenario were to arise, but thankfully the book is still where he left it, and indeed, we can report that nobody has even entered this room in the time that has passed between his leaving work yesterday evening and arriving back there again today. Calmed and reassured by the image of the Alexandrian library on the cover, this image of ancient library workers and readers, which is itself displayed on a book contained in yet another and even vaster library (albeit in the break-room), he locks the drawer again and sets out as neatly and enticingly as he can the sweetmeats and treats he bought at the coffee shop; he recalls briefly that he purchased these things earlier from the girl with the big eyes, who always acknowledges him politely, we forgot to mention, she does so with a demure and charmingly feminine smile which illuminates, momentarily and with a ray of light, an unusually sad and serious face, but enough of that, he hangs up his coat, takes a sip of coffee, and off to work and to do the right thing. He rolls up his shirtsleeves, as they say, puts his shoulder to the wheel in a fashion that demonstrates the resolution he has made, to work tirelessly and without stopping, to make it up to himself as much as to the others, he thinks, to work off the odd sense of disquiet from which he was suffering during the whole of yesterday, which so haunted his sensibilities that it even seemed to follow him home.

He thinks again of what he might do should the owner of this book come into the library and ask whether it has been handed in; and of what will happen if someone looks on the dusty shelf below the reception counter to see that the book which had been sitting there for the whole of the previous day has suspiciously vanished. Perhaps they will say to whoever else is standing there:

Has anybody seen the book that was here yesterday?

Which book? comes the reply.

The one that Flynn said he found on the theology balcony.

Ah yes. No I haven't seen it.

Odd where things go.

Quite true, it was there when I looked.

It had no paragraphs.

More correctly, it had just one paragraph.

You don't miss a trick.

Nor did it obey the conventions of how you're supposed to do direct speech.

A strange writer.

A maverick, even!

Depends how you look at it.

Like so many things.

Nobody has called today.

Maybe he put it somewhere for safe-keeping.

Who?

Flynn of course, who else?

Flynn then thinks of what he might say in this scenario, whether he will immediately begin to blush and stammer, giving all the behavioural signals of one who is up to no good, or bearing the burden of a guilty conscience about the matter over which he is now, in the counter-factual case, being questioned. How embarrassing it should be if all this were to occur in front of the book's owner, who might then fix Flynn with a frozen stare, gorgonize him, and immediately pick up that something was not quite right with this librarian, even eye him with hostility. We can picture a flushed and flustered Flynn having to hand over the precious volume which at present is at the centre of our thoughts and concerns, sheepishly and unwillingly perhaps, such is the strength of his intention to prevent this from happening. Alternatively, thinks Flynn, maybe I am more cold-blooded and clinical than I am giving myself credit for, perhaps I will be able to say perfectly calmly, despite lying through my teeth, coolly, calmly, and collectedly burying my nefarious web of deceit beneath a stony exterior, and saying:

No I haven't seen it, but if you leave your name and number on this piece of paper, *we will be sure to contact you if we hear any news.*

It is with thought processes like this, and moreover thought processes which are relatively under control, that Flynn starts to open the day's post. Sorting it, he helps one of his female colleagues, an older librarian with an artificial voice-box, to unpack a large shipment of new arrivals for the Social Sciences reading rooms, a package which he lifts from the ground and deposits ready for sifting and sorting onto a table. By mid-morning Flynn has noticed that the cakes, mille-feuilles, pastries and *petite madeleines* he bought from the girl with the big eyes have been all but gobbled up by his colleagues, and that his simple gesture, so common in workplaces and offices the world over, a gesture so crucial for fostering a sense of camaraderie amongst people who are more or less locked up with each other all day like inmates held against their will, this gesture has, so to speak, gone down well with his workmates. As the morning strides on towards afternoon, he begins to feel that they are warming towards him once again, their bellies filled, they begin to exchange the usual knowing nods, winks, eyes-to-heaven and other little gestures of affection and solidarity, how fickle some people are.

The Chief Librarian, whose office sits on the very top level of the central rotunda, a sleek-looking and glass-fronted domain which extends the entire width of the walkway, thereby dividing the top level into two sides of equal length, is standing at the window and surveying the proceedings down below. Bartleby Flynn, who has been as busy as a bee, catches the attention once again of the watchful leader, because of the alacrity and punctiliousness with which he, Flynn, is currently working; nor has it by any means escaped the Chief Librarian's attention that Flynn was also the one who left so large and ambrosial a selection of pastries in the break-room, the Chief Librarian having of course eaten more than his share of them already and when he believed no-one was looking. The Chief Librarian returns to his desk and pulls out the personnel files for the staff which are kept in a red ring-binder, locked away at all times for reasons of confidentiality, and he perches his reading glasses at the end of his nose and reads through Flynn's records again, slowly and methodically, running through a mental checklist of Flynn's capabilities, skill-set and sickness record; the Chief Librarian pauses and with an air of great seriousness stares blankly for several minutes at the huge Turner painting of a ship at sea which is mounted on his office wall, we are unable to say precisely which Turner painting it is, at a glance, and after all, they all look the same. Turning his gaze from the Turner and back to the folder, the Chief Librarian lifts the lever arch and carefully removes the document wallet containing Flynn's file, closes the rings again and turns a number of pages. He then re-opens the arches and very deliberately places Flynn back inside, one or two places closer to the top of the folders within, which we may now infer must be a series of staff identities arranged in their order of importance, by name of the employee who is next in line for a promotion. The Chief Librarian neatens the pile of papers with his thumbs, admires his handiwork and reflects with satisfaction that his judgment was correct; then he solemnly closes the ring-binder and places it back in the cupboard, locks the door, and turns back to his desk to continue with whatever else a Chief Librarian does when at work in his beautiful office.

*

Because it is Friday, a rumour begins to circulate around the staff of the National Library that a group of them will be going out for drinks after the working day is done, to celebrate the end of a long hard week, and to spend a few polite hours with one another in a more relaxed and unconstrained setting than the workplace, an atmosphere of conviviality and small-talk which will no doubt be lubricated, so to speak, or made less excruciatingly unpleasant, once the first flush of wine begins to work its magic in their cerebellums. The librarian with the tracheotomy, and from whose throat comes a phlegmatic whistling sound whenever she speaks, asks Flynn in her deep and robotic voice if he would consider joining them for a while that evening, it has been a long time since they last had a proper chat, thank God for pastries:

I'm so sorry, could you repeat that?

I said would you like to come out with us for a drink tonight?

Thanking her for the kind offer, Flynn says that he has some personal matters to attend to, affairs which preclude his spending any precious free-time in such a fashion.

Thank you for the offer, I have some personal matters to attend to this evening.

Maybe next week then, she says.

Say again?

I said maybe you'll join us next week then.

Oh yes, how kind, I'm looking forward to that already.

Flynn, naturally, is really bursting to turn his attention back to the book of the unknown author, who mentions Wittgenstein so readily, Billie Holiday and Schubert, and climate science, aphorisms, and the film noir cycle, as much as he does the greyness of cats and his:

`'deadly thought-processes!'`

and (thus the unknown author), what he calls:

`'this intolerable, nerve-destroying crisis of `**`everything that exists, or has ever existed, in all of world history.`**`'`

Flynn is beginning to be increasingly amused whenever the unknown author goes off on one of these tangential paroxysms of impotent rage, and it strikes him that designing sentences of extreme hyperbole in fact lends a peculiar artfulness to the unknown author's rants, raves and ramblings.

Flynn must now decide whether tonight he will breach a very strict library rule, rule number two in fact after the primary one about not kindling flame nor tinder on library premises, lest one bring about a depressing repeat of the conflagration that consumed and destroyed the Alexandrian library, the rule that no book may be withdrawn or removed from any library without due record being made of the details of the book, the time of withdrawal, and the personal particulars of the borrower. If this rule does not strictly apply in this case, since the book does not belong, in a fiduciary sense, to the library, and even if it did would be impossible to categorise and record because of its unusual features, anyway as we were saying, if this rule does not apply in this specific case, then it should also be pointed out that it is certainly frowned upon in a moral sense, to take from one's place of work, library or not, any piece of lost property, even if one fully intends to return the item again later. To do such a thing would look to all intents and purposes of course like an act of the purest larceny, since if we were in a court of law, the defence would not be entitled to infer what was going on in the defendant's mind and enter it as evidence, the defendant Flynn in an orange Guantanamo jumpsuit, his head bowed, with hands and feet securely shackled:

And at the time, did you believe Mr Flynn intended to return the book when you saw him take it?

Yes, I did.

Your Honour, this witness says she believes that Mr Flynn fully intended to return the article in question.

Objection Your Honour, may I remind the court that the defence *cannot* ask the jury to make an inference into the *workings. Of. His Mind!!*

Quite right, Lead Prosecutor, quite so. That objection is sustained.

Putting aside the thought of a trial, of being served a writ of replevin or some such for a moment, Flynn begins to wonder what could happen if the Chief Librarian has noticed the book in the drawer whilst on an excursion to procure another of the pastries. Perhaps he tried to open the desk in order to look for a napkin with which to wipe some powdered sugar or custard from his chin; perhaps he unlocked the drawer with one of his master keys, which he keeps at all times on a silver chain fastened to his waistcoat, and thereby discovered the book sitting in there and as he was poking about inside. It is not hard to imagine the Chief Librarian opening the desk for a second time, during a later trip to the cakes, and noticing that the book had been removed, this is precisely the kind of mastery of detail he possesses. No doubt he would then wish to know why a piece of lost property keeps moving around the library so mysteriously when nobody is looking, no doubt he will start to ask questions about whether it has been lost, stolen or collected, and what precisely anyone intends to do about it. It should be clear by now that Bartleby Flynn was born equipped with a rather visual and overactive imagination, and he turns over such possible scenarios as these all day long, but he is so fixated on making a study of *The Book of the Unknown Author*, that he decides he will not deviate from his plan to remove the book that night and take it home, that his nerve will not fail at the last minute, whilst smuggling it out in the inside pocket of his gabardine raincoat. And aware perhaps that he is the least likely smuggler in the entire history of bibliography and contraband, he makes a solemn vow to return the book by Monday morning. The Library is closed on Saturday afternoons, he thinks, and if the book's owner should come during the three hours in the morning when it is open, he will have to leave empty-handed, following an interaction with library staff that could not in principle suck Bartleby Flynn into compromising himself or his nature or his thought processes.

Before Flynn can leave however, there is the urgent and important matter of a staff meeting, presided over quite naturally by the Chief Librarian, and which all staff members are expected to attend. The subject matter of this meeting is a little unexpected to all of those present bar the Chief Librarian and his Deputy, a small wiry-looking man who assiduously enforces all directives to the letter, and whose rimless spectacles lend a rather hawkish and puritanical impression to his thin face and demeanour. The Deputy Chief Librarian is well-known in library circles as another pair of eyes and ears for the Chief, and he is the only other person apart from the Chief Librarian's wife who is admitted to the inner sanctum, the circle of board members and trustees who appoint this leadership team, with the priority of safeguarding the long-term future of the library and making important collective decisions on matters of policy, finance and future strategies. How often it is that someone is deep in the stacks, walking along an empty aisle, believing for all the world he is alone with his thoughts, before rounding a corner to find the Deputy standing before him under a naked light bulb, arms folded, as if expecting to meet whoever it is that has bumped into him:

Oh hello, you startled me.

Just seeing how things are looking, you can go about your work.

Thank you Deputy Chief Librarian, I will do that.

It is for this reason that the little man has become known by the unfortunate nickname of The Lurker, which nobody says to his face, but which he has often overheard, to his anger, at moments when people have been whispering about him and he has inevitably jumped out of some corner or other and caught them red-handed.

Another responsibility that the Deputy Chief Librarian has taken on in this strange and fragile tapestry of lives, which criss-a-cross one another within the walls of the library, is seeing to it that the Chief Librarian always has the things he requires for his lunch, usually a foul-smelling and unappetising-looking combination of vegetables, spices and bananas, either prepared by the Chief Librarian's wife or bought from a so-called health food café a few minutes' stroll from the library. The reason why this lunch duty has fallen to the Lurker is rather whimsical and amusing, the story being that one day the Chief Librarian had been sitting in his office, a huge cloth napkin tucked into his waistcoat, preparing himself for the banquet of incomprehensible food that was sitting in front of him. He was about to begin eating it when he realised that the dish was missing the essential ingredient of pine-nuts, a foodstuff by which the Chief Librarian swears, for its healthful and youth-preserving properties and which he therefore consumes in vast quantities at each and every meal. Aghast at the intolerable prospect of a lunch without pine-nuts, he threw down the napkin and went downstairs to the break-room, and then to the Post Room, asking every member of staff he encountered: 'Excuse me do you have any pine-nuts?', an odd and unexpected question which caused some bewilderment and puzzled looks amongst the workers as he went from one to the next, asking each one if they had any pine-nuts, why on earth he should have thought that a Post Room worker would be likely to have a ready supply of pine-nuts is quite beyond our comprehension. The lunch of a Post Room worker, after all, is far more likely to be something hearty like goulash or stew, whilst that of a librarian is more likely to consist of something simple like a baguette or perhaps a salad, and it was during this failed quest for pine-nuts that the Chief Librarian happened upon the Deputy, lurking behind him as one would expect, and asked him the same question. The Lurker was forced to confess that he too did not have a ready supply of pine-nuts on hand with which he might avail and placate the Chief Librarian, who was now becoming desperate, but immediately offered what management types the world over refer to as a *pro-active solution*, by offering to go on an errand, a field mission, to purchase a quantity of pine-nuts from a shop in town, and on his Chief's behalf. As might be expected, the Chief Librarian now regards the Deputy as some kind of Messiah figure and universal Genius in cases where there is something remiss with his provenders and victuals, and summons the hapless Lurker by a special pager as soon as he runs out of pine-nuts or plastic forks or tablets of garlic or anything else he might wish to consume.

On his downtime, the Lurker is also something of a hopeful inventor, who draws diagrams and writes up patents of things for which, in his opinion, there is some type of vacancy in the world, and which ought to be filled by a new convenience, mod-con or product. He has never been successful in registering a patent, to his continual bitterness and disappointment, and we recall how he flew into a violent rage, throwing things and jumping up and down incessantly, his cheeks scarlet, upon the discovery that his idea for chewing-gum stuffed with analgesics, intended for people who need urgent pain-relief but do not have any water to hand, was an innovation that had long been patented by a rival inventor. To the Lurker's astonishment and chagrin, he also discovered that this was an idea that the marketing people of the painkiller and chewing-gum companies considered a proposition of dubious commercial potential, and who is to say this was not a wise decision on the part of those executives? Perhaps they, like us, have often watched films where characters swallow fistfuls of tablets and painkillers by gulping down an enormous glass of tap-water, and perhaps these marketing people simply had the same private thought as we always have, namely, *we could easily do it without that.*

Although this Lurker may seem to be rather unlikeable in several of his aspects, at least that is the way he seems to be developing, it can be said – it must be said – that he is also someone who has had his own fair share of sadness, and not just because of his failed inventions either. (In Parentheses:

> `'If you cast a cold eye,'`

says the unknown author,

> `'If you look at anybody closely`
> `enough to examine the details,`
> `the purple eruption of lesions`
> `on skin perhaps, the dark cavity`
> `of a missing tooth, what you`
> `will find there is an entire`
> `universe of stories and sorrows`
> `if you want to, things which can`
> `turn your heart brittle, and`
> `leave you broken, splitted and`
> `snapped.')`

To apply this observation to the case of the Lurker, we can see that the unknown author may have a point here, for there was once a woman whom the Deputy Chief Librarian had loved with all of his being. One day he had received a telephone call from one of our embassies abroad, and upon hearing the message, his hands began to shake uncontrollably. The purpose of the call was to tell him that the body of the woman against whom he had so often lain, whose head he would cradle in his arms, had been blown into a thousand pieces by the bomb explosion that ripped through a train she was travelling on, along with the friend with whom she was vacationing. Nobody at the library knows of the Lurker's private loss, after all why should he, or indeed any of us, feel obliged to bare one's soul to all and sundry, to reveal the most inward and tender fragilities of the mind and spirit? As a consequence of his reticence, with respect to his colleagues, it is easy to see why they are unable to account for his chilly disposition, or make use of this insight in order to draw more far-reaching conclusions about his character. For the sake of accuracy we owe it to him to say at this point that there are reasons why the man is the way that he is; there are reasons why he behaves as he does, just as there are reasons for the unappealing things we ourselves do, without always knowing or understanding what they are – which is to say that there are reasons why this Lurker feels that nothing, ever, can come to any good.

*

So, equipped with these new facts, we return to the staff meeting, the Chief Librarian standing at the front, the Lurker sitting next to him with his legs firmly held together and clasping to his chest a folder full of different documents, into which he reaches every now and then in order to hand over some piece of information that the Chief Librarian's outstretched hand is demanding. The workers are sitting in rows facing the management, and the subject of the meeting provokes an air of tension to gather and form somewhere above their heads or about them, because the Chief Librarian is explaining that, given the recent and terrible cuts made in all areas of the public sector by our splendid government, the library itself is now facing far harsher economic weather. It has therefore been determined by management that it is necessary, in order to ensure the continuing renown and prestige of the institution as one of the world's great libraries, by keeping it stocked with every book and publication ever perpetrated, that it will be necessary, as he puts it, to *downsize and consolidate the workforce*, a euphemism to be sure for the word that every working man dreads to hear, or have hanging over him – Redundancy – often expressed by the powers-that-be with a 'I'm very sorry, but we may have let you go.' As a consequence of this sudden and unexpectedly pressing financial need for heads to roll, and as a consequence of the efficiency of the library computer system and automated accounting methods, the Chief Librarian says he has decided to implement a system of performance reviews for all staff; he has done this, he says, in order to determine as precisely as possible their areas of expertise and also their weaknesses, to quantify numerically what he refers to as a *skill-matrix analysis of competencies* (SMAC), which will yield *wholly scientific* results. These objective indicators, says the Chief Librarian, will show just how well each person is working at all their various duties, how skilled they are in comparison to the rest of the staff, and most especially it is a method which will introduce a little competition, perhaps it will motivate the ones who have been swinging the lead to improve their performances; strictly speaking, on the other hand, if we allow the lexicon to shift from road worker to that of a peasant, this is also a method to *separate the wheat from the chaff*, as the Lurker broodingly says in his head.

The details of this system are too boring, badly conceived and incomprehensible to be worth relating in any detail, trust us when we say that you do not need to know, and so we leave you with the image of the Chief Librarian standing before his worried staff, holding a large wooden stick, with which he points furiously at projected images of flowcharts, graphs and spreadsheets, as he explains to everybody how his assistant will be watching closely to see how everybody is performing. Flynn is a little alarmed at the mention of the forbidden word redundancy, but he is also comforted with the thought that he has always been looked upon favourably by the Chief Librarian, more favourably it has to be said than by the deputy, who thinks privately that Flynn's quirks and additional time in the library may be some form of plot to try to oust him some day from the role of deputy, a role which, given its importance with regards to such things as supplying the Chief Librarian with his pine-nuts, or emerging like a spectre from the shadows to terrify the wits out of a female member of staff, he guards with understandable vigour.

Flynn thinks to himself that there are others who will be in the firing-line before him, other more likely victims of this staff cull – his dedication to the world of the National Library has always been total. Total may be too strong a word to use at this stage, since Flynn's devotion has not been quite so total as it used to be, now that the matter of the unknown author has caused him to become unusually rebellious and distracted from his work, but in any case this new spirit of defiance and individualism has only been over the last couple of days and he now has plenty of time to ensure that he is no longer dragged down by the weight of such a millstone before the blade hanging over all of them comes so brutally down through the neck of one or other of their number. How humiliating it will be, thinks Flynn, to be summoned to the office and asked to leave the employ of the National Library, whether one wants to or not, to be stripped of one's security pass and employee privileges, even to be escorted to the door of the building by former comrades and ejected from the premises, for good measure.

It is here that a new thought begins to nag and torment Flynn, because he suddenly realises that the world of the unknown author and the world of the Library in which he works are starting to seem chillingly antagonistic to one another, the gravity of one world pulls him in this direction, the gravity of the other tugging him in that, and as a consequence he is beginning to feel a little jittery at the idea of having on the one hand to ensure that he ticks all the boxes of the Deputy Chief Librarian's flowcharts and matrices in order to move upwards, and on the other that he is still able to have the time to think about how the resources of the library might be best put to enable him to travel inwards, towards the voice of the unknown author, whom Flynn longs to observe and learn more about, a voice which he has come to think of as having become inexorably tangled with the thread of his own destiny.

Quite why Flynn feels so strong an urge to investigate the unknown author for such fatalistic reasons is not completely clear to us, and it is not completely clear to Flynn either, such is the nature of the compulsions which occur in us at unexpected moments, all of a sudden and out of nowhere. Flynn has fully acknowledged the insistence of this new presence within himself, *a question in his nerves is lit* as the unknown author would put it (almost quoting Dylan), and this is not completely illogical. After all it was he, Bartleby Flynn, who happened upon this book, rather than some other librarian, it was purely by chance that he had chosen to return books bound for the theology balcony as opposed to the literature section, or to the room that contains the books about medical science, the ones with diagrams of the various organs and apparatuses of the human body, the ones with pictures of skin lesions, sphacelated limbs and horrible burns, or the ones which describe the process by which lactose in milk is converted by the body into sugar by the action of enzymes. This book and this unknown author came to him, presented themselves to him alone, as strange things sometimes do; and who can say that one ought not to feel curiosity, a burden of responsibility, when presented with contingency and causality, as they dance their unceasing waltz?

The meeting is over, and Flynn and his colleagues make their way as a group towards the exit whilst the Chief

Librarian and his ghoulish deputy stay behind, deep in a discussion about some of the technicalities or the finer points of how the plan will be implemented, and there arises the sort of solidarity which always gathers amongst workers after hearing distressing news from upstairs, and they mutter to one another about how times are changing and how the old Chief Librarian would never have allowed such a thing to happen, and the apocalyptically-minded technician known as the Socialist gloomily predicts that all human labour will one day be replaced by machines, and that the machines may one day become sufficiently aware of everything that they will start to conspire against these human beings crawling over one another in search of their pine-nuts, pension pay-outs, or unknown authors, these people with their crushable skeletons and soft skin, their inexplicable tears of sorrow or howls of mirth, their need for understanding, their subterfuges, hysterical laughter in the face of certain death, and the limited imaginary powers such things naturally confer. These machines, proposes the Socialist, may yet wise-up and turn against us in exactly the way they do in the science-fiction movies, he says he thinks we would be well-advised to watch our backs when it comes to machines, and maybe he is right in his pessimism, after all he is a technician.

Flynn, whose mind wanders from fanciful thoughts of killer robots destroying the world, back to thoughts of the unknown author, hangs back a little and stops suddenly.

Oh, I think I've left something in the break-room, he says, I'll have to catch you up.

He leaves the group and walks back through the central rotunda, to the drawer in the break-room where the book is sitting. He sees from the corner of his eye the Chief Librarian and the Deputy deep in conversation just down the corridor, leaning close together and looking at a document, pointing things out to one another. Flynn sees his opportunity and quickly slinks into the break-room, he unlocks the drawer, shoves his hand inside, and extracts the book; closing the drawer, he slips the book into the waistband of his trousers. He is breathing hard, and lets out a yelp because he is not expecting to see someone else in the room when he turns around, he suddenly realises he is face to face with the inevitable form of the Lurker, who has been staring at him from behind. Flynn does not know whether the Deputy Chief Librarian has witnessed him stuffing the book into his trousers in so shifty a way, and there is an awkward moment as they face one another whilst Flynn is processing his options.

Not working late tonight, Flynn, says the Deputy Chief Librarian, his eyes never leaving Flynn's face for a moment.

No not tonight, says Flynn,

I was leaving with the others but I remembered I left something behind.

What have you lost?

Flynn now finds himself confronted with a dilemma, because there is nothing of his in this room whatsoever save the clothes on his back and his conscience, nor can he be truthful about his removal of the book which is lodged against his belly, and which he now realises is beginning to slip down slowly towards his crotch. Flynn blurts out the first thing that comes into his head which is,

Pen!

and he scrabbles around and picks up a chewed ballpoint from the table. He holds it up,

Ah, found it.

Surely that's the library's pen?

So it is, I don't know what on earth I was thinking.

But even if it is not the library's pen, continues the Lurker

(and after all, who knows where all those cheap pens are coming from?)

In any case, *it looks to me as though the ink has run out*.

Flynn had been hoping to extricate himself as quickly as possible from this predicament, rather than getting bound up in a discussion which could plunge him into hot water. He pretends to look at the pen more closely, shaking it a few times for good measure and peering at the end.

Goodness, so it is, he splutters, I wonder what happened to mine. As you say, quite empty.

He quickly places it back on the table and turns; he mentally rolls his eyes, as he hears the inevitable sound of the pen rolling along the table-top and falling on the linoleum floor with a hollow click, and he stoops to pick it up once more, placing it this time against the edge of a book. He turns, and tries to move briskly and nonchalantly past the Lurker, who is standing in the doorway as if to block Flynn's exit. The Deputy Chief Librarian does not budge an inch while Flynn is squeezing past, the book poking awkwardly against a thigh, and Flynn tries to ignore the fact that the Lurker is looking at him so closely. Then Flynn looks at the Lurker looking at him, to which the Lurker responds in kind by looking at Flynn looking at the Lurker looking at him.

See you next week then, Flynn, says the Lurker.

Yes, goodbye Lur… I mean Deputy Chief Librarian, see you then and do enjoy your weekend.

The book is now starting to slide down Flynn's trouser leg, which would spell disaster if anybody should witness it dropping out over his shoe and onto the ground, most of all if that witness happened to be the Lurker. It is because of this uncomfortable protuberance that Flynn is now forced to walk along the corridor with a wildly eccentric waddling gait, which for all the world makes him look like a drunkard, or an invalid, or a lunatic to the Deputy Chief, who turns with a shake of his head back towards the interior of the library, muttering to himself as he goes, *What a strange fellow.*

An unfortunate thing, we might remark, has just happened with regard to Bartleby Flynn, because although the truth of it is that nobody at the Library knows he has removed the mysterious book in order to take it home and consume it, an action moreover which is hardly a serious transgression of the rules governing acceptable human conduct in comparison with some things we might think of, Flynn is nonetheless now in the invidious position of wondering whether or not the Deputy Chief Librarian, this Lurker, is now onto Flynn's game, and will therefore be monitoring his activities even more closely in the future with a view to destroying and thwarting whatever devilish plan Flynn might have designed. Bartleby Flynn once again feels the force of the world of the book, the voice of the unknown author which is currently located down his trousers, starkly pitted against the force of the world of the library, his paymaster, pulling him in different directions by separate limbs, stretching them unbearably. Or perhaps it is gravity, that universal attraction, which is pulling him, down towards the earth, as far as possible, only for him to feel that the ground itself cannot support him, gravity would pull us down further if it could do, and as Yeats rightly says, in the end, even the centre cannot hold.

(In Parentheses:

> `'The universe would kill`
> `you at the slightest`
> `opportunity!'`

thus the unknown author,

> `'Indifferent!`
> `Healthy!`
> `Strong!')`

If it seems a little melodramatic of Bartleby Flynn to be thinking this way, there is nevertheless a sense in which he is justified in feeling that he has been caught between two conflicting forces. What is the cure, the eirenicon for this conflict? It could not have happened at a worse time, thinks Flynn, it could not have happened in front of a more delinquent person, as if there are appropriate times for everything good or bad that happens, *in der Nacht sind alle Katzen grau.*

6

Bartleby Flynn is sitting bolt upright in his bed, and holding *The Book of the Unknown Author* against an upright knee; he has read the long paragraph that comprises it twice the way through, and from cover to cover. He closes the book after finishing the final shattering sentence for the second time, stares blankly at the wall for several minutes. Realising he is soaked in sweat and that it is now the middle of Saturday morning, he tears off his pyjamas and walks to the bathroom, to clean the body, as his uncle used to say, *to ablute*, and he hurriedly and distractedly dresses in the nearest clothes to hand. He sits down at his table, which is in the window of this room, we shall not bore you with details of the furnishings as they are perfunctory and much as would be expected in a place like this, the reader is therefore invited to imagine any details of it exactly as he or she fancies, you can picture things for yourselves far better than we can. Flynn looks down at the sprawling sweep of the library with a perplexed look on his face, and now he reaches for a notebook and a pencil and begins to write down some of the things that he now knows.

The first thing to say with respect to the unknown author is that he or she is capable of conveying images with considerable brevity.

'Bus. Dog. Frightful.'

Or,

'The smell of despair and divorce that becomes immediately airborne in the reek of dreadful perfume.'

And,

'Tuesday. Fog.'

The unknown author also calls himself,

'*A Raskolnikov of workplace transgressions!*'

and as we are now beginning to diagnose, he also has a superb eye for italics; and he also seems very well-informed about a dazzling array of disparate topics, writing with the authority of a polymath. The second thing to say, as it should by now be clear, is that the unknown author is extraordinarily bitter and resentful, and if his words are anything to go by, which we have no reason to suspect they ought not to be, he finds there to be a great deal at fault with this world, faults he finds either completely unbearable, or unacceptable in principle, and very often both at once. The third thing to say is that the writer intimates at one point that he writes anonymously on the internet pages of *The Correspondent*, which as we know already is Flynn's newssheet of preference. This is something Flynn has inferred from various references within the text itself, to:

> '...the ink-pissers of that paper who shamelessly steal ideas they see written by more perceptive minds below the line, as well as the revolting array of right-wing trolls and lurkers who descend like vultures the minute anything is published with the slightest suggestion of humanity.'

and also,

> '...the ludicrous invented persona of *Gaunt* whom I never hesitate to report for abuse the minute he writes anything and whom I ridicule as violently as

```
            possible for the brainlessness
            of his "thinking" processes.'
```

The unknown author, it may be fair to assume, is perhaps someone actively involved and familiar with the phenomenon of internet message boards, and their attendant memes and customs, and if this is the case, thinks Flynn, maybe it is possible to scour the comment threads of *The Correspondent*'s web pages for clues as to the unknown author's online persona ('the characters of the threads glow like faces in the meadhall') – a persona which may well be an anonymous secret identity, of course, but whose postings may nevertheless be distinctive, given what Flynn has picked up about the author's prose style. Further, thinks Flynn, these thoughts and responses on the threads may contain further clues for him to follow, as he attempts to dig more deeply into the mystery in which he is finding himself ensnared. Flynn also has the idea that, should he indeed be able to find in the chaos of these threads the precise internet identity of the unknown author's so-called sockpuppet, he may be able to leave a message or a sign, maybe not by being so bold as to introduce himself by name, but nevertheless find some way of acknowledging the existence of this person with a voice that roars across the pages like the bellows of a bound and shackled bull. Maybe, thinks Flynn, I will even be able to communicate that I have in my possession this unusual volume and try to return it. If this book appeared in any library catalogue, it would of course be filed in the drawer marked Author Unknown, a category of books which includes such epics as *Beowulf*, *The Book of A Thousand Nights and One Night*, tales such as *The Song of Roland* and *Chicken Licken*. We must include along with these works the myths, legends and also proverbs, such as *in der Nacht sind alle Katzen grau*, with its intriguing figurative suggestion of nyctalopia, so-called *night-blindness*, its evocation of the sense that in the dark places of the world, our vision reverts to some kind of monochrome. The implication is not that our own unknown author is any more or less important than the shadows which remain of these storytellers of old or even roughly comparable, merely that the impulse to write, classify, codify the things that torment our minds at Godforsaken hours, is an impulse which is not peculiar to time and place, and one whose urgency remains today as it always has, we can't live with it yet norcan we ever really live without it.

Not only, thinks Flynn, are there lots of forms of words by unknown authors which are justly famous, there is also the matter of texts of questionable or disputed authorship. This category of writing includes certain plays within the Shakespearean canon, the Homeric epics, the poetry of Sappho, along with *The Book of Lemmas* attributed to Archimedes and which consists of numbered propositions about the nature of circles, a book which is thought by some to be apocryphal because the author refers to Archimedes in the third person, although, were Archimedes a postmodernist or connoisseur of meta-fictional observations such as this one, a reference of this sort would in no way rule out the possibility that he wrote the manuscript himself, but for some whimsical reason decided to refer to himself in the text by name as opposed to the personal pronoun. This book, *The Book of the Unknown Author*, is difficult to categorise, if for no more than the fact that it would naturally need to be filed in the drawer marked *Author Unknown*, for the reason that although compelling in a certain sense, it is neither autobiography nor novel, nor history nor philosophy; it is simply a torrent of words, in which the author jumps haphazardly and helter-skelter, from one topic to another, without rhyme or reason. Given our own fondness for capriciousness, this should not bother us unduly, but it makes it all the more difficult for Flynn to infer from the text who or where the writer is, and why the book was written. Pursuant to observations such as these, we might add that the unknown author may also be one more voice amongst all the other unknown voices who haunt and inhabit the corridors of internet comment threads. It is from the kernel of this thought, then, that there is a reason for Flynn to hope that the unknown author may live in our country, which after all is not so very large; and given the sense of urbanity expressed in the writing, who knows, he may even live in this city or its environs. Maybe he is even the person who lives downstairs.

Flynn has decided therefore that his next port of call must be the web pages of *The Correspondent*, and given the fact that the unknown author conveniently mentions a fellow poster with whom he has had cause to quarrel and issue remonstrations, a poster who calls himself *Gaunt*, it occurs to Flynn that an entirely sensible starting point might be to look up this individual first and begin a survey of his profile and posting history, in an attempt to locate the threads upon which Gaunt and the unknown author may have crossed words with swords. The principal difficulty, by no means an insurmountable one, proceeding as it does from this latest idea of Flynn's, is the one of not having ready access to a computer, because up until now it has simply never occurred to him that he should ever need one for himself. He ponders for a minute whether to withdraw some money and then go and buy one, but thinks to himself that this would be no good for the task immediately at hand, because he has no means of connecting to the internet in his home, and he has heard tales of woe concerning the tardiness and unreliability of internet service providers and their burly installation men, who seem to be a law unto themselves, and who can often be totally unreliable. Flynn cannot wait two hours let alone two weeks, to absorb himself more deeply, and given his technological naïveté, and the crumbling infrastructure of this country, which irks and inconveniences us almost daily, it does not occur to him that he might take a new computer to a café offering wireless internet access. Wi-Fi is a technology that for some reason has not yet reached the National Library, and it is therefore a system with which Flynn has never had the chance to become acquainted.

Flynn's options then, to summarise, are these. He can try to find a so-called cybercafé which has public computers that can be rented for the purpose of web-browsing, or he can find some other public computer, of course the ones in the library, where he might sit undisturbed in order to proceed along the course where logic is inexorably leading him. He looks at his watch and sees that it is already half-past eleven, as we noted the library will close at noon, and he thinks to himself that if he goes down there now they will soon be locking the doors for the weekend. He certainly does not wish to arouse the suspicion of the Deputy Chief Librarian who is on duty today by showing up just before closing time and then staying behind to use the computer equipment for mysterious private purposes on his day off. It then occurs to Flynn that, as one of the several secondary keyholders, he can simply enter the library whenever he wants to, secretly unlock the enormous wooden door and sneak inside once he knows that everybody else has left, the Deputy Chief Librarian in particular, whom we shall suggest may spend the rest of this Saturday in casual clothes, perhaps corduroy slacks and a Faroese sweater, and working intensely at home on his latest ideas and inventions. Another problem now presents itself to Flynn, quite simply the fact that using the key that has been entrusted to him in this manner, whichever way you look at it, would constitute an enormous breach of the trust that has been placed in him with regards to his role within the hierarchy, and if he should be caught entering the library at a time when he has no business being there, he would be instantly disgraced, his keyholder status revoked and his personnel file quite possibly placed at the back of the binder, putting him firmly in the crosshairs as quite possibly first in line for dismissal. Flynn once again begins to weigh up the odds with the evens, and he feels the tension we spoke of earlier, between the voice of the book and the face of the Deputy Chief Librarian, and for some time he deliberates upon exactly the best way to proceed. He will be able to see from home when the final person leaves the building and locks it, but the question is whether it would be safe for Flynn to go down immediately, to let himself into the library, only to be caught by a returning Lurker perhaps, because he had either forgotten something important or, God forbid, had somehow guessed what Flynn might be intending to do.

Flynn resolves therefore to wait until nightfall, when he can be as sure as is possible that he is unlikely to be caught entering the building and using the computers. However, there is also the possibility, he thinks, that he may find himself in even hotter water should a police officer or well-meaning member of the public notice him furtively slipping into the library, and assuming that he was some kind of cat burglar, believe he was intending to deprive or divest in some way the library of its world-famous and valuable contents, and therefore try to have him arrested. The shame, the sorrow, the pity that would follow, were Flynn to be led out of the library in handcuffs, have his head pushed down by some sergeant as he was bundled into a police vehicle, the radios crackling and the blue lights flashing in the night. The disgrace would be such that he would never again be able to show his face at the only place he has ever worked, and which no doubt would also cause him all kinds of trouble when seeking alternative employment. Although he is prone to such fancies, Flynn concludes that this eventuality is rather unlikely, after all, he can wait till the square is empty, and who would notice or be expecting to see a man opening the main door of the library a crack, and quickly and quietly slipping through? The remaining question he has is the same one that arose when it came to the possibility of it being noticed on some kind of computer report. Should it transpire that Flynn secretly logged into the library system late at night, in order to read his way through historical articles from the web pages of *The Correspondent*, he would undoubtedly lose his right to hold the keys, in the worst case he might even be instantly and summarily dismissed. Flynn tells himself he has never once heard of an employee being disciplined for misuse of the library's computer equipment, even though he regularly sees people slumped back in their chair, and blatantly looking at non-work-related web pages for hours at a time, and then he thinks perhaps no such report of the staff's computer behaviour even exists; I am brooding too much, he then thinks, maybe I am simply dreaming things up.

Whilst we are waiting for the library to close and for night to fall so that we may accompany Flynn on the mission he has set for himself, a mission which he feels he has had no choice but to accept, it is worth saying a little about the nature of comment threads and the subterranean cultures which exist below the line of internet discussion forums and message boards. It will become necessary for a while for us to abandon the tone in which we have been speaking, in order to provide examples of the dialectics and conversations which take place in this domain, a hermetically sealed world like the one which exists beneath the vast ice-shelves of our polar regions as far as Flynn is concerned, the torrents of written words and personal avowals which are combined by unknown authors the world over in response to articles or phenomena, avowals which may take the form of platitudes or ingenuously simplistic expressions of personal belief, or anarchic thoughts, or blazing insights, a zone of moral neutrality and anonymity where members of our species try to be as offensive as possible, or where they despairingly attempt to form bonds and coalesce at key points in the historical narrative in order to establish forms of intimacy. One thing to say, although the humble librarian Flynn would never put it this way, is that there is an interesting question of identity at the heart of internet personae, an identity which is most unlike the identity of whichever body constitutes our own metaphysical continuity and ontic horizons. For unlike the human animal, the fictional or meta-identities of anonymous authors surround not the material conditions governing the persistence through time of organisms or objects extended in space, but rather the intriguing and difficult relationship between packets of information which emerge within an enormous and not quite physical amphitheatre. The identity of the unknown author, which is significant both because of the question which surrounds the relationship between his writing and his physical self, not to mention the relationship between these things and whichever online persona he has chosen to adopt, in Flynn's mind this is the identity of an individual who uses things to stand in place of what he is, in the actual world; this is to say that 'the unknown author' is the unknown author of the book, or that his symbolic avatar is that of 'the unknown author', which is to say there is at least one sense, and very probably many, in which it is a metaphor.

Flynn has yielded to temptation and bought a packet of cigarettes while he waits for darkness to fall, and in order to evade the smoke detector and the strict non-smoking rules which apply to properties rented in his apartment building, he smokes one of them furtively and clandestinely in the bathroom, lifting up the lavatory lid and blowing the fumes he exhales down into the pan. He is surprised and alarmed when he hears loud thumps against his front door, and he discards the cigarette, which extinguishes with a little fizz of the most perfect compression. He walks to open the front door. He sees his next-door neighbour standing outside looking rather puzzled, he has passed this neighbour many times on the stairs or outside the building and they have always acknowledged one another with a nervous and friendly nod, although neither has ever formally introduced himself and so it is a little awkward as they stand face to face on the threshold for the first time.

There is cigarette smoke coming out of my toilet, says the neighbour, a tall thin man with round glasses and a curtain of silvery hair, who (unbeknownst to Flynn) works his day-job as taxidermist. The reason for the smoke coming out of his toilet of course is that this building, in which private tenants live cheek by jowl with one another, nevertheless shares such infrastructural essentials as pipes and plumbing, not to mention the wires and cabling and air vents which run under the floorboards and behind walls of all such buildings, just because we can't see them doesn't mean they are not there, and Flynn realises he has inadvertently intruded into the private home of a neighbour by the simple act of blowing his cigarette smoke into the commode, which has through some connection or other made its way to the next flat whose bathroom is, in an architectural sense, back to back with his own.

Goodness how strange, says Flynn.

Are you having the same problem?

I don't think so, come in for a moment, and we'll look. How's life treating you at the moment anyway?

Between you and me, it's terrible.

Flynn tries to appear as innocent as he can, as he leads the taxidermist through the flat, to his own bathroom; as soon as he opens the lid of the lavatory, of course, clouds of smoke billow out from it, smoke Flynn himself has breathed. He tries to look as baffled as he can, even though he is not baffled at all, about why this preternatural phenomenon should also be happening here. The neighbour, who doesn't know that Flynn has just taken up the smoking habit he gave up so long before, and therefore has him privately pegged as a non-smoker, says he suspects the younger people who live downstairs, whom we have often seen standing conspiratorially in the front doorway at night with cigarettes ablaze, and whom the neighbour therefore assumes smoke continually.

It must be the people downstairs, we must confront them, says the neighbour, and looks a little put out when Flynn tells him that he thinks this measure unnecessary, a little over the top, not just because the people downstairs will be as baffled as the taxidermist, but also because he thinks anyway, and as a matter of principle, that such neighbourly disputes are generally better settled politely, rather than with potentially ugly confrontations. Not to be placated, the neighbour is now furious with Flynn, in addition to being furious with the innocent young people downstairs, furious that Flynn has not forged an allegiance with him on this point, furious with Flynn's *sang-froid* and his recommended omerta.

If it happens again, I'll most certainly join forces with you.

You must agree that this is unacceptable?

Yes, absolutely, I do see. Smoke coming out of our toilets is not acceptable, says Flynn, shocked at the feculent exhalation of the bog, and privately vowing never to smoke into one again.

*

During our meandering speculations about identity and the time-period in which this rather odd incident has been occurring, the day has occluded. The street lamps have begun to smoulder and blush, in readiness for their nocturnal vigil, and the sun is making its way slowly downwards to share for a while its life-giving warmth with peoples and vegetation which inhabit other regions of our planet; the sun is harsh but fair in this matter above all others, how else could anything work? Flynn dresses in black, and walks down the stairs, through the door, across the square towards the library. He has seen all the other staff leaving and observed the Deputy Chief Librarian lock the front door some while ago, and looking around quickly he puts the key into the lock, turns it decisively, and slips through the crack like a shadow, closing the door behind him. He quickly enters a security code into the panel by the door to switch off the library's intruder alert system and stands for a second as he waits for the atmosphere to gather around him and make itself palpable. The central rotunda is itself very dark, but it strikes Flynn that the silence which greets his arrival reminds him of an enormous weight pressing down from the dark vaulting high above him, or perhaps from the books themselves stacked in their shelves all the way along each of the levels and which in the daylight seem to stretch as far as the eye can see. His vision is becoming adjusted to the gloom, and he sees the silhouettes of familiar arrangements of tables and bookcases which are lined in an orderly fashion across the floor of the central rotunda. He turns suddenly, half-expecting to see the helminthoid silhouette of the Lurker standing behind him, and ready to demand what exactly Flynn thinks he is doing clad in black in the National Library at such an hour? All he sees behind him caught in a beam of moonlight is his own inevitable shadow, that faithful companion which from time to time also appears as if from nowhere to remind ourselves of our presence and which is perhaps not so ephemeral a thing as one might think, for in the wrong circumstances, shadows too can become indelibly imprinted on walls.

With his heart beating so heavily that he is sure it can be heard echoing in the great chamber by the books, by mice and other vermin, or indeed anybody else who should happen to be present, Flynn makes his way quickly across the central rotunda and towards the accounting office where there are several computers through which one can access the internet. It suddenly strikes him as it has not done before that he need not use his own name to access the system at all, because this library like all libraries has public computer facilities with which to access the internet. These facilities are of course available to anybody who cares to join the institution, therefore he can simply sign into the network using the public guest profile and password with which every library employee is familiar. He suddenly feels relieved, as the worry evaporates that the Socialist or anyone else in the hierarchy will be able to identify him by name, should they happen to notice that someone was using the computers at such a peculiar hour. He sits down and switches on the machine, and it clicks and whirrs and its green lights flash, and it suddenly emits an enormous electronic beep into the silence, a blast of sound which makes Flynn's heart skip a beat and leads us to consider the grave eventuality of a stiff and dead Bartleby Flynn, dressed in black, sitting at the computer with a rictus of terror on his rigid face under his woollen hat, being discovered in macabre fashion on Monday morning by a screaming cleaner.

The screen lights up, brightening the room a little, and lending Flynn's face a deathly pallor and revealing to us the little studs of perspiration gathering on his brow. He goes to the homepage of *The Correspondent* and sees a text box where it is possible to search the site for content or to look for the profiles of their community members. He types the name *Gaunt*, immediately bringing up the page of that person or syndicate of people who use that suggestive name to signify virtual activity. Flynn is able to see the commenting history, stretching back over several years and at first he is unsure where to start looking. He slowly scrolls down the page, and he looks over the words on the screen in front of him as they reflect the light, sometimes he sees short comments such as 'GENERAL ELECTION, **NOW**!' or long comments in which more complex ideas are adduced, ideas surrounding free-market ideology, the moribund inevitability of democratic socialism's historical mission, the assumptions of atheists, the dogmas of anthropogenic global warming evangelists and so forth, and Flynn looks at the names of the other posters whom Gaunt speaks to and his mind begins to hum like a bee-swarm. We see such names as BifidusRegularis, Weathereye, ThomPayne, AMGatward, Silas.T.Comberbache, BlindBoyGrunt, Comrade Jenny, all there in the mix, names like JesterJinglyJones, Constable-Growler, Clamjouster, InformationSilo, Flaubert Flaubert, Mook and twenty more such names as these, which perhaps no man ever saw before, and as Shakespeare rightly asks, what's in a name? Some of these names have photographs or pictures of internet memes such as cats or unicorns next to them, and there are others who have not bothered to make use of an image at all. Gaunt's picture is that of a Puritan in portrait, and Flynn looks over this poster's comments more or less randomly and at one gulp, searching for the comments addressed to particular people as opposed to ones which are merely outpourings of an individual private manifesto, and all of a sudden the finger with which Flynn has been rolling the grooved wheel of the mouse, freezes at the point where he sees the comment dated November 27th, 7.54pm:

'@**ThomPayne**: *all cats might be grey in the dark, but in the daylight they show their true colours.*' (👍2👎2)

Flynn's stomach tightens, and he feels suddenly cold. He is holding his breath, and moves the mouse-arrow to click back through the pages of his browser to the initial text field where he searched for the name *Gaunt*, now he enters the name *ThomPayne* instead and clicks <search>. The computer needles and wheedles in its plies and nasal grooves, it hawks and hums in its clicks and clacks, and suddenly in front of Flynn's eyes appears a black and white picture of the cat which appears at the shoe of Harry Lime in the film *The Third Man*, a still from that timeless moment where Orson Welles' face appears suddenly illuminated in the darkness of a post-war Vienna doorway. Flynn sees a new vista opening up before him, the words comprising the commenting history of this new individual, a history which extends, like that of Gaunt, voluminously into the past and possibly all the way back to the time when the managers of *The Correspondent*'s web pages first had the idea of allowing people to leave comments on the internet threads following their articles. He scans these postings for signs of a calling card, a phrase or expression or syntactic beacon of the unknown author's writing style with which he is familiar from the book, and if the reference to the German proverb was not enough already to set the pulse racing, Flynn feels an excitement which takes him to an even greater depth of fascination, when he stumbles on expressions such as:

'recruiters and HR manag-
ers, whose *ghastly adenoidal
voices* make you think their
nasal cavities must be somehow clogged with faeces,'

(👍 2 👎 2)

and,

'having multiple addictions myself, I love to
see a lapsed celebrity swigging from a
Champagne bottle in the tabloids; it's the only
recovery system I aspire to,'

(👍 2 👎 2)

and,

'the smell of too much cheap perfume
reeks to me of loneliness, desperation and the
grave,'

(👍 2 👎 0)

and finally,

'a fishmonger once told me that when a fish rots, the decay starts at the head. Such is also the case with the unbearable stench of fecklessness that comes off the people who run banks, governments, and call centres. I too shall die, as Swift had it – *from the head downwards.*'

(👍4 👎1)

Flynn sits back in his chair for a moment, and ponders the implications of the connections between the strands that are emerging in his mind. He notes that the postings are made at all times of the day and night, and how they range over a bewildering variety of subjects, such as cinema, literature, particle physics, politics, classical music, popular music, and that they make continual use of elaborate metaphors or personal anecdotes, 'I was locked in a Spanish hotel for two days. Eventually I was saved by a butcher, dripping with blood and offal', who, according to ThomPayne, 'was the only one who had it in him to reply to my screaming.' He sees references to being:

    'lost in Chinatown, way the fuck out on Highway 61,'

(👍1 👎0)

(which Blind Boy Grunt famously revisited); and he sees phrases like,

`hosepipe jobs`

in connection with the horrific deaths and accidents that are always reported in the papers. I have found the unknown author, thinks Flynn, the unknown author is ThomPayne, who posts obsessively and according to his own pers   onal credo, on the internet pages of *The Correspondent*.

Flynn notes that ThomPayne's comments are sometimes sufficiently incendiary to have been removed by the editors of *The Correspondent*, the precise contents of which we will therefore never know. He notes how this person veers wildly between extreme sensitivity to some things and extreme misanthropy towards others, by virtue of the way in which he chooses to express himself. Furthermore, it is possible to tell through the website's use of a recommendation system, that involves thumb symbols, up for approval down for disapproval, that ThomPayne has acquired as many admirers as he has detractors amongst the people who participate in this virtual community, and that he appears to enjoy the heat of debate and the living fire of thought immensely, admitting openly to have

> 'found a way past the firewalls at my cowshed of a workplace to go about,'

what he calls,

> *'my vitally important work for The Correspondent,'*

and operating whilst he is at work,

'beyond the bounds of all

accepted professional norms and standards.'

(👍3 👎2)

He likes to do this right under the noses of his supervisors and colleagues, he says, *to rub it in their faces,* and furthermore finds the fact that he gets away with it,

'highly amusing.' (👍1 👎0)

It is with:

'100% metaphysical certainty,'

(👍0 👎0)

that they see him concentrating intently and assume he's hard at work,

'(I'm the greatest shrike and shirker imaginable),' (👍1 👎1)

and, just for emphasis,

'Writing is how I cope with the day job,' (👍1 👎0)

and also,

'the first thing I do is prioritise any work I am given, often by shredding it, and I then set about my obligations – *to put into words what is really the case.'*

(👍1 👎0)

'I write at my best when I'm amped up on amphetamines,' says ThomPayne, and Flynn then thinks back to the book, and back to what he is discovering. He decides to print all of ThomPayne's comments and to work on the assumption that ThomPayne and the unknown author are one and the same person, the stylistic similarities and coincidences too great to be dismissed as simply paranoia, coincidence or the result of any maladjusted assimilations as might be occurring in Flynn's brain. Page by page, comment by comment, word by word, he hears the office printer go about its work. Following the enormous paper-jam which quite naturally grinds everything to a halt, midway through the printing process, Flynn finally has a pile of pages, writing that covers more than an entire ream of paper, all left by ThomPayne over the past few years on the comment threads of *The Correspondent's* website, quires which Flynn places with solemn and careful devotion into a coloured plastic wallet.

Bartleby Flynn is unsure what to do next. Should he attempt to engage ThomPayne in the febrile arena of the comment threads, partly in order to find a way of returning the book and partly to communicate that he, lonely Flynn, has recognised in the words of a stranger a kindred suffering spirit and connoisseur of the unusual, and who seems to have been gifted so singular and questionable a talent? Or should he come no closer and just walk away, simply let this stranger go about his business anonymously and unperturbed by any unwanted interference? Flynn is now feeling what Freud, following Schopenhauer, explained in terms of the fable of the porcupines, an imaginary scenario in which a group of the creatures come together on a cold night and must work out how to balance the communal warmth necessary for survival with the fact that their sharp spines will inevitably cause one another physical pain if their proximity becomes too close, an absurd and gloomy situation into which these figurative porcupines are locked and doomed to repeat, they come together for comfort and then they must spring apart again from one another when the pain becomes unbearable, they need one another yet in so doing they inevitably wound one another; and it strikes us that this underlying question of a balance between a longing for warmth and intimacy in our own lives on the one hand and an instinct for self-preservation and safety on the other, is a convenient parable for the problem of intimacy that presently confronts Flynn and maybe even all of us, just by the fact of existing we can wreck others beyond salvation just as we ourselves can be wrecked forever, and it is with this consideration that we conclude the present chapter.

7

L AST NIGHT BARTLEBY FLYNN left the National Library of Books and Publications well after midnight, *in der Nacht sind alle Katzen grau*, and carrying under his arm a document folder filled with the writing of ThomPayne from the internet pages of *The Correspondent*. He re-armed the security alarm and skulked across the square, let himself into his building, climbed the long staircase up to his apartment, and went inside locking the door firmly behind him. We join him again on Sunday morning, he has spent much of the night reading steadily through the foolscap pages of commentary that he printed, and he is now adamant that the unknown author and the writer ThomPayne are one and the same grey cats in murky light.

There is much here for him to digest, because the unknown author is nothing if not a prolific writer, often spouting thousands of words of commentary per day, words evidently written extremely quickly if the timings are anything to go by, and so it is quite some task for Flynn, who is a librarian, rather than an academic scholar or private gumshoe, and therefore unused to sifting through the finer points of texts with an eye for every last detail of syntax or style or reference, to get to grips with things; but we must say also that he is learning on the job very quickly and that there are certain new things that he now knows about the unknown author that he certainly did not know before. For example, ThomPayne claims to be facially scarred, the result of a late-night attack with a knife, and also to have endured a:

'wretched violent childhood,'

($👍_1$ 👎$_0$)

at the hands of:

'hysterical fanatics,'

($👍_1$ 👎$_0$)

('*psychopathic fantasists,*')

and also to have:

'received a very poor level of for-mal education,'

(👍1 👎1)

although to read the polymath content of his writings, one would not know it. He also appears to use social media, if the references in his comments to *Friendspoke* are anything to go by, and Flynn notes down the contexts in which these references occur, contexts such as:

> 'I'm a follower of the **Anarchist Collective**, you have to laugh, they're incredibly well organised.'

(👍1 👎1)

Then, following an article about the movies, there is:

> '*Angels with Filthy Hearts* is one of the greatest and bleakest of all the great and bleak films in the noir cycle. The sad thing is that *Angels with Filthier Hearts* was never

made as a sequel.*'*

(1 1)

These little plums of information have suggested to Flynn additional strands of investigation to attempt to untangle in the course of his enquiries, and which even if he cannot, are nonetheless enriching his sense of the unknown author's character.

It is well known that there is often a perceptible void in our lives, one that separates the expectations or hopes of one day and the fears and material realities of another, and this is the feeling that gives rise to such a platitude as that which states that things do not always turn out the way you had them planned. Flynn is not a person for whom this futilitarian sentiment runs particularly deep, such has been the nature of his untested time so far on earth and the inborn or so-called natural features of his temperament, but the unknown author in his writing appears to be extremely well-acquainted with this specified despondent sense, this mental and emotional dissonance, and as might be expected, the unknown author is outraged, and even disgusted at the very idea of entertaining the possibility. Reading the ramblings of the unknown author, Flynn has resolved to go back to the library tonight, once more under the cover of darkness, in order to see whether ThomPayne has been spending more time writing on the web pages of *The Correspondent* today and to see which news articles and commentaries are currently sparking ThomPayne's interest. Flynn also intends to try to establish an identity of his own, and if he does not do this with a view to joining political debates with all guns blazing, at least he will have begun the long and difficult task of marking his territory. If the unknown author were to happen upon one of Flynn's comments, we might interject, perhaps he will see that Flynn also has an identity and conative world of his own, one which he almost certainly has the need to bring into closer contact with others, or at least to pull them into the orbit of his words, ideas and spheres of feeling.

Waiting for darkness to fall once again, Flynn re-reads a section of the book where the unknown author suddenly talks about onions, which is also consistent with a remark that Flynn found on the threads:

'Onions have to do with the centre of things,'

says ThomPayne, and,

'Peeling an onion can seem a little like strain-ing to find your way to the centre of a labyrinth, as anybody would know had they ever been forced to

work in a kitchen,
peeling onions non-
stop and for hours at a
time.'

According to the book, the unknown author once worked
in such a place where he would be given 'a vast and
mouldering sack of those abominable things', and would
spend his working day grimly tearing through the skins and
the epidermal layers and strings, with a sharp cutting knife
over a stained plastic chopping board, with his perspiring
head bowed low, running great sweating chunks of these
vegetables through the blades of a steel chopping machine
of industrial-scale dimensions and power, 'at all times in
the most unbearable heat and working conditions
thinkable.' His hatred of all forms of work and
management structures stems from this time, he says ('I
was still a child when first exposed to it'), and he found
such experience not just hot and uncomfortable but also,
'tedium beyond all description. David Copperfield, with no
redeeming narrative provided.' He says that this work
'caused my eyes to stream all day long, from peering into
the soul of the chopper', in order to 'dig out asymmetrical
segments of onions whenever the blades got jammed up,
which obviously they always did constantly, and for no apparent
rhyme or reason.' Even after stringent nightly ablutions
and applications of moisturiser and cologne to his hands
and person, 'my fingers and clothing would stink to high

heaven all through the night, making sleep impossible, therefore exhausting me physically and mentally even more than I would have been anyway,' and he says that as he was chopping them, 'the onion juices would acquaint me with all the paper cuts and scratches on my hands I didn't know were there,' stinging them, 'perpetually', leaving his hands chapped, 'raw as a pulp of exposed nerve endings.' The main thing that the unknown author thinks his performances in this limelight did for him, why he mentions it again and again in the threads, and the reason he now, with the benefit of hindsight, 'happens to respect onions more than possibly any other form of vegetation or life-form', what he considers to be, 'more or less, their grand evolutionary significance and purpose', is that for all their weight and apparent insubstantiality, for all the tears and sourness and the hours of pointless servitude that being employed to chop them elicits ('endured the world over by people whose lot in life is only ever to chop onions for survival') and, immortally, 'only ever dreaming of promotion to mushrooms', onions chopped to go in the quiches and the stews or the soups, stroganoffs and salads eaten by anonymous others, an onion is nonetheless ultimately the most peculiarly and intriguingly delicate of mysteries. 'You peel away at an onion,' he writes, layer after layer, hour after hour, day after day, '*onion after onion*', with the eventual realisation that 'you never once find anything in the middle when you eventually get there.' The onion, he therefore concludes from these experiences has '*philosophical* significance', it simply disintegrates, disappears and collapses into piles of unbelievable wreckage, leaving behind not a smile or some kind of *sine qua non* but a useless and ghastly mess ('Oh! how we onion choppers longed to find a pearl one day, buried somewhere within that hideousness!'). If there is a God or creative being, and the unknown author says he has no good reason to suppose there to be such a universal providence or controlling intelligence, if there were a God, 'He could not have designed a better or more eloquently apposite metaphor', nor could He have been '*a more elaborately malicious comedian*' in the design of things in His creation, and all of what they might be thought to stand for. After all, if for one second you think of the onion 'as metaphor for this world of ours,' and 'our violent, contrarian place within it', you are forced to conclude that 'there's nothing substantial to the illusion, nothing to find in the middle, and further that the onion, *like this confounded blue orb itself*, compels you to weep bitterly.' If there were a God, the unknown author would think, He must have designed onions as a potent symbol for His work, and what better symbol could He have devised? 'Why didn't the snake tempt Eve with an onion?' he asks. The trusty apple, with all the stout robustness of its central core, 'has all kinds of other metaphorical connotations', which he is '*perfectly content to acknowledge*', but he thinks that these associations are 'misleading in implication, totally inaccurate', and also, 'there are as many different ways of thinking as there are mountains and fields full of onions.' The factory where he worked, says the unknown author, was right next door to an enormous brewery, every Tuesday the brewers would add the hops to the latest batch of chemical ingredients for lagers and ales he says, and the entire town would stink, 'like a dog's breakfast, a ghastly festering smell', which would linger until the following week, 'when as soon as the air was bearable, the entire process would start all over again.' It is this *'intolerable breathing atmosphere'* that explains for him the reason why the people in that town are 'taken in such an advanced and incurably continual state of drunkenness', they do it 'in order to escape the stench', he writes, and also, 'to escape the oppressiveness of *olfactory persecution.'* He of all people can understand this, says the unknown author ('I too have been drinking all evening'). The brewery workers had for all intents and purposes, 'a limitless supply of strong alcohol' with which to tank themselves up at work; in order to pass the time ('which by all accounts dripped with monotony'), they would play 'desperate and increasingly extreme drinking games', hide-and-go-seek or sardines, he writes, 'they would clamber inside the machines at night and use them as hiding places', where because of the brewery's size and unsuitability for such activities, 'they would sometimes fall asleep in the machines and be forgotten.' When someone turned these machines on again, workers would still be in the sleep of the righteous within, they would be 'ground up or boiled, therefore killed.' Many men lost their lives in this fashion, according to the unknown author, 'gratefully, without protest', a placid and stoical reaction that he thinks was:

'Perfectly natural. Entirely to be expected!'

The unknown author says he is 'a person of extremes (a *person of feeling!*)' and he says that although his brain is 'weak, and a shameless plagiarist', it is also capable of producing 'loud noises of unbelievably poor quality.' 'My amps themselves,' he continues, the amps through which 'these awful feedback loops' are fed, the amps themselves, 'go way past eleven *and all the way around.*' He says he is incapable of the drive and determination to fight his way out of whatever hole it is that he has got himself into, because 'the inevitable certainty of failure and the misery that would follow would crush me yet further.' His brain, he says, is 'like a loaded gun or pregnant stomach,' filled with the *'inevitable certainty of death'*, and although he is calm and anodyne on the surface when he is at work, and gives nothing of himself away for people to feed upon when he is out and about ('*If my thought dreams could be seen*, as Dylan says, *people would drop dead in horror if they knew what really goes on in them*'), he finds that everywhere he has ever lived, he has been always felt or been considered 'a circus freak, an internal cripple, *structural human waste*', because of his intransigent commitment to his ideas and principles, 'my genotypically conscribed aversion to nonsense', he says, 'even though everything I do is transparently nonsensical.' Finally, 'I dislike myself immensely. And the people I do like and admire seem to dislike me even more than I do myself, which may account for why I like them.' But he knows something that they do not, says the unknown author – 'the truth that everything fails in the end.' When he feels rejected and particularly low, 'I proceed from the assumption that the sun will one day burn itself out and all life will be extinguished. In death, we are equal and we are not equal', because he thinks that 'once tumbling in the void, even equality has no meaning.' When he is awake, he writes, 'I inevitably feel terrible', finding that 'the only solution to it is to listen for the rattle of the bones', quoting Eliot, and respond to it with *'demented and histrionic laughter.'*

Flynn pauses and turns again to look out of his window. He leans to the radio and switches it to the classical music station, the swirling sound of the Schumann C Major *Fantasie* greeting his ears, which is ironic, because it suits our purpose perfectly. He turns again to the book in front of him and reads again a longer passage concerning the unknown author's view of music.

Something to say for the sake of saying it is that a singing melodic line should be like the sea. As Basil Bunting put it in *Brigflatts:*

"A strong song tows
us, long ear-sick
Blind, we follow.
Rain slant, spray flick
to fields we do not know."

A melody gathers momentum and comes in, it breaks on the shore. But crucially – like the sea – it also pulls away at the right point, with a regular rhythm. There are monsters under the surface of that water and things which float up from beneath – and maybe you can find a treasure or two, down beneath those waves. But it needs relative calm and silence – or more probably solitude – for those thoughts to breach the surface of your conscious mind.

Flynn listens to the Schumann and reads through these words again, the skittish threads of sound of the first movement registering in his ears and soul, and he ponders these intertextual swerves in the unknown author's writing where he suddenly reveals a peculiar and unexpected tenderness of spirit. He looks to the foolscap printed papers on the table, and finds in them the thread of the unknown author's views about aesthetic taste and subjectivity.

People always want to explain things in terms of something else. What happens when you do that is something quite interesting. It's not so much the like/dislike aspect – rather it's wanting others to understand why something, like a harmony or a cacophony or some structure of words initially appealed to us in the way we assimilated it to our view of things. When you enter the community of feeling, you get the sense that somebody understands you – or at least a little part of the way you see the world. When you do your best to explain to someone what you hear in Prokofiev's 8th Sonata, then the success of your criticism is whether or not I come to share the feeling and hear it in the way you do. Something like empathic thinking is what is at the heart of things like this. Imagining what it's like to be somebody else. I'd call it figurative imagining – having the imagination to view the world from multiple angles or revealed in different types of light. Possibly there are moral consequences...if you imagine yourself as someone else it can be a very good way of working out what obligations you might have towards them. My personal view, what strikes me when I am at my most solitary, is that when we try to inhabit another subjectivity and peer into its ontic horizon – whether it's in understanding which movies they like or understanding the music they write or whatever else – simply thinking of yourself as someone else – is to do the same mental tightrope act as grasping a metaphor, where additional stuff is carried that you hadn't ever thought of before. It's a version of colour-blindness or tone deafness when people are incapable of accessing those appearances, those narratives. It's an insensitivity to the power of phenomena. I turn my collar to the cold and damp at that point. Everybody wants to be heard and understood – when your situation reaches the point where you are no longer understood, where your life is over because of the insolences and absurdities of what surrounds you, that's the logical point when you are lost in Chinatown. That too is a metaphor for something else, and if you understand that, to misappropriate Wittgenstein, then you understand me. In the Polanski film *Chinatown*, the place of the title is someplace in which people fundamentally do not understand each other, and where the really bad things therefore happen. It's a place where you do as little as possible when you end up there, as the Nicholson character says twice, a town you do not go to, where you should not be.

*

Flynn waits once more for darkness to fall. He is not hungry, and he paces up and down the floor of his bedroom, the ideas forming, fermenting, and foaming in his mind, as the Schumann continues to whirl about him; this music, with its coded references to Clara and even Beethoven, and its ruins, trophies and palms, finds us moved to quote a translation of Friedrich Schlegel's words, the stanza of poetry which was placed at the head of the score of the *Fantasie* by poor Schumann himself, as an epigraph.

> Through all the notes
> In the world's many-coloured dream
> There echoes a soft stretched sound
> For the one who listens in secret.

Flynn does not know these words because he has never seen the score to this music even though he loves it dearly. As he waits in a state of nervous excitement and listens, and thinks, and the words of the unknown author continue to tumble over one another, playing hop-scotch and beating like drums within the cavity of his cranium, it seems to us now in our capacity as the torch-bearer through this maze, that these lines of Schlegel are a highly appropriate way in which to try to characterise what, at present, he is going through. If you can think of anything better, please feel free to consider that now; that was merely the best we could do, given the present circumstances.

Night falls on the city, and once more Flynn makes his way downstairs, clad in black, and if we linger in the flat a little and watch him from his high window for a few moments, we can see his tiny figure flitting darkly across the empty square in the moonlight. If we look more closely, we can see that almost all traces of blue have been hounded from the horizon of a Cimmerian sky; far below, Flynn checks quickly and stealthily to see whether anybody is looking, as if the human eye were in any way discerning enough in such circumstances and light conditions. And, once more, he goes back into the library to access the computer system, to look for further clues about the unknown author on the internet. Perhaps Flynn might begin to plant his own footsteps on this landscape in the hope that they too will somehow be traced, or that his being may emerge as a new and interesting feature of an ever-growing tapestry of lives. We do not get to choose what life offers to us in its pale palm, any more than we choose the people and voices that emerge before us; it is better put that sometimes these things discover us or reveal their light with the inevitability of a young morning sun. The choice has been made for Flynn that today he will not go to a concert, or go to the café to see the girl with the big eyes, or spend the night brooding, or planning a holiday. Rather he will once more slink into the National Library of Books and Publications to follow the thread that has been handed to him, to access once again the computer systems to search for ThomPayne, whilst everyone else is sleeping.

Flynn has disabled the alarm by the time we join him sitting at the computer terminal in the office, he has navigated himself to the pages of *The Correspondent*, and is looking for signs of new activity on the part of the unknown author. Indeed Flynn is not let down, ThomPayne has evidently been extremely busy in the writing sense: there are several new pages of writing which have been left recorded below the lines of newspaper articles, multiple new threads and lines of enquiry have been created and emerged during the time in which Flynn has been waiting for them and reading about onions. Now that Flynn has become familiar with the strange book and has worked his way through more of the printed written history of the unknown author's comments, Flynn feels as though he has brought himself up to speed, and that he is now far better placed to follow all new developments. Indeed, from the perspective of the threads comprising our own narrative, it will now be easier for Flynn to decide his next move; he has come a long way since he first discovered the book on the theology balcony. The unknown author is evidently in a foul mood when Flynn joins him, perhaps someone has upset ThomPayne during the day, because he fulminates against,

'...the

direness of working

as a **factotum**,'

The:

> '*...immoderate deprivations I endure* (in both a material and inter-personal sense,'
>
> (👍0 👎0)

privations which would be:

> '*...farcically funny, if my mind could stop racing, and I didn't have to be continually reminded of them.'*
>
> (👍2 👎0)

Flynn also sees that ThomPayne has been oppugning the '*unctuous thieves*' (the '*impertinent brigands*') of the National Library itself,

> '**worthless troglodytes**, who yes-terday managed to find and immediately lose a book of mine,'

(👍1 👎0)

(…instead of:

> 'establishing for it a category, *if necessary inventing a new one –*
>
> *sui generis,*
>
> somewhere in their **irresponsible head-fuck of a filing system.'**
> (👍0 👎0)
>
> …)

This book, according to ThomPayne, is a work 'neither of fiction nor non-fiction', and 'a message without a bottle'; a tract that he,

> *'left in there deliberately because I can't get it published,'* (👍1 👎0)

and,

> 'for no particularly good reason,'
> ('I did it to see what would happen,')
>
> (👍0 👎0)

especially in order to annoy and beguile them, especially to:

> 'set them the challenge of categorising **something that does not fit happily within a system**.' (👍1 👎0)

This volume he refers to as,

> 'my incunabulum, *my written exception to conventional literary rules.*' (👍1 👎0)

> '(I call it **The Diabolicon,** but nowhere within the manuscript or on any form

of paper is that title mentioned.)ʼ

This is one of the few books ever composed, he says, which cannot ('in principle', *'in esse',*) be found in their:

'terrifying brain-crash of a catalogue.ʼ

Flynn reads this most recent comment and once again feels a tingle of excitement run through his spine and spirit, the path of his own trajectory has now become intertwined yet more closely with that of the one who is the focus of his thinking and upon whom he has been directing so much of his attention, and it strikes him suddenly that the unknown author must have virtually crossed paths with him yesterday – that the unknown author who calls himself ThomPayne must have stood at the library reception and asked one or other of Flynn's colleagues whether a book had been handed in, only for a physical search to be carried out which resulted in perhaps,

No, I am sorry nothing like that seems to be here.

Or perhaps,

Yes, it was here the other day, but I'm not sure where it is now.

(*Or even:*

I'll ask the person who found it when they come back in.)

Flynn has with him a notebook in which he has written certain important points which emerged through the tangle of threads of writing which he printed off yesterday in the library, and he takes it out of his jacket pocket. He divests himself of his coat, hangs it over the back of his chair, and opens the notebook at the first page upon which he has written down references to things that the unknown author mentions in relation to social-networking websites and his tastes or peccadilloes, which in Flynn's mind constitute further clues to be researched. Flynn reaches for the telephone directory, and looks up the surname Payne, yet there is no Tom or Thomas Payne listed, it doesn't follow that ThomPayne is a false name from this fact alone, after all he may have chosen not to appear in the telephone book or not even have a telephone, or he may live with people listed under the name of the telephone account-holder, whose identities are in principle unknowable at this stage, given the limitations to the information at his disposal. Flynn types the name ThomPayne into a search engine and he scrolls through pages of results, there are many ThomPaynes and Tom Paynes in this world, and it occurs to Flynn to try alternative spellings Thom Paine, Thomas Pain, but nothing immediately stands out to him in the mass of data, the cricket player from Australia, the other sports professional, the business people and teenagers. Next, he tries to search for the name with a few key phrases, inevitably the phrase *in der Nacht sind alle Katzen grau*, which only yields for him the circular result of linking him back to the pages of *The Correspondent* where it appears, and hence to information he has already acquired. Flynn then performs the search on a variety of social and professional networking websites, and finds hundreds of Thomas Paynes and Tom Paines, but there is little by way of a clue to suggest which of them might constitute a lead or a new strand of enquiry with which to initiate new searches. He wonders whether the letters 'N.O.' of the book's cover stand for the true initials of the author, and whether ThomPayne is merely the pen name of someone else, a Neil, Nathan, Newland, Nick, Norbert, Noel, or Nimrod, an Olsen, Osbourne, Ostler, Owen, O'Doherty, Oswald, or Olds. He knows already that the possible permutations and combinations of names beginning with these letters is unfathomable, that guessing would be all but impossible, and we might wonder whether perhaps the unknown author does not want to be found.

Thinking further, he looks again through the notebook and remembers the comment, made on the pages of *The Correspondent* some years ago, which states that within the connections and workings of *Friendspoke*, his preferred social media service, there is the lead that the unknown author is, or was, a follower of the updates of a group calling itself the Anarchist Collective. Flynn returns his attention to *Friendspoke* and he searches for the Anarchist Collective's profile page; it may be worth saying in parenthesis that it is always rather surprising when anarchists bother to organise themselves like this, anyway, he finds a group dedicated to their principles, and which contains only around four hundred members. Flynn looks down this list of people for a Tommy Payne or Tomas Payen, or Thomas Paine; finding nothing, he looks for somebody with the initials 'N.O.' – a Norbert Omen, a Norris Oiler, a *Noddy Obama*. Instead he finds nothing but a cascade of countless other unidentified and possibly fictitious people, on reflection *unidentified* may not be strictly the right word to use there, since he knows what these people call themselves, and even *fictitious* may, in the wider context in which we are dwelling, be somewhat misleading. Instead of thinking about that, however, Flynn is speculating whether perhaps the unknown author simply no longer follows or takes an interest in the material that these anarchists produce, even whether the unknown author is no longer a user of *Friendspoke* services at all, but Flynn prints the list of names anyway, and places it next to the computer, thinking perhaps that he will begin the painstaking process of looking up each of these four hundred individuals, one at a time. Bartleby Flynn looks back to the notebook and sees the name of the film *Angels with Filthy Hearts*, a movie which as we saw, the unknown author unreservedly approves. He has the idea of looking for a fan page of this movie within the *Friendspoke* site, once more with a view to retrieving a list of the people who have signified that this is a film which they rank amongst their favourites. There is no Thomas Payne, no person with the initials N.O. on this list either, although there are fewer results than the one for Anarchist Collective, perhaps twenty or so for the movie, and once again Flynn prints the list; his evidence assembled, he begins to cross-refer these names with the earlier list to see whether they have any names in common. He looks at each name on the shorter list, and then across to the longer list, crossing out any names that fail to appear on one but not the other, as he comes to them. Near the bottom of the list of people who like the film is the name Barnaby Totten, and Flynn is a little surprised to notice that the name also appears on the longer list, the list of people who are interested in receiving disseminations of ideology, or otherwise wish to follow the updates of the political group known as the Anarchist Collective. He looks closely at the photograph next to the name Barnaby Totten, but there is hardly anything to see. It is a tiny black and white picture of somebody standing with their face turned partially away, who appears no more than an outline etched against a backdrop of dazzling city lights. Flynn attempts to open up the page belonging to Barnaby Totten to find it comprehensively sealed for privacy, without any option whatsoever for members of the *Friendspoke* community not linked to Barnaby Totten personally, to send him a private message directly or attempt to initiate some kind of communication.

It is at precisely this point that Flynn hears a sudden noise come from the central rotunda, the sound of the front door being opened, and he hears footsteps echoing rhythmically through the hall. He switches off the computer monitor immediately and darts behind the door, peering through a crack as a figure walks past the office and continues down along the corridor. Now Flynn hears the footsteps suddenly stop; there is a pause, and then we hear the sound of them re-approaching the office. Someone looks around the door, perhaps hearing the sound of the fan of the computer which has been left switched on, and he enters the musty little room and walks over to the machine. Flynn presses himself further against the wall, his breath still held, and he watches as this other nocturnal visitor switches on the monitor and initiates the shutdown process of the machine; will the information that is still on the screen be noticed, or will this person simply switch the monitor off again and move on? He doesn't pause or seem to take any interest in the information that is on there, he simply shuts off the monitor and leaves the room, walking briskly down the passageway. Flynn hears the footsteps click-clipping down the hall and finally breathes free, he is unsure whether the presence who entered the room is the Lurker or some other keyholder or perhaps somebody else entirely, although it then strikes him that whoever it was, they were very likely a library employee as opposed to a random intruder, given the interest that they took in turning off the computer which was still running. Flynn peers around the doorway and sees that a light is now shining from one of the rooms further down the hall, and realises that he must decide whether to make a run for it and escape from the library at pace, or alternatively slip into the central rotunda and walk in the opposite direction of the front door and retreat deeper into the library through the long line of reading halls that extend backwards from it. Flynn finally has the courage to move, it's now or never, and he thinks of the silent moon as he makes his way stealthily along the corridor on tiptoes, towards the side-entrance and the deafening silence of the main rotunda. Feeling suddenly lost and trapped and incredibly small under the weight of all that emptiness, we always feel dwarfed and somehow supplicant by redundant space, be it the sky domes of shopping malls, high-vaulted churches or even cinemas. He momentarily freezes in the middle of the floor, wondering whether to turn left or right, towards the way out and the city or towards the darker interior of the library. A tiny sliver of light is visible from the door to the corridor from which he has just emerged, the light from the office that the stranger switched on suddenly goes out without warning. Flynn darts behind a bookshelf and hears the same regular footsteps making their way back along the corridor towards the central rotunda where Flynn is now hiding. Flynn realises that he has left his notebook next to the computer in his haste to avoid being caught, and he peers around the edge of the bookcase to see the dark figure making his way towards the front door again and carrying a briefcase. He unlocks it, activates the alarm, and dissolves outside and into the night.

Flynn stands frozen to the spot, listening to the beep as the alarm activates itself, terrified whether the front door will open again, perhaps whoever it was might have forgotten something, we could all do that; suddenly he realises that if he makes a move, the motion sensors will detect him and initiate a forty-five second countdown before all hell breaks loose and the alarm starts howling into the night, thereby telling the police and anybody nearby that the library has an intruder, so-called *persona non grata* skulking within its walls. Flynn hears the bells of the cathedral chiming the midnight hour, and he is suddenly emboldened by this cacophony, which seems to him to be masking the sound of his thumping heart, the gaze of the books and his shallow breathing. The bells overpower the sound of the alarm's arming procedure, therefore seeming for a moment to disguise his unauthorised presence and his very existence within the building. He sprints across the central rotunda and once more disables the alarm, its pips steadily increasing in intensity during the forty-five seconds he has to enter the code. Having disabled the alarm, Flynn dashes back to the office where he was conducting his enquiries in order to retrieve his notebook, and upon reaching the computer once more stands there as a slow wash of further horror dissolves over him when he sees that the notebook is no longer where he left it on the desk. Flynn looks under the table, under piles of paper, but the notebook is nowhere to be found, and he is forced to conclude that whoever it was who came into the library so late in the night and switched off the computer must have seen the notebook, wondered why it was there, lying open next to a running computer, and taken it away for further investigation or locked it somewhere, perhaps to give to the Chief Librarian to investigate personally.

Flynn feels a wave of nausea come over him, I am into this far too deeply, he thinks, what will happen tomorrow when I come into work? Will the Chief Librarian call a meeting in the morning and gather the staff together to say, 'There was an intrusion into the library overnight, nothing was taken, but it appears a computer was accessed and this notebook left behind,' as he holds up the exhibit in the air for all to see? How will Flynn comport himself in such a scene, since although the notebook does not contain Flynn's name, every word is in Flynn's handwriting? Will the Chief Librarian then demand to see samples of everybody's handwriting, in order to ascertain whether he can find the match or compare it to written records, or will he state that he wonders how it was that the security system did not pick up the intrusion, the intruder must have therefore been a person familiar with the entry system, and Flynn's mind turns now to the realisation that the stranger who entered the library will also have wondered why the alarm was switched off, did he perhaps set it once again in the belief that the intruder was still in the library, is he now waiting outside to see if anybody emerges, or is he speaking on the telephone already with the police and asking them to come and perform a sweep of the library?

Flynn is paralysed and he waits for half an hour, pacing up and down inside the office like a caged animal, wondering what he should do next. Should he wait all night in the library and attempt to sneak out tomorrow, or will the police arrive and find him hiding somewhere, or should he open the front door, set the alarm and attempt to sneak out only to find himself clobbered by a team of commandos, waiting for that very moment, or is the mysterious stranger sitting in his car, parked discreetly on the far side of the square and invisibly waiting to see who it is that emerges? It occurs to Flynn that he cannot solve these puzzles in a way that is wholly satisfying or with the relief that certainty brings, nor is he in a position to come up with a definitively correct course of action, and eventually he feels himself becoming tired and exhausted with the weight of such mighty considerations tumbling over one another in his mind. I must report to work tomorrow as normal, he thinks. If I have another day of peculiar episodes they will have rumbled me for good, they will know I have been up to something, he thinks, I have to make everything seem perfectly regular, as if I am unaware of any of this when I first come in, and pull down the lever on the machine which punches my timecard. He is standing by the front door of the library, and all of a sudden he is punching the numbers back into the alarm panel and the alarm is armed, his decision has been made for him, and he opens the door and goes outside into cold air. He pulls the door shut again and fumbles with the key to get it locked as quickly as possible, he now has his back to anybody who might be approaching and about to put a firm hand on the shoulder:

What do you think you're doing?

I think you'd better come with us, sir.

(Or, *What time do you close?*)

He drops the keys to the floor, feeling he has been caught naked in the giant square in front of an enormous unseen audience, all those darkened windows like eyes scrutinising my every action he thinks, feeling acutely that somebody could easily be watching him and that he is therefore at a considerable disadvantage. No hand seizes his shoulder, when he turns towards open territory, he is not surrounded by a team of squad cars, and no helicopter appears suddenly from the sky to capture him guiltily holding up a hand to protect himself in the wind and glare, caught in a spotlight as a voice over a loudhailer screams out above the din and dust of the rotors:

You there! Put your hands in the air where I can see them and stay where you are.

Instead, Flynn turns and the square is silent, save for the odd howl of traffic from somewhere in the city and a distant siren. The bars and cafés are closed, and there are only a few empty-looking parked cars lining the roads which surround the quadrangle. Flynn determines to stay away from these, lest he unwittingly be seen by anybody who might be sitting silently in one of them, and he walks away from the library and does not proceed directly to his house. Rather, he takes a circuitous route which leads him down side-streets and along the alleys that run behind the terrace of buildings in which his flat is situated, and as he turns off the square, no headlights come on in one of the stationary cars, no vehicle slowly pulls out, to follow him with some kind of unhurried and sinister purposiveness. Flynn walks the back streets for fifteen minutes, and re-emerges at the other end of the square through an alleyway; he is now facing the library and walks as casually as a man dressed up all in black like a cat burglar can get away with, over to the front door of his building and lets himself inside.

8

A WRITER, ACCORDING TO the book of the unknown author, should think of himself when he is writing as:

> 'A hit-man; a cold-blooded killer who comes in the night.'

He tries to inhabit this role himself, he says, in his comments about politics, and culture and so forth; he holds the view that anybody with the least aptitude for metaphor – (a capacity which 'leads the brain to conceive and assimilate new semantic possibilities at light-speed', and also, 'immediately, in a way which should fizzle and explode like fireworks between my synapses') – anybody with this potential within themselves should be able to see immediately that

> '...the reader,'

(according to the unknown author's metaphorical logic,)

> '...must be the victim in the cross-
> hairs of the telescope, the
> unsuspecting target in the flight-path
> of the assassin's bullet.'

Critics and intellectuals, by the same token, are the mortuary assistants or coroners, he suggests. They chop, frown and diagnose; they investigate organs for signs of latent illness.

> *'They look for the cause of death.'*

Flynn's dreams are uneasy and he awakes several times during the night, gets out of bed and goes to the sink to drink a glass of water, before getting back under the covers in order to listen to the clock ticking in the dark. The unknown author says he is waiting for the arrival of:

> 'an inverted Novalis – I want to witness the
> veil of order shimmering through all this
> chaos',

just as much as he admires this idea the way it was put originally (*'chaos shimmering through the veil of order'*, thus Novalis), a maxim which the unknown author believes is an epoch-defying one in its permutations, a statement which describes 'simply everything of value.' These words and ideas, Flynn thinks, they are bouncing in all directions within my head; and at the back of his mind also lurks the dread of what he will face when he arrives at work tomorrow morning, whether the unauthorised access of the library has been reported, and is in the process of being investigated by the powers that be. It is around six, and with heavy eyes, with the lethargy and the queasiness that attend broken sleep boiling and churning within him, Flynn decides he will certainly not doze now and therefore decides to go out early, perhaps sit for a while in the café and eat a hearty breakfast, or wait a little while on a bench before going into the library, and trying to battle through the day ahead. He showers, he shaves, he sees his own pale face staring back under the whiteness of the foam. He dresses, he makes the bed, trudges down the stairs, a little light-headed and with weak aching legs.

Outside, the air is gelid with a forenoon dampness that aches in Flynn's nose and makes his bones feel porous or as though they were made of porcelain. He hears the cries of a querulous jackdaw somewhere within the cypress trees, and is immediately aware all over again of his lack of sleep, in the way that we always are when trying to confront the early morning, after a restless night, we try to deceive ourselves that the act of washing can somehow sponge away the insomnia, expunge the queasy jangle from our nerves in the hope of leaving us feeling as normal as we would do, had we spent the night sleeping soundly and easily within our dreams. This nausea gathers itself apace into something that feels like a fist, punching at the walls of his stomach, a monster trying to get out, and Flynn walks to the café and orders a cup of coffee and a plate of thick toast. He is the only one in there at this early hour, save for the girl with the large eyes, she looks so fresh and rested this morning thinks Flynn, she probably only awoke half an hour ago, and it has not escaped her attention how haggard and careworn Flynn looks today, how he arrives earlier than usual and seems distracted when he takes his change. If we look at her face closely, it appears as though she wants to ask him if things are quite alright. Yet she does not do so, perhaps in order not to be seen to breach the shell around Flynn, perhaps because it would not be quite the done thing in such a relationship as this, or perhaps because she is simply too nervous to ask. Flynn on the other hand is becoming slowly and ominously aware of a world that is waking up to its own youthful wildness in the early morning light; it strikes him suddenly how young morning light has usually yawned and stretched and bounded from the house, long before we ourselves walk into it. Today, it is Flynn who got out first, and he watches as the buses, the deliveries, the men and women, seem to follow the emergence of the light, dragging with them their burdens, and filling the world with their energies and echoes, their songs and screams.

Having walked through a deserted square to the café, he sees increasing numbers of people emerge from different directions and in double-file, maybe they have come into town on underground trains, or shared lifts, or ridden bicycles, maybe they are rapists or the unknown author, or perhaps like Flynn they have emerged from the apartments where they live behind closed curtains, and slipped out unnoticed into the humdrum human stream. Fatigued Flynn finishes his breakfast, and decides that it is time he faced whatever music it is that awaits him in the library; he walks from the café, and even though the high sun is now shining bright and harshly upon him, it seems to give out no comfort, no warmth, rather it is simply laying bare and exposing for him the tightness of his newly shaved skin in the cold, and the bilious and somnambulant feeling which his breakfast has not shifted, the soreness of his eyes, the dryness in his throat, as if all the power with which our indispensable star sustains us, has been suddenly withdrawn and focussed elsewhere, simply gathered up and bottled, or sealed away in a jar.

Flynn walks into the building, and he sees that a few of his colleagues have already arrived, there is nothing unusual so far in the way that they are behaving, though his nerves are almost as frayed and tattered as they were when he was standing with his breath held behind the mysterious stranger last night. He goes to the cloakroom and takes off his long winter overcoat; next he puts his head around the door of the break-room, says hello to the librarian who has the artificial voice-box, and who is sitting reading *The Correspondent*. He walks out onto the floor of the central rotunda, and stands behind the reception desk where there is a pile of books which need to be taken back to the stacks.

What happened to that book you found that was down here the other day?, asks one of the librarians, a man with a devilish little goatee and a crooked nose, and who is sometimes known as The Shirker, on account of the fact that he will often disappear into the stacks for hours at a time, and presumably hide down there, whenever there is a lot to be done. Flynn replies airily, without looking up from what he is doing, that he does not know where it went.

Is it not down there? Why do you ask?

The Lurker was asking about it on Saturday morning.

What was he asking?

He wanted to know where it is.

Any idea why?

I think someone came in for it.

Did you see how they were?

No, I didn't. What a strange question.

Flynn considers this new development; should he now pay a visit to the Deputy Chief Librarian, or more properly, should he simply remain where he is and wait for the Lurker to appear inevitably, in a puff of smoke out of nowhere, and ask him:

I hear you were looking for the book that was left behind.

Yes, do you know where it went, Flynn?

Was somebody looking for it?

Yes they came in and asked about it on your day off.

Did you see what they looked like?

Yes, I imagine we did. What's the relevance?

Just curious.

Never mind that, how about giving me a straight answer?

I haven't seen it since the other day.

Well keep an eye out. What would people think of us if they thought we lost the lost property?

They might think all kinds of things.

Quite right. *And we don't want them doing that.*

Or, should Flynn act as though he knows nothing at all about the fact that the unknown author, who may or may not be named Barnaby Totten, had at some point on Saturday morning asked a library staff member for the return of his book, indeed that someone had physically walked up to the very same reception desk that we are floating above, and made the enquiry?

It is while this is going on in his mind that the Chief Librarian sends a message by way of the Lurker that he wishes to see all the people currently at work who are keyholders. Flynn follows the Lurker up the stairs and along the topmost gallery of the central rotunda towards the Chief Librarian's office; the Lurker knocks on the door before opening it, knock knock, '*Come in.*'

The Lurker turns the handle and holds the door open, watching Flynn's face closely as he passes; once Flynn has entered, he closes the door again and follows inside. The Chief Librarian's office, handsome though it may look, is a dry and airless place once you get up there, thick with stale breath, old coffee and either mildew or the contents of his lunchbox, it is hard to tell a difference. Flynn stands before the desk slightly awkwardly.

You wanted to see me?

Ah yes, have a seat Flynn.

The Chief Librarian gestures to one of the chairs in front of his desk, and the Lurker makes his way over to the lawn-green leather settee which lines the window overlooking the central rotunda, and sits down wordlessly. The Chief Librarian removes his reading glasses, closes them, and looks straight at Flynn:

We had a *troubling incident* over the weekend, he says; and Flynn wonders whether he is referring to the disappearance of the book of the unknown author, or to the intrusion, or to something else entirely. Then, he muses whether anybody has made a so-called leap of thought at this point, and proposed that the unauthorised access and the disappearance of the book might in fact be somehow connected. Flynn rejects this conclusion as somewhat unlikely, given what he knows about the way things are run, but he has noticed that the Chief Librarian has before him the notebook which, as we know, Flynn left in the office last night. Flynn's eyes have registered it with the barest of perceptible flickers, and he continues to look into the face of the man sitting before him, in the most oblivious and innocent way that he can:

Oh dear, what happened?

An intrusion. Someone entered the library and appears to have used a computer.

An intrusion, says Flynn, trying to keep calm. How could that have happened? Somebody would need to have a key and know the alarm code?

We know all that, says the Deputy Chief Librarian, putting down his pen. This is why we are asking.

Was anything taken?

It wouldn't appear so, but we are asking each of the keyholders what they know.

Flynn can feel the hot stare of the Lurker boring into him from behind, but he does not turn around. There is a pause, and Flynn notices the Chief Librarian's eyes move ever so slightly to his right, as though he is exchanging a glace with the Deputy.

Any ideas, Flynn? After all you live across the square. See anything unusual?

I wasn't at home last night.

We didn't say this happened last night, says the Lurker immediately; and once more Flynn notes the slight shift in the position and tone of the Chief Librarian's gaze.

What we are asking, continues the Lurker, is whether you are aware of anything suspicious going on. Whether you have heard any chatter. You know, *amongst the troops?*

Flynn stares into the Chief Librarian's face with a look of the purest despair that he is not quite able to disguise, studying and staring at the features as though this face were the last remaining life-raft, floating in a heavy sea.

Not in the least, everything normal. I left work on Friday, I was off on the Saturday, and yesterday I travelled to visit a friend. I got back to town rather late, around midnight.

And then, nonchalantly:

So, what time did the intrusion occur?

(Aha! Flynn is learning.)

We think it was at around ten thirty, judging by the logs of the security alarm. The Deputy Chief Librarian had to come into the library last night on another matter, and found this.

The Chief Librarian gestures towards the notebook, and Flynn allows himself to acknowledge it at last.

You found a notebook?

In an office.

What's in it?

All sorts. Mad as a bag of cats if you ask me. Can't make head nor tail of it.

Do you recognise the writing?

No, and the chap who wrote it looks like he might have a screw loose too.

It could have been a woman.

Well, that's the truth.

It couldn't possibly have been me. As I said, I was out of the city.

Of course, I'm sure that you have your alibi, and quite frankly you are not really a suspect. But what we need you to do is to keep your eyes skinned. Stay sharp. And I do not need to remind you that the keyholder status is a privilege which can be revoked at any time. So, and I am saying this to everybody, if you see anything at all suspicious, or hear something…round the campfire, we trust you will do the right thing.

You can count on me.

I'm sure we can.

How's your wife?

Funnily enough, she's taken up golfing.

At her age?

What are you implying?

Forgive me, that came out wrong.

You're a funny sort.

It's what I've been reading.

And what would that be?

Oh, this and that. Is that all?

Yes, well quite. *A-ha.* Mmm, right. Carry on then, Flynn. You can go back to whatever it was you were doing.

The Lurker gets up, as if to usher Flynn from the office, and the Chief Librarian puts his reading glasses back onto their perch at the end of his nose, and begins looking back at the papers on his desk; Flynn can see the tiny movements of his fountain pen as they follow the lines of whatever it was he was reading, the occasional flourish, as the Chief Librarian writes his notes, somewhere in a margin. Flynn takes the cue, stands up and he is escorted to the door by the Deputy. As he is leaving, the Lurker tells him to send up the Shirker.

Flynn does as he has been instructed and passes on the message, and goes immediately to the computer to look at the web pages of *The Correspondent* and the profile of ThomPayne, who seems to be named Barnaby Totten in his civilian life, if Flynn's detective work is anything to go by, and we can read this person's views on employment.

For the past ten years I have felt as though my overlords have been farming me like a piece of livestock. Any mediocrity with the right connections, the right kind of gormless smile can make it to safety, and the idea that hard work and dreams and aspirational thinking are the difference between people who drown and people who stay afloat and get to have conspicuous holidays is pure mythology. The reality is that the harder you try to clamber onto the lifeboat, the more these people will bite your knuckles, stamp on your finger ends or try and unpick them one by one from the rot of the rim, the lifeboats are full, and they could not care less if they see your face sinking slowly and vanishing beneath the waves. And even if the puppet masters, the ones who hold all the strings, are not meeting in basements or smoky backrooms, drawing up the plans to keep their kind where they are by the ruthless purchase of political power or loyalty, they still look shifty. I don't trust them.

(👍21 👎1)

Throughout the day, Flynn goes back and forth between the reading rooms, the Classification Room, and the central rotunda; back and forth between the stacks and the computer room, and when he thinks no one is looking he takes a brief glimpse at ThomPayne's page to see whether any further comments, and comments about comments, have been added. Flynn finds nothing, and once more the Deputy Chief Librarian asks about the intrusion last night, he has it on the brain, might he perhaps have given the alarm code to another employee, or written it down and left it lying around carelessly. This Flynn denies, just as he denies all knowledge of the missing book, and which somebody came to try to retrieve on Saturday morning.

The Deputy Chief Librarian is standing at the front desk, his briefcase with him, which is open. Flynn walks over and clearly notices in the open bag the notebook from last night sitting next to the Deputy Chief Librarian's lunchbox; for once the Lurker has himself been lurked, so to speak, and Flynn watches as he proceeds to put on top of it a sheaf of reports he has just pulled from the reception's printer. The Lurker closes his briefcase, announcing that he is off out to pick up some ingredient for the Chief Librarian's lunch, perhaps some raisins, some granola, a four-bean salad, or something organic, he tells them that he will be back in twenty minutes or so; can everyone hold the fort until he returns, 'The Chief Librarian does not want to be disturbed', since Monday (as everyone knows) is always busy, and in any case and as we all have felt, it is also the most difficult as well as the most wretched day of the week. The Lurker has left his briefcase on the floor behind the reception desk and Flynn looks at it, wondering how to retrieve the notebook that contains an undeniable record of his handwriting, if he can get at the thing and make it disappear, then that will be one less incriminating item of evidence for him to worry about. Flynn cannot very well simply open this under the very noses of his colleagues, start rooting and rummaging, extract the notebook in the hope that nobody will notice his furtive ways. A spot of good fortune is about to come Flynn's way, the Chief Librarian is hungry and for the past few minutes has been wandering around the reception area like a lost child. Suddenly, he picks up the Deputy Chief Librarian's briefcase somewhat gingerly as if he fears it might explode, or that he is implicated in something nefarious by the simple act of picking up another person's property, and Flynn watches him take it across the central rotunda towards the side door. Flynn calmly drops what he is doing, and, glancing at the front door, he follows the Chief Librarian down the corridor towards the break-room; he turns and walks in the opposite direction the moment he sees the Chief walk out again with empty hands. When the coast is clear, Flynn proceeds towards the door and sees that the Lurker's briefcase has been placed squarely on the break-room table, ripe for the taking, things could not have transpired more perfectly if we were trying. He strides in, closes the door behind him, locks it, and tries to open the briefcase; the left lock springs up but the right one will not open, it must have the wrong combination number. He pushes up the middle dial of the lock which is half way between the seven and the eight, still it will not open, and so he pushes it down again to the numeral below, and this time the right hand lock opens too, he lifts the lid and pulls out the notebook, stuffing it as he had with *The Book of the Unknown Author* into his trousers. He closes the briefcase, pushes the clasps shut and returns the combination to the position he found it in, he unlocks the door of the break-room and walks out into the empty corridor, grabbing a trolley of books bound for the old chapel and where, as we know, the theology balcony hangs serene above the shelves and tables.

There is more to the life of a librarian than simply putting things back on shelves and taking them off again, thinks Flynn whilst he wheels the trolley, as we saw from the last incident which involved a book being stuffed down his trousers, this time he has the volume in question lodged firmly against his stomach, pressed against the trolley so there is no way that it can slip out down his trouser leg and onto the floor, in front of an onlooker, who would no doubt immediately wonder why on earth Flynn has such a thing as a notebook down there, and undoubtedly mention the matter to somebody else, at some future point. Should this catastrophe obtain, it will surely get back to the Chief Librarian eventually that this is what Flynn has been doing, which is precisely what we want him to avoid; if he is not careful here, we might add, it is in the nature of things that this is precisely the kind of disaster that could so easily happen. He wheels the trolley along the passage that winds past reading rooms to the chapel, and he parks it at the bottom of the stairway to heaven; it could quite easily be described as the stairway to hell once you look at it from the perspective of being at the top now we think of it, and he picks up a pile of books that belong there, and ascends the metal steps, pausing and looking from left to right as his head emerges through the hole in the floor. Seeing that the balcony is empty, he puts the pile of books down on the ragged, threadbare carpet which has been laid over the old black floorboards.

Flynn looks over the edge and down into the reading room, and sees the bright beams of sunlight scattered in different directions through the stained glass, they seem to hold clinquant particles of dust hovering in the air, as though the light contained them somehow in a tangelo mist. He sees another librarian below him facing the opposite wall, arranging books on the low shelving that runs under the stained glass window, he sees the heads of people in the reading room bowed over the books they are studying, and he turns towards the ladder to place the books he has carried back onto the huge shelving unit that has been constructed where the organ pipes used to be. He reaches for the notebook that he has lodged in his trousers and quietly pulls out the pages that are in his handwriting, he places these pages on a shelf and lays the notebook on the very top of the shelving unit which is covered in a thick coating of the dusts of time. He replaces the library books where they belong with one hand and furtively pushes the edge of the notebook further and further towards the back of the top shelf and feels it disappear over the edge, where it falls and lands on the stone sill of an old window which has long been bricked up and painted over. He descends the ladder with the pages he has torn out from the notebook, and once he has reached the floor of the balcony he folds them carefully in half. He descends the stairway to hell with the folded pages in his front pocket, walks back through the library towards the little room which contains a photocopier and a shredding machine, and seeing it empty, he takes out the folded pages and rapidly runs them through the blades of the shredder which consume the paper authoritatively, they are gone in an instant.

*

Flynn is surprised at how calm he has felt throughout this entire mission, and he can't help feeling a little amused at a thought he has of the Deputy Chief Librarian: perhaps the Lurker will pick up his bag and take it into his office, adjust the combination, open the lid and look under the piles of paper, under the lunchbox and run the flat of his hand through the document compartment fixed to the inner lid, ransacking his way through the briefcase, looking for the notebook, only to find it no longer there. Perhaps the Deputy Chief Librarian, piqued and perplexed at the disappearance of a prime piece of evidence, and furthermore surprised at such skulduggery as this which has brought his investigation to such an unexpected impasse, after all his is not a magic briefcase or the kind that glows mysteriously when you open it, perhaps he will even then pick up the briefcase in the realisation he has been bamboozled and bushwhacked and hurl it to the floor in exasperation, jumping up and down and stamping on it in foiled frustration. We do not know if this will happen eventually but Flynn has walked past the break-room twice and thought about it each time, even though the briefcase is still exactly where it was before, on the table.

From the idea of the Lurker getting a taste of his own medicine, Flynn's mind turns to the more pressing and potentially hazardous issue of the notebook. They will really think something funny is going on when they discover that it has vanished into thin air, thinks Flynn, but they did not know it was my notebook and I can simply deny all knowledge should they ask me, even though it appears that the existence of this exhibit in the case to determine the identity of the intruder was never mentioned to anybody other than the Chief and Deputy Chief Librarians and the potential suspects. He thinks of the computer system and the traces he may have left behind him; I have to stop, I must go in the opposite direction to untangle myself, thinks Flynn, I cannot go further into this under the eyes and ears of the Chief and Deputy Chief Librarians, all the time at risk of possible surveillance and being caught in the act by the Socialist or some other person who is onto me, or who could have been craftily watching these nefarious and devious things I have been doing all along. At this moment in time he is resolved to stay well away from computers and the web pages of *The Correspondent* whilst he is at work, to abandon this senseless parergon, to find some other means of continuing to investigate this chain of events without the risk of a huge net being brought down on him when he least expects it – a net in which today he very nearly found himself caught. Before returning to the central rotunda and his duties however, Flynn must first pay a visit to the office where the local telephone directories are kept. He checks that the coast is clear, softly closes the door, and then thumbs through each one, until he reaches the letter 'T'. He looks up the name Totten, but nobody of that name is listed in any of them. Nor is he able to find anybody with this name listed in the membership database of the National Library itself; and he will linger in this office a little longer, as he thinks about that.

Advice Columnist Sacked Over Q&A Web-Meltdown

The Correspondent on Sunday, February 7th

The Globe's advice columnist Warren was sacked this week, after posting what editors described as a series of 'grossly inappropriate responses'.

Should he have?

- ○ **Yes**
- ○ **No**

Here are some extracts:

Dear Warren,

Leaving for work yesterday, my car wouldn't start immediately because of the cold weather. My hair was still wet from the shower, and I got very chilly as I sat waiting for the engine to turn over. After a few hours at work I could tell I was running a temperature, and so I decided to go home early because my nose was running and I had a sore throat. When I got home, feeling exhausted, I was shocked to find my husband kissing another man on the lips in our living room and watching a mucky film. He immediately confessed that he has been secretly bi-sexual since he was a teenager, and feels helpless about the strength of his feelings. We have been married for twelve years and I love him very much. He recently lost his job and has been feeling worthless and depressed. I don't know what to do. I broke down in tears when he told me,

and went straight to bed. Now I just feel so wretched and confused.
Mary

Hello Mary,
Don't worry. Delirium and confusion often accompany the high temperatures we suffer from when we are ill. It is unlikely that the cold-like symptoms you describe were caused by an infection caught whilst going out with wet hair, as both the common cold and influenza are caused by a virus and not a bacterium. If the symptoms do not go away in a couple of days, see a doctor. Depending on your general health and the extent of your immune-weakened state, you may also be at risk of pneumonia or pleurisy – more serious ailments which require treatment by a medical professional. It is also possible to get Bell's palsy if you go outside with wet hair, a neurological ailment which without treatment can lead to permanent collapse and numbness to one side of your face. This in turn can lead to ulcerations on your inner lip, and burns on your chin skin, if you try to drink hot tea (think novocaine). I'm sending you my leaflet called *Coping with Fevers*, but for now, remember that a hat or hairdryer is a good way of avoiding going out with wet hair. For that pesky problem with your engine I recommend you put anti-freeze in your car radiator; be careful though not to ingest any of it, as anti-freeze is highly toxic, and can lead to blindness or even death from liver failure within approximately 72 hours.
Sincerely,
Warren

Dear Warren,

I am 32 years old and have been married to my husband for eleven years. We have an active healthy life, a strong chemistry and a lot of mutual friends and hobbies. About six months into our relationship, I started to notice that whenever I cooked a quiche for a bourgeois picnic or dinner thing, he would always refer to it as a 'flan'. I corrected his mistake immediately the first time, but he has consistently failed to take notice of my correction, continually referring to quiches as flans, and using the two words as if they were interchangeable. I am finding his insensitivity to linguistic nuance increasingly depressing, to the point that it is affecting our sex life, and our general lives. He keeps asking me what's wrong but I just feel all buttoned up. I am terrified that he will pass on this terminological ambiguity to our children, and as a result I have been feeling increasingly distant from him, and abusing methamphetamine. I am now considering asking for a divorce and starting again with someone who knows shit from shinola. The thing of it is that I just don't know how much longer I can go on listening to him refer to a quiche as a flan.

Susan

Hello Susan,

Try explaining your feelings to your husband and telling him how much his lexical mistake is upsetting you. Try asking if he would mind starting to refer to a quiche as a quiche and not as a flan in his everyday speech – not for himself but out of respect for your wishes and private feelings. If he continues to be so selfish, use a recipe book to gently explain that a quiche is a baked dish that is based on a custard made from eggs and milk (or cream) in a pastry crust whereas a flan is actually a rich custard dessert with a layer of soft caramel on top (as opposed to crème brûlée, which is custard with a hard caramel top). Prepare a sample of each, and force him to repeat the words *'This is Not a Flan'*, when he eats a piece of the quiche. If this fails to work, it may be that he has a learning difficulty, which can be easily cured by hypnosis or astrology. Arrange for the two of you to see a therapist so that you can talk through your issue in a safe environment, where you both feel comfortable with expressing your feelings. It may be that he will be quite receptive and understanding once he realises how badly his louche semantics are affecting you. If the first strategy fails, have a look at the leaflet I'm sending you on *Semantic Insensitivity*, but from the sound of things you might well find yourself better off without him. Therefore, to avoid the inevitable emotional trauma and financial strain of a divorce, or to cash in on any life insurance policies he may hold, you could simply lace a piece of quiche with anti-freeze (or a piece of flan – it doesn't really matter); this strategy invariably leads to irrevocable blindness and death from liver failure, usually within 72 hours.

Yours ever,

Warren

Dear Warren,

I am a 34 year old office worker. I live a so-called atomised existence, in a faceless city with which I have very little personal connection, following a series of personal disasters and feckless life-decisions. I am highly

imaginative and artistic, but have always been a lonely sort of person, and have great difficulty finding meaningful work, establishing friendships, and attracting women. I've seen most of the films there are and read a hell of a lot of books, but I believe I may have developed a serious drinking problem as a coping mechanism for my extreme solitude, my sense of disillusionment, and in order to get through the episodes of unrequited love and depression which follow my continual romantic rejections. I can't really see the point of getting drunk by myself night after night, or sitting in empty cinemas, or cutting myself with knives, or watching happy, smiling couples through the windows of pretentious restaurants, steaming them up with my face all pressed up against the glass. I am being treated with a number of unhelpful anti-depressants, and find myself seriously considering suicide, even though I'm terrified of death and find it hard to imagine. I've got more scars inside than a bypass patient in a road pile-up. Can you think of any way, or imagine possible states of affairs, in which I could be saved?
Chollis

Hello Chollis,
Joseph Conrad once said: *'We live as we dream – alone.'*
In your solitary brooding state, you have discovered the grim truth that lies at the heart of living, which is the truth of the world's blind and complete *indifference to fucking everything*. The world is an encyclopaedia of the unacceptable, a theatre of disappointment, a circus – filled to the brim with a brutality that not only leads to our own annihilation, but which will also bring about the complete destruction of the planet itself, once the sun begins to burn

off the helium in its outer layers, and expands to approximately twice its current size. The oceans will then boil away, and all of earth's atmosphere and elements will be violently sucked out into the vacuum of space, to be reclaimed by nothingness for all eternity. If you think you're in hell now, I can assure you that the only possibility facing you is further annihilation – and the inevitability that things are going to get worse.

You clearly have a delicate temperament which is ill suited to becoming easily reconciled to this kind of harshness, let alone an emotional makeup that is fit for coping with all the shit, all the disappointments, and the unending river of heartless, *dead-eyed dancing bastards* who are everywhere; a cheering consequence of this, perhaps, is that it is unlikely you will survive on your own for very much longer, since I have grave doubts that you would ever find comfort from throwing yourself into some kind of life of reckless abandon. It is also unlikely that you will find a life partner, because let's face it, *nobody likes a sourpuss*. To take Schopenhauer's dictum – anybody who thinks that the amount of pain and pleasure in the world balance each other out, has only to consider the spectacle of two animals – 'the one of whom is eating the other.' Doesn't bear thinking about really, does it? Suicide by anti-depressant is relatively difficult, owing to the low toxicity of most anti-depressants (doctors don't prescribe poisonous compounds to the depressed, because anti-depressants often cause people to feel worse). I'm sending you a leaflet called *Coping with Failure By Means of Addiction*. Owing to your drinking problem you may have already begun to damage your liver; a quick way to finish things off might be to lace your Southern Comfort with

anti-freeze – which reliably causes death from liver failure within 3–5 days.
Yours truly,
Warren

Dear Warren,
Yesterday at work I accidentally dropped a fistful of loose change into the soup tureen as I was serving myself in the café area. Unobserved, I was able to slip away quietly while colleagues continued to fill their polystyrene beakers with the tainted soup mixture, feeling pleased with myself for not being caught and at having managed to avoid a conversation I didn't want with the catering duty manager. Then today I overhear this gap-toothed prole of a kitchen worker mentioning that he found some coins in a soup container as he was washing up, and wondering aloud to his friend how they got there, claiming it was his so-called '*lucky day*'. I am disgusted that he did not have the honesty to hand the money in, and appears to have kept it for his own gain. It makes me sick to think that he's probably selfishly spending my money on things for himself at this very minute, maybe even as we speak, without so much as a hello or a thought for the concept of property rights and due entitlement. It's as though these feckless hillbillies didn't learn a damn thing at school. Do you know how I should go about making him give me my money back?
Yours,
Blind Boy Grunt

Dear Grunt,
You have a heart of blackened teak.
Warren

Dear Warren,
I was unable to start my car this morning in the freezing weather and the windows were all covered in frost. I shredded my wiper blades and ruined a Mastercard when I tried to use it as a scraper. What should I do?
Sally

Dear Mrs Boomerang,
A plastic window scraper is a crucial addition to the glove compartment. You should also try adding anti-freeze to your radiator and spraying it on the windows before you leave in the morning. Be careful that you don't get any anti-freeze in your mouth as it is highly toxic once ingested, usually causing irreversible blindness and death from liver failure within 3–5 days.
Warren

Dear Warren,
I am so confused about the middle east. My husband was in favour of the Iraq invasion of 2003, and repeatedly points out that there are signs of nascent democracy starting to take hold in the hearts and minds of the Iraqi people, following the reduction in suicide attacks in fish markets. He uses this to justify the long occupation by our armed forces, and also the accompanying loss of civilian

lives, which I think might be a compelling argument. However, I am still upset by the Jelly Inquiry, and by the fact that we were blatantly lied to and misled over the issue of weapons of mass destruction. I am also embarrassed by our government's blatant disregard for popular opinion and international law, and their faintly sickening toadying about with the USA and the erstwhile Bush regime. On the other hand, I can see that Saddam Hussein in his role as leader of the Baath party was effectively the sadistic leader of a murderous crime family, who had flouted international regulations for many years; and I am open to the idea that this is what ultimately led his country to the brink of economic and military catastrophe. Now there's talk about declaring war on Iran. I just don't know what to think any more.
Ruby

Dear Ruby,
There are no easy answers to this one. The issue of not having any weapons of mass destruction may just have been left-wing propaganda in the liberal media. For example, do you ever hear it mentioned that in 2004, chips were found frying *unattended* – in the kitchen of an Iraqi palace? Of course not. Yet this could easily have caused a scald or burn to the hands of an American soldier; or it might have spat hot fat in their faces. It could also have been used by the regime's evil henchmen to torture Kurdish political prisoner – behind the smokescreen that boiling oil can have a so-called *civilian purpose*. Further, chip pans are chemically volatile – and can explode if they overheat, causing sharp shards of metal to fly in chaotic directions, which could also lead to unexpected eye

injuries to waiters and kitchen professionals. Have a lively exchange of ideas about the subject with your husband and see if you can come to some sort of agreement. If not, you may just have to agree to disagree! Have a read of my leaflet about *Holding Different Opinions*. My own view is that it is important we resume trade relations with Iran and negotiate sensible oil prices, as oil is an important base product in, amongst many things, the anti-freeze industry. Warren

Dear Warren,

My girlfriend has had sex with another man but isn't interested in sex with me.

I'm 27 and my girlfriend is 26. We've been together five years. We've had a few problems but I thought our relationship was heading in the right direction. Then I started noticing oddities and things just didn't add up. In the end I checked her mobile and sure enough found a text from another man saying it had been 'so amazing'. Being 99 per cent sure she'd cheated I checked her emails too. It seems that while I've been out at work he's been round here shagging her. They'd then gone so far as to email and joke about it. I doubt this was a one-off and I'm unable to understand why. We've not had much sex recently as she's never in the mood. She's always had a low sex drive since I've been with her so why sleep with another man? I've always considered myself unselfish during sex and I also do more than my bit around the house. She's asked me to forgive her but I'm completely heart-broken. I can't look at her without getting images of this guy in my head. I really wanted to spend the rest of my life with this woman but she's made it feel impossible. Now she's asked if she should move out but I just don't know the answer.

Yours sincerely,

Jeremy

Hello Jeremy,

Most commercial anti-freeze formulations include corrosion inhibiting compounds, and a coloured dye (commonly a green, red, or blue fluorescent) to aid in identification. A 1:1 dilution with water is usually used, resulting in a freezing point in the range of −35°C to −40°C, depending on the formulation. In warmer or colder areas, weaker or stronger dilutions are used, respectively, but a range of 40%/60% to 60%/40% must be maintained to assure corrosion protection and optimum freezing prevention. Glycol anti-freeze solutions should generally be replaced with fresh mixture every two years. I'll be sending you my leaflets on gambling addiction and STDs when I get round to it, these people I have to respond to are driving me increasingly bat-shit.

Warren

Dear Warren,

I couldn't help noticing the theme here, so maybe you can answer me this. I read in a magazine that Ethylene glycol anti-freezes are poisonous and should be kept away from any person or animal that might be tempted by their sweet taste. Apparently in order to prevent ingestion, denatonium benzoate could be added to engine coolant as a bittering agent to make it taste more unpleasant. I was shocked to find out that in 2005, a bill was initiated in the

United States Congress that would make mandatory the use of a bittering agent in the commercial production of anti-freeze, but that this legislation failed to pass.
Jonty

Hello Jonty,
What a great question. Anti-freeze is indeed highly toxic to animals (cats especially), and can cause death from liver failure within 72 hours in human beings. In rare non-fatal cases of ingestion, it can also cause irreversible blindness, and paralysis. I agree that the failure of the 2005 bill proposing the addition of a bittering agent to anti-freeze may seem puzzling. Unless you want to kill yourself from liver failure within 72 hours however, bittering agents or not, you should avoid ingesting anti-freeze at all costs.
Warren

Dear Warren,
I can't help noticing that your advice Q&A make frequent reference to anti-freeze in puzzling contexts. This might be a silly question, but I have been wondering why this is the case.
Yours,
Uncle Fester

Hello Uncle,
All is hopeless, and we don't know the why. Stop trying to attach meaning to everything. A man who has never killed is like a virgin, as Malraux says in *La Condition Humaine*. The killer awoke before dawn, and he put his boots on.

He took some anti-freeze from the ancient toolshed…and he marched on down the hall.
Warren

Comments

BifidusRegularis

February 7th 6.19pm

Looks like old Warren finally lost the plot.

ThomPayne

February 7th 6.25pm

I can't in all honesty say, at any point, that he's wrong. A lot of his advice above the line here is better than the stuff these people usually say.

BlindBoyGrunt

February 7th 7.05pm

Not sure that some of the questions are genuine either...

Gaunt

February 7th 7.25pm

@ThomPayne – He's not so much wrong, as an asshole. Pretty disgraceful that you can get moderated for shooting your mouth off, and then they print this for a laugh. I suspect though that you're liking it for the shock value as much as anything, or because you are some kind of twisted contrarian.

Weathereye

February 7th 8.04pm

It must be hard, dealing with a sackful of shit each morning. What's in those leaflets he does, anyway?

JesterJinglyJones

February 7th 8.09pm

laJester wholly approves of this radical performance.

Warren, like laJester, is a destroyer of worlds, a revolutionary conqueror of cities. What begins with a custard pie and a glass of anti-freeze ends with a handful of dust dispersed across barren landscapes by the four winds. laJester longs to instigate the revolutionary terror. The counter-revolutionaries will be so terrified by her acts of mayhem that they will beg, beg, beg to be forgiven, but la Jester will reply 'no' – and continue with the shocks and thrills and tortures of her craft d:-O)

ThomPayne

February 7th 5.08am

I can sympathise too, **@Gaunt**. Who knows why he lost the plot – maybe he'd had enough of things, like that pissed off air steward, who swore at all the passengers and then exited the aircraft down the emergency chute, drinking a beer.

I'm in a rancid mood today, and Warren's new methods have struck a certain resonance with me. So listen, allow me to share with you a truth about the world and human life. The world is full of bastards. They run and control everything, they exploit your good intentions, and then they let you down. I could go on and on about it. These people: they do not care about what is true.

They just care about their material lives and their own nefarious bastardising.

If Warren lost his mind, I can't say I am surprised. In fact, we should have expected it. Had it not happened... *we should have demanded it.*

And you know, if I'm wrong, at least it was artful.

THIS THREAD IS NOW CLOSED

A M Gatward

Part Two

Below The Line

.

9

'WHAT'S IN THE BRAIN *that ink may character?*' asks the unknown author at one point in the book, quoting Shakespeare. A fine question! And so, the second thing Bartleby Flynn has decided, in the meantime, is that even if there were not an unknown author, it would probably be necessary to invent one.

The first thing Flynn decided to do was to acquire for himself a laptop computer as a research tool, having earlier found a solution to the knotty problem of how to establish an internet connection in the flat. The day before yesterday, he happened to observe a girl in the café accessing the so-called interwebs, tricked out with what turned out to be a cellular modem, flashing and radiating vigorously from a USB port; a few judicious questions later, and his vocabulary had been expanded to incorporate the word '*dongle*', along with an enriched sense of the potentialities of mobile broadband technology. Later that evening, he signed up to a contract for just such a service, along with buying the laptop itself.

Since we left him a few days ago Flynn has, by day, been beavering busily at the library, trying to impress everybody afresh with his fastidiousness; by night, when all cats are grey, he has of course been reading at leisure more and more of ThomPayne, on the assorted web-fora of *The Correspondent*. Flynn has continued to comb and scour the threads, in order to piece together for himself as detailed a picture as he can of the life of this stranger, whom he consequently only imagines, whom he senses has somehow found him, and whom he therefore feels compelled to seek out. The precise reason for this compulsion remains as opaque to Flynn as ever it did, we do not always know why it is that we are doing what we do until someone happens to ask; in fact, the question itself has remained un-raised, at least with respect to Flynn's own self-knowledge and streams of thought. It has not even occurred to him to wonder whether any reasons exist at all, such has been his absorption in the subject; and in consequence, your guess is as good as ours at this point as to his reasons for action, it is almost certainly for the best that we do not know everything.

Nobody has returned to the library to pick up the mysterious book, and it has been sitting in lost property ever since Flynn left it there, along with a few other odds and ends that have gathered there over the years, patiently awaiting collection.

'I was raised by my grandparents, '

(👍1 👎0)

wrote ThomPayne several years ago on a thread.

'My parents would leave me with them until it was well into the night and would only pick me up when they felt like it. I spent weeks there, sometimes months, and I was happy during these periods away because I was able to avoid school. I mean, shit and fuck it, with my grandparents, you would never get someone holding your face under the hot tap at lunch hour or taunting you with chants

on a daily basis until
you were terrified of
ever going near the
place.'

(👍 1 👎 0)

Flynn has also begun to research quality book-binding and typesetting, for he is proceeding from the assumption that the book he found is one of a small run of books which the author has had printed for himself. He has performed internet searches and made a list of the printers he considers it likely that the unknown author may have used, by eliminating the most expensive and also the cheapest, and trying to look for the printing houses which advertise quality book-binding and typesetting at the lowest prices. He has a list of some four companies in and around the city that look promising, since he has made the additional assumption that the unknown author would have had it done locally in this computerised age for the reason that a run of even as few as one hundred books would incur considerable shipping fees, a cost which could be circumvented were the unknown author to be sufficiently close to be able to pick up the books himself. The weather is extremely cold, and as Flynn makes his way across the square from the library he realises that it has grown dark, night is rending and riving once more at the edges of the world and in the midst of unleashing the full force of her majesty and dominion, how strange it is, Flynn suddenly thinks, that it has to be dark enough in order to see things as bright as stars.

Flynn ascends the stairs to his little garret, unlocks the door and takes off his winter coat. The flat is chilly, and he puts on a lamp before making his way over to the inadequate electric heater; how solemn a little ceremony it always is in the late autumn when we first have to put the heating on after a hot summer. We catch the first reek of burning dust as the bars of the electric fire begin to glow first red, then amber, and recalling this moment, Flynn begins to wish that spring would come, and not just because the weather will save his electricity bill either. He sits down at his new computer and begins to search again for the telephone numbers of local printers, writing down any promising leads on a notepad. Now that he has a computer of his own, he feels more relaxed in his searching than he did on those clandestine evenings in the library, and he looks once more for web pages containing the name ThomPayne or Barnaby Totten, trying to search for them along with other words, such as politics, music, *The Correspondent*, cats, *in der Nacht sind alle Katzen grau* and he looks again at the social networking profile of Totten, with its strange and ill-defined picture of him fading into the cityscape. He narrows his search by restricting it to the domain of this website, to see whether he can find any public comments or postings. Sure enough, he finds the following words from Barnaby Totten on a forum about cat ownership:

'A legend of the times when the Black Death swept across Europe: the Church believed that all cats were agents of the Devil. The Church spread this rumour, and all the cats across Europe were strangled and flung down wells. It has to be said that the cats had the last word – they weren't around to hunt the rats. So the rats spread a plague across Europe that killed every-body...and since then we've had to rely on Pied Peter Pipers.'

(👍3 👎0)

A further comment he finds concerns genetically modified crops.

'I don't know why people are so worried. In the 1950s they used to use radiation on seeds. They'd plant the seeds to see if there were useful mut-ations. The horror films of the day, think of *The Fly* and *The Incredible Shrinking*

Man, were born of people's paranoia about radiation. Sometimes mice and insects would get into the machines when nobody was looking. It was a big problem. The mice and insects would be zapped into ravenous mutants (which ripped all the scientists apart and ate them).'

(👍2 👎0)

He finds a further comment concerning vanity publishing.

'I once had a book printed (I should have had it published print on demand). I thought of it as my *novum organum*, or New Instrument, as Francis Bacon had it. Or since he was riffing on Aristotle, maybe I should have called it my *novissimum organum*, because I like to go one further. You can have a book done quite cost-effectively (*no publisher would ever take me on or give me anything in advance, they know I'd squander the money and not produce anything worthwhile*). You could have it done some-where like Irvine's outside the city, they always do a good job. You can't simply replace the book with a digital text. It isn't an even exchange'

(👍1 👎0)

Flynn stops and re-reads the sentence. With a shiver of excitement, he now realises what the 'N.O.' of the book's cover stands for. He looks at his list, to see whether the name of this printing company is on it, and he notes that it is not. He searches for the company website, and sure enough, he finds Irvine and Son located on the outskirts of our city on an old industrial estate which can be reached by a journey on the Blue Line bus. He writes down the address in his pad, with the intention of going there tomorrow afternoon, for what reason he cannot say, perhaps he will take the book with him asking,

Excuse me did you make this?

Or, perhaps, he will go so that in some sense he can continue following the shadow of the unknown author, trying to inhabit the footprints of this person with his unknown story, private hopes and fears, to see what new things he will be able to unearth. Flynn wonders what the people he will meet will be like, will they be like picture-framers, with their curious way of insisting upon the exact type of frame that their customers buy for a given picture, will the printer be such a person who takes one look at a manuscript, for example a manuscript of one long monstrous paragraph, and already have an idea clearly in mind of the exact format, typeface and texture of paper from which such a book should be made? Will he be the type of personality who suggests an image for a cover, having dipped into the vanity author's writing for a sneak peak, and put pressure, this way or that, upon the composer of those sentences as to what the book should look like? Or does one simply show up and say, 'Hello I'd like this manuscript printed please, about so big, yes **Bookman Old Style** is fine because I hate *sans-serif typography.* I'd also like to know whether you could do me a nice glossy cover with this picture I found.' Flynn returns to the web pages of *The Correspondent* and looks once more for ThomPayne, to see whether he has written anything new since early this morning.

*

Flynn sleeps sporadically once again, waking up several times during the night, finding himself wondering about the circumstances of the unknown author's relationship with his very own:

> 'Irene Adler, as it were. To me, just as that woman was to Sherlock Holmes, the one I have

in mind was always *the woman,* therefore one whom I incessantly think of as a person of *distinctive and idiopathic rhythms and resonance,* and who was possessed with a clarity of gaze you'd get lost in.'

(👍4 👎0)

Flynn also wonders who the unknown author's tormenters were ('I still wake up from screaming nightmares!'), and his regular situations of 'astounding social awkwardness', situations in which he is unable to express himself, 'struck dumb by beauty and feelings of tenderness which burn like a raging inferno.' Flynn has planned to take the 3.15 Blue Line bus, to pay a visit to the printing premises of Irvine and Son, and he asks the Lurker if he may finish early, 'as I have some important business to attend to,' and, 'yes of course Deputy Chief Librarian, I will be sure to make up the hours later in the week.'

At lunch-time, Flynn slips into the room where the lost property is kept, the uneasy smell of other people's lunches hangs heavy here, the garlic perhaps in some ratatouille that has been heated in the microwave; he unlocks the drawer, once more removing *The Book of the Unknown Author* from where it has been waiting, and he slips it quickly into a shoulder bag he has brought along especially. Flynn is no longer furtive or hesitant in his manner of proceeding, rather he removes the book and places it under the leather flap of his bag in one deft and elegant movement, a manner that could almost be described as professional, before turning decisively, and purposefully walking out into the central rotunda, and towards the exit. It feels strange to Flynn to be outside of his place of work at such a time on a weekday, for he rarely leaves early save for the occasional dental appointment, and as he is very often the last to go he feels a strange sense of guilt at leaving behind a library still very much a hive of activity and with important work still left to be done. He walks across the square, in the opposite direction from his building, and goes to one of a cluster of decaying bus shelters that line the busy road which makes up the opposite side of the quadrangle. Flynn rarely ventures very far from home or the library these days, after all most of the things he needs are within easy walking distance, living as he does in the centre of our capital city, and as a consequence, on the occasions that he does venture further than usual by public transport, he is sometimes surprised at the sudden changes which naturally occur in all human environments, shops which have closed down since he was last there, new graffiti, other signs of vandalism, and on this occasion he notices in the gutters some of the pamphlets and fliers of the protest marchers which have been dropped on the street, and left behind to be trodden, torn and trampled.

He is resisting the urge to give in once more and buy himself another packet of cigarettes, after all it is a filthy and fatal habit as well as an anti-social and expensive one, and he nervously paces up and down the pavement as he awaits his bus. Sitting under shelter is a dumpling-like woman with a walking stick, clutching two or three bulging bags, she is eyeing him suspiciously and when he finally sits down next to her he catches on the air the smell of grease in her clothes and the smell of a cold when she coughs, and he notes with distaste the wiry hairs which are protruding from her chin. Presently enough, and not too late, he sees the unmistakable shape of the bus emerge over the top of the hill, and he stands up immediately with renewed vigour, reaching into his pocket for some loose change. The bus pulls in, and he buys his ticket to the old trading estate, and sits down next to a young man with a shaved head, who is listening to music that must be deafeningly loud inside his skull, because Flynn finds himself able to make out not only the lyrics of the song but also recognises the tune, which we are not always able to do in such situations, and which is certainly rare for Flynn who has very little interest in popular forms of music. Holding his legs tightly together, Flynn is gripping the bar in front of his seat with both hands, and we can observe if we look closely that his knuckles are white, such is the way he is clinging on to it. The bus mumbles its way onwards, irritatingly slowly as far as Flynn is concerned, pausing to pick up new passengers at virtually every stop along the way, and slowly but surely filling up until there is standing room only, this is why buses in our city are always late, and if only the drivers would step on it a bit, a lot of useless waiting could be avoided.

We are leaving the city behind us and moving through suburbs, Flynn can see tower blocks and bungalows, the leisure centre, the enormous supermarkets, the car dealerships, the out-of-town multiplex cinemas; presently we arrive at a junction, the bus turns into a short stretch of dual carriageway, struggling to accelerate to a respectable speed. Threadbare hedgerows furl and furrow past the window, and we turn off at the first exit, and onto a main road that leads through woods on one side and farmland on another; an occasional pub flashes past and we see a sign to the industrial estate coming to us over the horizon like an offering. It is spitting with rain as the bus turns onto the main road of the development, and all around us are large warehouses and dilapidated office buildings, depots and units: Flynn rings the bell, and as it slows down, he gets up from his seat. Standing on the narrow pavement, Flynn watches the back of the bus moving slowly away from him, and he can smell the black hotness of the diesel fumes pouring from its rear end, cars and articulated lorries streak past us at speed, while he waits to cross to the other side of the road towards the first buildings on the estate, in order to consult the sign which points to where the different business premises are located. The sign displays directions to a company that makes components for servicing the railroad industry, a paper mill, a sugar refinery, a cheese dairy, a rendering works, a vodka distillery, a meat-packing plant, a cannery, a bread-baking combine, a garment workshop, and a factory making feather and down articles, but nothing to indicate the presence of a printing house. He knows the road where Irvine and Son is supposed to be located, and looks for Marine Way, but he is unable to see it on the map, and he decides to walk across a dismal patch of waste ground strewn with litter, towards the front door of a parcel delivery company in order to ask for directions.

The door is locked when he tries the handle, so he rings the bell and waits. He was unable to hear the bell tintinnabulating inside the deserted-looking building and is now beginning to think that the place must be unoccupied, when suddenly a small hatch opens and a man with a crooked nose peers out suspiciously.

Can I help you?

I'm looking for Irvine and Son, somewhere on Marine Way.

That'll be the old printing place, eh?

Flynn nods his head, and the thin-faced man leans out of the window, pointing Flynn in the direction he has just come from. Looking hesitant, the thin-faced man disappears and then re-emerges with a piece of paper and a blue ballpoint pen, and contortedly leans out and draws Flynn a perfunctory map, using the brick outer wall as a surface. The strokes of the pen are unsteady and unsure of themselves against the crenulated texture of the brick, but Flynn thanks him, and holding the map in front of him walks once more across the litter-strewn patch of scrub and back along the road, towards which the thin-faced man has directed him. There is no pavement on this side of the road, save for a small oasis of concrete that marks the spot on the waste-ground where the bus stop stands; Flynn halts to read the timetable, but the paper inside has become eaten away with rain and mildew, and the plastic face is cracked and covered with jagged writing. Lorries yowl past him as he makes his way along the rough ground, this is no place for a stroll, and the wind has picked up, throwing the rain into his face in great handfuls. He sees that the street lamps have just come to life, they are glowing red and dim but have not yet reached full lambency, and gathering in the collar of his coat, Flynn presses on towards the second building on the right, the printing company called Irvine and Son. Exactly what he is going to do there, he has not yet decided. Like the parcel depot, the front door is locked and this unit has a silver box covered in buttons in place of a keyhole, a box into which one can only suppose a code must be punched in order to unlock the door. Here too there is the button for a doorbell and so he presses it, an aggressive metallic sound rings out, of the sort that could make your teeth hurt, if you stood too close to it, and presently an elderly man comes to the door; Flynn hears the lock release before it opens.

Hello, may I help you?

I have a few questions about printing.

Did you make an appointment?

No, actually.

We don't usually see people without an appointment.

But I don't have one.

You know, you really should have called ahead.

I'm sorry, I didn't think.

And *that's exactly why* we have all these problems today. People showing up without appointments, ignoring rules, wanting everything on demand.

Well, I can relate to that.

Then, you have the foreigners, all the country people. The wheel-kickers.

The printer shakes his head.

No good will come of it.

I take your point, Flynn replies. But if you could possibly spare me a few minutes, it won't take long. I came all the way from the city to see you. To make some enquiries.

Muttering under his breath, the old man relents; he unlocks the door and leads Flynn down a sour-smelling corridor, the carpets are threadbare and there is a sharp chemical fetor to the air which Flynn can only suppose are oils and inks, and from somewhere in the building can be heard the insistent rhythmic noise of machinery. The old man arrives at a rinky-dink reception counter, behind which there are photocopying machines and guillotines, he lifts up a battered wooden panel and walks behind the desk, replacing the barrier once more and turning, looks fully at Flynn. He places his hands on the countertop, and Flynn notes that the cuticles of the man's finger-nails are blackened by ink, there are fine white grooves and creases on the skin of his palms and epithelia, and his thumbprints are clearly visible in the low light. Flynn takes out *The Book of the Unknown Author* and places it precisely on the counter in front of the old man and he asks quite simply,

Do you remember printing that?

The old man picks up the book and looks at it, and runs his thumb down the pages so that they rifle from front to back, and Flynn notes that a slight ink stain from the printer's thumb is now visible on the white edges of the pages.

Not quite sure, says the printer. No markings on it. We certainly use that paper, and that typeface is as common as whores.

Can you remember anybody ever submitting or requesting something like this?

Not personally, I can check with the typesetters. Hold on.

He walks away through a back door, and Flynn catches a glimpse of what looks to be a large warehouse or factory floor filled with primeval-looking heavy machinery. The man comes back moments later with a younger man in work clothes, who is drying ink from his hands on a filthy old rag, and who stares at Flynn from the moment he catches sight of him.

Sure, I remember doing this one, he says.

The thing of it is, I'm looking for the person who wrote it, says Flynn. Do you recall who it was – a face or a name perhaps?

It was a while ago, not sure they ever came in. Think this one was all done by email. I remember it because he only wanted one copy. We would have posted it to him afterwards.

Do you remember where you sent it? asks Flynn, barely able to contain his nerves and excitement, and the younger man's eyes narrow suddenly.

It would all be in our records, he says, indicating an old filing cabinet behind the reception desk. But what would you be wanting that for?

I found the book and I need to return it to its owner, says Flynn. I'm a librarian at the National. The book was left in our building.

Evidently there is something in the way that he says this that comes across as *not quite right*, a little suspicious perhaps or excessively eager, and the young man pauses again to scrutinise Flynn, who after all, has just emerged out of the rain on this windswept afternoon, and who probably looks a little wild and unkempt from all his exertions.

We can't give out the names and addresses of our customers, says the younger printer... But, I can put it in the post and send it out to him myself?

No no no, that's no good. I have to return it personally, I need to give it to him myself.

The young man looks at the older man, and they both look back at Flynn, who looks at them as they do so.

We would be unable to help you with that, says one.

If you want to return the book, you have to leave it here with your details, says the other.

Flynn hesitates, cursing how our data protection rules and so forth should extend to so antiquated an operation as this, and he extends his hand to take back the book.

No, I'll have to find another way.

The older man instinctively hands the book back to Flynn, who replaces it in his shoulder-bag.

Why did you think it was us who printed it? We're not the only printers in the city, says the young man.

I had a hunch, replies Flynn, backing away.

More than that, I think?

Maybe so, but I need to get going.

As you wish, I'll let you out.

Thanks.

It is evening and Flynn makes his way back towards the bus stop in order to return home to the city. As he walks, he sees the spectral image of a bus sailing past the bus stop he has been heading for, and curses his luck as he realises there is no way he will be able to make it there in time and will now have to wait for the next one. It is still raining, and he feels oddly naked standing solitary in the tiny square of concrete that marks the bus stop, as a convoy of rattling trucks and cars rumbles and speeds past his face, their headlights catching frozen instances of the momentum of rain. The sun is setting and the light now appears weary under this firmament of Prussian Blue, now the lamps have attained their full potency, and Flynn feels exposed to the elements under these lights, which stand tall and stern and weatherproof in the early evening. It occurs to him that he might call Irvine and Son the following day and pretend to be Barnaby Totten, but what would he say? He could hardly ask them his own address, and who knows maybe Totten has moved in the meantime. It occurs to him that the conversation might run,

Hello this is Barnaby Totten – you once printed a book for me.

Why yes Mr. Totten, how strange, a man was here yesterday evening clutching that very thing.

If he comes back could you send it to my home address?

Yes of course, let me check we still have it, are you still at 3562 Broadgate, Flat 6½B?

Yes that's the one.

Ok fine, I'll leave a note.

Sir, you really are too kind.

Next it occurs to Flynn that such a conversation would represent the best of all possible worlds and outcomes, but that it is also really too contrived a dialogue to be very likely to happen as easily and naturally as we have just imagined. Flynn then thinks that he also might ring up and ask for Totten's address by telephone, in the hope that he might speak to somebody a little more willing to bend the rules than the two men he encountered this evening, after all they must have other employees not all of whom will be such upstanding and punctilious citizens, and a telephone conversation is much less personal than looking into somebody's eyeballs and having them size up every feature of your body language to determine by animal instinct whether the individual before them is to be trusted or whether he appears to be someone who is up to no good.

It is with such thoughts as these that Flynn notices a small car pulling away from the road where Irvine and Son stands, and he notices inside it the hunched figure of the older of the two men, peering intently over the wheel, accelerating the vehicle away from his place of work and one can only presume to his home, or to a bar, or to a Master Printer's meeting, or to meet an illicit lover, or to do any kind of thing since we haven't asked him where he is heading. Flynn notices that it is a red hatchback car and that there are now no more cars in the forecourt of the building. Squinting his eyes through the rain, he can no longer see any lights on inside the building either, and it suddenly strikes him that this trading estate is really rather remote, a man could lose his life here and not be discovered for quite a while, and he sees how the evening darkness looms behind the print warehouse from the cow-fields and farmland which divide that row of manufacturing units from the main road. Flynn turns once more to look into the oncoming traffic for signs of a bus, and sure enough the friendly sight of one is now visible, trundling towards him in that methodical way they have. For a few moments it seems as though it is not moving at all, but it strikes Flynn that the bus has suddenly made quite a bit of ground along this long straight road, and he leans out from the kerb and signals with his hand, and presently the orange indicator on the side of the vehicle tells Flynn that he has been spotted, that he will not be marooned here forever on the roadside, that he will soon be heading back to his home and his thoughts about what to do next.

We can see Flynn getting onto the bus, the doors make their pneumatic sneeze and the bus pulls away from us, Flynn safely on board, and we can watch as the bus disappears down the road. We can linger for a few moments longer in this unconsoled place, time enough for us to feel and convey the new thought which Flynn has had and which suddenly burst into his mind with the hyper-mania of a train that is speeding away from you in the opposite direction to your travel. The thought that has arisen within Flynn is that he can simply return here under the shadow of night, when everybody else has left, in order to break into the firm of Irvine and Son and look through their paperwork himself, perhaps he will shimmy up a drainpipe and crawl catlike along a ledge to an open skylight, or perhaps he will take a cushion and smash a window with his elbow, reach through and open a door from inside, there will be a way of getting in there, he is persuaded, he feels sure there will be, and we can re-join him on the bus as these things rush through his head. What will he need, how will he cover his tracks, and he is well on his way to resolving these questions, almost back in the city when his thoughts turn to other things.

Cyber-Stalking: A Dark Side of the Internet

The Correspondent on Sunday, February 7th

Comments

Weathereye

 17 3

February 7th 5.32pm

> Her repeated complaints were not dealt with by the police until he physically attacked her, at which point it was of course too late.

This is frightening on any number of levels, although you want your head looking at if you make your details visible for everyone.

To the sub-editors – it's a dark side of the internet, not the only one.

BoiledMouse

 9 3

February 7th 5.43pm

Somebody once got hold of a video I'd made and did a number on me, and if I catch that bastard I'm going to make them pay; they linked the tags in it to some pretty nasty pornography. It was a nightmare to get it sorted out and I have been more careful ever since. It was near the top of the page rankings when I did a search on my name, and I can tell you that it is not easy getting a website hosted in Argentina to pull a page down in a hurry.

MopDog

February 7th 6.01pm

It's what you should expect if you're dumb enough not to be anonymous, and paste your life where anybody can find it.

Eusebius

February 14th 2.10pm

You can find out all kinds of things on people. A girl I sometimes see has these big eyes you could get lost in. Not that I'd want to harm anybody, but I'm stuck working with the *direness of being a factotum.* I'm nothing, but there's part of me that wants to see how people live and what illuminates them; I have screwed up and died inside so many times, I'm not sure how much of me is left; if I can *live vicariously*, on the other hand I find I can make the *unbearable...bearable.*

BlindBoyGrunt

February 7th 6.04pm

There was a story in the New York Times about this in relation to freedom of speech. Some guy used an array of usernames and posted 8000 tweets about a woman in a Buddhist group. The question is whether doing that is simply having your say from a speakers' corner like we do here or whether it is closer to something private like a letter, when it's directed at an individual. He was writing horror film descriptions of what he was going to do to her and saying things like 'Do us all a favour and kill yourself. P.S. Have a nice day.' Bit much, I'd have said.

I have spoken.

BifidusRegularis

 0 0

February 7th 6.07pm

Why anybody makes themselves known to the world via careless talk on the f'ing internet is a mystery to me. Then if online gaming is your thing, you get the fucking griefers; the ninja-looters and kill-stealers – not to mention the trolls on these threads. When I was young and a bit of a cunt, I used to log into chat-rooms, in the days of those Geocities homesteads – if your java applet was working, you could wind people up like crazy. It was pretty funny, but I used to shock even myself, with the heinous things I would type.

Gaunt

 14 1

February 7th 11.10pm

The stories are well known. There was the case of this 12-year-old Australian girl, whose friends made up rumours involving her and the lead singer of some god-awful emo boy-band. She was naïve, and she replied, so it got worse. Here's one comment from that thread –

> even if that douche was a pederast he wouldn't fuck her with a ten foot pole – even though that bitch looks like a whore.

She responded with an angry video, which 4Chan got hold of and it went viral. Encyclopaedia Dramatica doesn't help given it specifically has an entry on 'How to troll' with such recommendations as 'Tell her to kill herself', etc. The final video was of her sobbing on camera, as her dad screamed impotently at the screen. Some people genuinely think that what we need is censorship.

Eusebius

February 12th 3.21am

Posting under your own name is possibly the sign you're an incipient psychopath. That said, it's surprisingly easy to track people down.

ThomPayne

February 12th 4.09am

@BifidusRegularis

You are as addicted to wanting to reveal yourself as any of us; but I would say it is a safer thing to do under the safety of being in deep cover.

@Gaunt

I'm speechless. And, for once we agree, as I wouldn't risk provoking Anonymous either. But there's something else to say. Used to be the case…back in the day… that there was this big white book that freaks and pervs could get their hands on, and in that book were things like your name, where you lived, your telephone number. *It was insane.* Serial murderers would run a greasy finger down the listings, choose a name, give them a call to see whether they were home and if they got an answer they'd do a heavy breathing and chilling silence routine, then pop over and slaughter the family, but I don't want to put ideas in your head. But. It's easy to do all kinds of unpleasant things if you know you're not going to be identified and because you covered your tracks. Maybe you're the submissive kind who would prefer to be shot in the back – as opposed to being executed by a bullet in your head, facing up to your killers with grim resignation. Humanity has not evolved or become worse because of the internet. People are just as amoral and scummy as they've always been. It would be hard to become more evil or plumb the depths of depravity any further than we had managed to do, centuries before people had computers where they could post outrageous personal attacks. If you're talking about calling people names on a message board, it's playground stuff. In my opinion the most depraved psychopaths in this world are the people you brush up against in your daily grind – the ones who are friendly and then try to have you sacked or steal your thunder because they're concealing the fact that they can't stand you or because they envy your talent. Thick people with no empathy who do not understand some harmless comment you made – and then construed it automatically in the worst way possible as some kind of personal attack. I should know – I have worked with them and had relationships with them. Dull people, humourless people. People who take things literally. Just because you know them, had a Christmas party thing with them where they were civil, feigned some interest and were possibly friendly to you whilst you were all dressed up – this does not mean that they do not intend to harm you. They probably do, and what makes it worse is that in your innocence, you do not even realise. Plus, pantomime villains are not real villains. If I, once I have posted this comment, were to look up your phone number in the white pages, make a chillingly silent call to see if you're in, hack you to pieces with a claw hammer and eat you for dinner, that would be pure Hollywood. For the reason that you would probably make me violently ill. If on the other hand I were to start a thread somewhere on 4Chan, and ask the b/tards to do a number on your real world name and identity – whoever you are – it would probably be far more serious for you. I'd say something like, *Hello I am ThomPayne and I write for The Correspondent* (which is all true) – please make Gaunt's life a living hell. It would be so easy, it would be hard to fail. Gaunt you are lucky that I am an ethical person and too weak to move at the moment. There's no telling the things I could do if I felt like it.

What's that noise Gaunt?

And, **@Eusebius**, you too sound a little paranoid, a seeing your reflection in the knife kind of thing. I don't want to alarm you…could it be though…that down the hallway……… footsteps are a-coming for the Jack of Hearts? ♪♪♪♪

THIS THREAD IS NOW CLOSED

Protests at Spending Cuts: Open Blog

The Correspondent, Friday February 12th

Comments

Weathereye

February 12th 1.58pm

These anaemic suggestions from the OCB will not stop the banks stumbling into another crisis. It's like giving the keys of the jailhouse to the convicts and then wondering where everyone went. You'd be an idiot if you thought they would simply police themselves.

If you look at how they laugh in the face of the tax payer in awarding huge bonuses and ridiculous salaries to senior management as any kind of barometer, it's very much business as normal. We've had 4 years of jibber jabber, a judicial enquiry, and what good has that done? Unless there's a major paradigm shift – away from the way in which this government is in thrall towards the financial sector – and towards the establishment of an independent and stringent regulatory body, the s**t will inevitably hit the fan. That will be the point when we'll get to test the idea that everybody is in this together.

BoiledMouse

February 12th 1.59pm

When the mess kicked off and the banks started squealing, what were they actually squealing about? They weren't making a loss – it was fractional reserve banking which dictated that they had to hold onto a percentage of their deposits or capital as a reserve. What they had really done was to lend ridiculous sums of money to people who were unable to repay or service the debt, and then covering the loans with the 'collateral' of artificially overpriced properties. When the property bubble burst, which every intelligent person said it obviously would do, the banks were in a position where reserves of capital were marginally less than the outstanding debts. A slew of foreclosures caused further drops in value and the banks had to face a huge margin default. They needed capital to bring their reserves up to the point where bad debts could be covered. That was the point when the State had to step in. Most governments are in piles of debt anyway, so the bail outs were financed by borrowing.

So, banks have jacked up the values of assets artificially, in order to lend money that did not really exist, and which only ever became money when it was entered in the book as a debt. Now they've had to borrow more borrowed money, which everybody else has to work off, when we didn't have it to lend anyone in the first place. On top of that, we have to pay interest for lending us something we didn't have and with probably some nice administration fees thrown in for the final insult. If I did this I'd be sharing a jail cell with a corrupt politician or a sex criminal.

MopDog

 21   1

February 12th 2.00pm

Slavery is a crime against humanity and therefore illegal. So is financial slavery, yet it's allowed.

NathanTheProphet

 5   0

February 12th 2.04pm

Retail banks should be split from the gambling side of it because they have been given the opportunity to create money by lending far more than they have on deposit – and this has ultimately been sanctioned and backed by the state. Effectively they are using the opportunity to lend to themselves and use the cash for further large and probably risky punts. The upshot of that is cuts, because government borrowing has to be curtailed, and the upshot of the spending cuts will be the protests.

BifidusRegularis

February 12th 2.07pm

Getting them to split casino and retail operations into separate divisions is wholly different from forcing the establishment of separate companies which is what the US imposed in the Great Depression. The right wing party receives over half of its funding from the city. It's really a case of purchasing political capital. This government would never risk damaging that source of funding or antagonising the people who represent it.

Gaunt

February 12th 2.10pm

@MopDog:

> Slavery is a crime against humanity and therefore illegal. So is financial slavery, yet it's allowed.

Pray tell us what kind of metaphor that is.

Financial slavery?

@NathanTheProphet:

> Retail banks should be split from the gambling side of it because they have been given the opportunity of creating money by lending far more than they have on deposit and that this has ultimately been sanctioned and backed by the state.

No that's not right. A bank cannot create money out of nowhere in surfeit to what's on deposit already.

Effectively they are using the opportunity to lend to themselves and use the cash for further large and probably risky punts.

That also is not right. Splitting it is a little strange. You look at them and see them doing things you like and can follow. Then you see them doing things you do not like and do not follow. It's more complex than that, and the dependencies are more complex than just splitting banks' operations into discrete categories of good or bad.

JesterJinglyJones

14 1

February 12th 2.12pm

laJester will instigate the revolutionary terror. The counter-revolutionaries will be so terrified by her acts of destructive mayhem that they will beg to be forgiven – she will reply no and continue with the shocks and thrills and tortures of her art. She has no wish to boast about her fees on here, she is in it for the terror d:-o(

BlindBoyGrunt

11 1

February 12th 2.16pm

@MopDog, neo-feudal serfs we surely are. Slave-owners have always tormented their serfs for kicks, pricks and the lulz.

@Gaunt

A bank cannot create money out of nowhere in surfeit to what's on deposit already.

Gaunt you do not know what a deposit is. It is not just cash on hand in an account. You can list any loan you make as an asset, and it gets classed as a deposit. The point is that when you take away the cash on hand deposits from the loans made that are based on them – the cash on hand is loads less than the value of what's been lent.

You should read up on fractional reserve banking and economics before posting nonsense and wasting everybody's time with stuff you haven't researched for yourself. In any case, the spending cuts are down to the bail-out, whether you have a simplistic view of banking or not.

I have spoken.

InformationSilo

 20   1

February 12th 2.30pm

Jebus Christ Gaunt, do you seriously believe that recent events suggest that the regulatory system that was set up to safeguard the financial system was anything like watertight or robust? JesterJinglyJones – troll.

ConstableGrowler

 79   14

February 12th 2.35pm

It makes me think of how the National Socialists pilloried Jews in the '30s. Labour camps for bankers and economists is it?

JesterJinglyJones

 2   2

February 12th 2.38pm

troll

laJester is not a troll, but a jester, and that matters greatly; the clowns and jesters of the world are a family – dedicated to their art in all of its delights and terrors. You dogs can hunt in your packs, whereas laJester hunts alone. My caravan door is always open to those whose purpose is not humour but chaos.d:-oD

Mook

February 12th 2.58pm

One easy thing they could do – no bank should be rescued but all deposit accounts should be backed and insured by the Finance Ministry.

Cryptorchid

February 12th 3.56pm

> One easy thing they could do – no bank should be rescued but all deposit accounts should be backed and insured by the Finance Ministry.

Yes and they should have a new insolvency rule which states that any recovery of assets should go to the treasury until the refunds are made. Pretty clear, if these eunuchs only had eyes.

FlaubertFlaubert

February 12th 3.56pm

> This comment has been removed. *Click here* for FAQs regarding moderation

ThomPayne

February 12th 3.43pm

ConstableGrowler we were thinking more along the lines of a mass public lynching ceremony or the bastinado over a death camp. Click here to read about a practice called *scaphism*.

Maybe a few people in cages suspended from the ends of all the lampposts. Although the smell of barbecue does have an appeal now you mention it. Yum yum yum, let's cook up some banker and have us a tasty roast. Try reading Charles Mackay's *Extraordinary Popular Delusions and the Madness of Crowds* of 1841. It is not just about a tulip bubble.

From the book: *Men, it has been well said, think in herds; it will be seen that they go mad in herds, while they only recover their senses slowly, and one by one*

The failure of fiscally conservative economists to own up to the fact that their free-market ideology collapsed with the bailouts is nothing short of a conjuring trick where you can see all the wires and secret compartments. The root of all the banking problems is not really an economic issue. It's a political one that is screamingly apparent from the way that private debts have been transferred to the public purse. It's a form of extreme socialism for the elite classes – these scummy people are perfectly happy with communism if it benefits them.

It's very simple if you're lucky enough to have access to capital: the so-called risk-taking entrepreneurs spend a massive amount and get themselves indebted. Their enterprise goes tits up because they have no business skills, and then they get normal people who do not take risks or own capital and who were therefore not entitled to any profits when the banks were in clover, and force them to foot the bill. The nihilist in me can't help but admire the ruthlessness of it, but do not follow the madness of King George Bush II…and *misunderestimate* the human cost. If I went to Vegas and gambled your house on the spin of the gambling wheel, would you sign over the deeds to the property? With the cuts and the protests which will come, I can only hope that it will result in bloodshed of some kind. I have been chewed up and spat out by the recession along with the rest. I am sick at the minute and flat broke. When I fall over, which I inevitably will do, I think I am just going to stay wherever my head hits the ground.

It's like Dylan sings about patriotism being the last refuge to which a scoundrel clings: *steal a little and they'll throw you in jail/ steal a lot and they'll make you king.*

The people who swallow this kind of kool-aid are the kind of people who would amputate all of their limbs if it became fashionable to do so.

BlindBoyGrunt

 3 1

February 12th 3.56pm

Thanks for the Godwin violation, **Growler.**

I have spoken.

Mook

 1 0

February 12th 4.01pm

@Grunt – electronic banking, from benefits to bonuses saves a huge amount across the economy. Having a bank account is virtually a mandatory requirement of citizenship these days. They shouldn't be able to slap us with fees as a consequence – particularly when they're financed by the taxpayer anyway. You could ramp up corporation tax a bit and fund the spending cuts that they've got planned from that and from slashing the bonuses.

@ThomPayne – Why are you so cynical? If you want bloodshed, speak for yourself and not the rest of us.

Gaunt

 1 1

February 12th 4.59pm

Mook, people like ThomPayne are leftist misanthropes. Pay his vacuous hyperbole no mind. Comments about cuts from those who have no solutions for deficit cure are depressingly predictable, especially when those people are either in denial over the guilt of the previous administration in causing all this with their credit card mentality or in denial over the structural emergency surrounding the deficit. Luckily these delusions are held by just a very tiny minority who read this newspaper. The cuts are not as swingeing as you seem to imagine **InformationSilo** – the plan is to cut back to the levels of spending we had 5 years ago. Things weren't so bad then. Why do I feel like a voice in the wilderness on this website? More seriously, the alternative that the leftists would have instituted is some kind of kolkhoz-filled socialist nightmare, the system that paralysed Russia and led to the extermination of vast numbers of people. Prefer that to free-enterprise, the system we voted for, would you? What we need to lift ourselves out of recession is growth.

Same with personal responsibility: the other day one of my sons smashed the patio window next door. I've paid for the damage, and he will have to pay for it from his allowance.

InformationSilo

 20 1

February 12th 5.30pm

Gaunt, you have to factor inflation in. I'd be very happy if everything were as cheap as it was 5 years ago, but it is not. The things they are cutting will have a direct impact on people's lives.

ThomPayne

0 0

February 12th 6.23pm

@Gaunt

> the system that paralysed Russia and led to the extermination of vast numbers of people. Prefer that to free-enterprise, the system we voted for, would you?

Here we go with the right-wing disjunction, the old spurious dichotomy. Let's give it a name – the *argumentum ad Stalinium* – or the Gaunt Violation – the internet rule that any criticism of capitalism will inevitably result in a reductio ad absurdum comparison to Soviet Russia.

If we don't have wing-nut capitalism we'd all be starving on collective farms and imprisoning writers. The stock market or the kolkhoz. *Freedom or the gulag.*

Don't you realise the number of people who starved or died of drinking meths once capitalism worked its magic, after the iron curtain fell? Your view is that we have to swallow down the way things are, where the 1% get to keep all the wealth or everybody will end up drinking themselves to death with meths, forced to give up what they own, and sent to the Gulag. You can see, can't you, that what you're saying isn't logical?

> the other day one of my sons smashed the patio window next door.

I wouldn't like to live next to you Gaunt. It sounds to me like you're one of those people with children who have 'gone feral.' They just seem to be operating beyond all known rules of acceptable conduct.

> What we need to lift ourselves out of recession is growth.

Well growth for the sake of growth – is the ideology and method of a cancer, isn't it.

@Mook

> Why are you so cynical?

Why should I tell you? Maybe I am drinking heavily today or maybe it's the blue shakes because I haven't.

> If you want bloodshed, speak for yourself and not the rest of us

You know, like the man says in *Henry VIII* – *if I chance to talk a little wild, forgive me.*

I probably get it from my old man.

But if I feel like making hyperbolic statements or grandiloquent gestures with which to accuse and indict the collective ethos that I have no choice other than to choke down, or if I simply feel a little whimsical and enjoy speaking on your behalf, then chaverim, just watch me do so. For your own good as much as mine, you know, to plant a few seeds in that parched and barren mental soil of yours. Without you knowing it, your mind will soon have adapted to being a mindless drone in the massive global beehive. My job is to let the bee out of the bottle and point people to the exit. So Mook, I suggest you bring yourself up to speed...*by joining me*. Refuse the urge to attach meaning to everything or anything. Join me Mook...*I am your father.*

THIS THREAD IS NOW CLOSED

10

BARTLEBY FLYNN IS WATCHING the Chief Librarian wholly absorbed in the act of eating an apple. Having munched his way to the centre of it, the Chief Librarian then holds up the moist core to the light, scrutinising and twiddling it by the stem for several moments, before poking the whole thing into his mouth with sudden finality, and swallowing it. Flynn has slept well since we saw him last, as he was making his way home on the Blue Line bus, and in the intervening time he has assembled for himself the tools he thinks he will need to force an entry. He has a torch, a pair of gloves, a balaclava, a brick, a thick towel, and a length of washing line which he bought from an ironmongery, earlier this lunch time. Also in his bag are spare batteries, a knife, and his grandfather's old telescope. He has returned *The Book of the Unknown Author* to the lost property drawer; nobody seems to have noticed it missing during its few hours of absence. All morning, Flynn has been doing his best to attract the good favour of the Lurker, with self-conscious and frankly rather ostentatious displays of zeal and solicitude, and rather to the irritation of his colleagues. A large shipment arrived at the library this morning, a delivery of volumes containing all the minutes and transcriptions of last year's political debates in the Senate, the legislation that passed, the legislation repealed, the interjections, the pleas for excuses, the irrelevant. For legal reasons as much as anything else, this documentation must be kept in the library for all posterity, as has been done for the past couple of centuries; these unlovable hardcover books are enormously heavy, even more so because nobody will ever read them, and it was decided a long time ago that they would need to be stored somewhere out of the way. There is an annual tradition which results from this, involving the casting of lots amongst the library staff; the losing worker, whomsoever they happen to be, must push trolley after trolley of these books down to the stacks, all day if necessary, in order to deposit them at the furthermost point, where they will be out of the way.

This year, Flynn volunteers for the job, and all afternoon wheels cartloads of these books down to the end of the longest of the subterranean corridors; there, the tunnel opens into a dusty and derelict little room, which still contains some of the builder's mess that was left when the stacks were extended this far some forty years ago. This room is rather damp and humid, and a lot of mortar has fallen from the exposed bricks at the far wall. As you make your way down the corridor towards this terminus of all reading, the metal shelving units running down the centre become increasingly Spartan and unpopulated. All of a sudden the vinyl flooring stops, there are entirely empty shelves, followed by another with just a few books on it. Finally the shelves themselves run out and disintegrate into ruin, even the National Library of Books and Publications must come to the end of the line somewhere with respect to the written word. Flynn finally arrives and begins to stack the new arrivals onto one of these empty units and, fully engaged in his library work, his thoughts turn once again to the more mundane elements of the only job he has ever known.

As he is making his way back with the empty trolley he remembers that there is another meeting this evening regarding redundancies, and emerging from the depths, he is reminded of how everybody has been in a state of nervous anxiety over what new developments may or may not have transpired, and remain yet to be reported. The disappearance of the notebook from the Chief Librarian's briefcase a week or so ago has also resulted in a level of suspiciousness amongst the library workers which had not been there before; one of us must surely have removed it, they mutter, this dark actor must also be the intruder who came into the library like a cat in the night. Nobody has owned up to any of it of course, nor does anyone have an idea who it might be, therefore everyone automatically suspects everyone else and each other.

Do you think it was her?

It could have been anyone.

A-ha, perhaps it was you.

An Outrage! For all we know, you were the one.

Now you're thinking.

Perhaps it was the Spaniard.

Hey you're right, he never says much.

It's a language thing.

He's a Catholic.

Like so many of them.

His wife is stunning.

A real princess.

It's a delightful country.

Great food.

What was his motive?

I expect they fell in love.

No, the thief.

Which thief?

The Spaniard!

What are you talking about?

Fucked if I know.

There is also a breaking news headline, which Flynn has not failed to notice even though he has been busy with other things, a headline which says that once more there will be protests staged today, protests over the largesse of the administration, the cronyism, the nepotism, the so-called pork barrel policy making, the nimbyism inherent in forcing, at least according to the organisers of the protests, we want no part in this one, forcing people who have done nothing wrong to pay for the inept mistakes, greed and financial mismanagement of others. Yesterday evening Flynn had seen a large group of protestors marching through the city to deliver a petition to the Senate. Although the march was peaceful, he had observed the cavalry of mounted police; he had watched as the officers in riot gear, bearing batons and marching in phalanx form, tried to marshal the chaotic demonstration, to settle flaring tempers and prevent things getting out of control. There were a few minor skirmishes, according to *The Correspondent*, and there was one arrest for drunk and disorderly behaviour after the police aggressively kettled a crowd of students. It is also reported that there is a sense of high tension on the streets this afternoon, keeping everybody on tenterhooks about what the night may unleash, when large crowds gather together who knows the things that can happen?

Now that Flynn has decided to take the law into his own hands and become a burglar, an offence which would carry a harsh penalty were he ever to be caught red-handed, he is giving much less of his attention to the front desk on the off chance that Barnaby Totten or somebody else should come in and ask for the book. The library appears to Flynn to be especially messy today. Scores of books have been left out on the tables in reading rooms and not returned to their proper places, left open in such a way that they remind him of vultures and carrion, this for the reason that the heaven of the librarian exists in an entirely different circle of Elysium from that of the bibliophile, the casual reader, or scholar. And so all morning Flynn pushes his trolley up, down, and all around the world, returning books to their correct places, only to find upon arriving back at an area that he had just so methodically sorted, that the entire place is once again in total chaos and in need of reorganising; sometimes we have seen men with leaf-blowers or rakes, carefully gathering and assembling piles of leaves for disposal, until a single gust of wind, for that is all it takes, sends the leaves into chaos once more, to the chagrin of the leaf blower who must start the whole routine all over again. Such Sisyphean occurrences are of course not encountered only by leaf blowers and librarians, and though harried by constantly finding that he has more work to do, Flynn nevertheless approaches the absurdity of it with general good humour. He exchanges many a knowing glance with his fellow librarians, who are beset with precisely the same problem.

At the meeting, the Chief Librarian gives very little away, only re-emphasising that redundancies are in the offing and that everybody is being watched. They must therefore, he says, be as careful as possible to keep their fingers out and their noses clean, in order not to be earmarked as the unfortunate one whose time is up and must therefore be put out to pasture. He asks once again if anybody would be interested in taking voluntary severance, no doubt a generous deal could be struck, and he encourages the older members of staff to think carefully about whether they would consider sacrificing a few years' extra pension benefit in return for a redundancy package, perhaps in order to spare a younger colleague the ignominy of being asked to leave, or perhaps by emphasising the tranquillity of the retired life compared with the working one: retirement sounds so very tempting. The atmosphere in the room is rather sullen, there is a feeling of resentment amongst the troops, for who wouldn't want to work in such a place compared with the call centres, sewers, assembly lines, chemical plants, building sites, triage units, breweries, after all, the library is so very civilised a place in which to work compared with the sound of all of those other places. The Chief Librarian does not mention the matter of the notebook or the intrusion again, quite naturally nobody is going to own up to having taken it out of the Lurker's briefcase and once the meeting has concluded the staff leave the building in wordless solidarity.

Not working late tonight are we, Flynn? enquires the Deputy Chief Librarian, Don't forget that you need to make up time from yesterday.

Not tonight I can't, says Flynn. I have a few things to do.

Still busy I see. Just do it before payroll.

I won't forget.

We won't let you do that.

I'd best be going.

Good-night then Flynn, have a pleasant evening.

Thank you Deputy Chief, and the same to you too.

Flynn is the last to leave the library, and returns home to pick up the bag of tools he has gathered for the break-in. In the planning stage, he had decided early on that it would be most unwise to bring cat-burgling equipment to work, what would anybody think if they thought he was off to the sticks carrying a bag containing a balaclava, some clothes-line, and a knife? He puts on dark clothing, *In der Nacht sind alle* Katzeeinbrecher *grau*, and makes his way across to the bus stop where he plans to catch the Number Seven at 6.15. Once more he finds himself mingling amidst a milling multitude, as he waits for the bus; once more he feels the urge to smoke cigarettes, to focus his thoughts into a singularity in plumes of fuming fug, but he resists just as he did last night, this urge to scurry over to the little tobacconist and give in to temptation. He turns his attention to the bus timetable, in order to see the schedule of the buses back to the city. We shall be there by 6.45, he thinks, ten minutes or so to get to Irvine and Son, possibly ten minutes to see whether there is an alarm, and to work out my entry and exit strategies. I can give myself half an hour inside to look through the records; so we need to find a bus returning around 8pm.

Once he has finished, Flynn's plan is to walk to the main road, in order not to be seen alighting a bus too close to the scene of the crime, and he runs his index finger down the timetable. He sees that one is scheduled at the industrial estate at 8.15 and thinks to himself, so it's between now and then, which is the duration of my mission. The 6.15 arrives, Flynn boards and sits alone with his thoughts, as the bus winds its way through the city. It deviates from its regular downtown route, in order to avoid the troubles which may erupt there; it could also be said, circumnavigation or not, that it is in the direction of trouble that we seem to be heading. Once again Flynn can see the protestors with their placards marching towards the government buildings, and he sees that the police officers have formed a line of defence behind their riot shields, although it is not clear whether this is a precautionary measure or whether there have already been any eruptions of violence. The bus is moving too quickly for him to catch any details of what is happening, he will have to read about it later to get the details, and in any case there is a lot running through Flynn's head, and as one might expect; whilst the bus grinds through the suburbs, past tenements of yellowed concrete and cooling towers, out towards the countryside, he begins to think of the tactics he will use to gain access to the building, how he will assess the situation, what he will do if a hysterical alarm bell starts shrieking violently into the night.

He alights from the bus at the stop preceding the one he used last night, and starts to walk. There is very little traffic on the industrial estate at this hour, and he goes around the block a few times to see whether there are police cars or security men on patrol; he is also on the look-out for the joggers or the dog-walkers who mysteriously always seem to be on hand whenever there is a dead body in need of discovery, or even a man streaking through the night and looking for an eyewitness description. Such people are always alert to one such as I, thinks Flynn, who it has to be said is almost certainly up to no good and very much looks like it too. There are very few vehicles coming and going and no sign of any pedestrians anywhere, he sees only the steel glimmer of a milk truck making its lonely way to the dairy, we drink milk yet have to reconcile its means of production with industrial machines, and just as he had faded like a shadow into the library, so too he now makes his silent way towards Irvine and Son, Printers. He puts his bag down on the grass and circles widdershins around the building, looking for a suitable door or window for his point of entry, and he peers through windows on all sides of the unit to check for signs of life or leverage. Satisfied that the premises are deserted, for no light is visible from within, he picks up his bag and moves around to the rear, spying a back door that appears to lead into a corridor. He cannot see any external evidence of a security alarm, that does not prove the absence of one, and he wonders whether the warehouse has an intruder alert system that is linked directly to the police or to a private security company. He decides nonetheless that he will break the back door window, to see what will happen, preparing himself for a sharp getaway if necessary through the cow-field behind the building, before he makes the bold step of venturing inside. He takes the towel from his bag, folds it double, and places it against the window-pane of the door; holding it in place with his right hand he lines up his left elbow and strikes the glass panel with as much force as he can muster, but the glass refuses to break or crack. He waits for a moment, no alarm sounds from within, and he tries again. He reaches into the bag and takes out the brick, and holding the towel in place with his left hand this time, he strikes the glass once again, but the brick is rather heavy and slightly unwieldy for such a purpose, he feels the sharp pits gritting against his clammy palm, yet still the glass will not yield. Flynn mutters to himself, something inaudible followed by, *Fuck It*, and more or less throws caution to the wind; he drops the towel to the gravel, and then hurls the brick with all his might. The window immediately shatters into a shower of sapphires, and sprinkled cadences of breaking glass puncture the bubble of night. He hears the cows behind him running in the darkness, disturbed by the unexpected noise, and he catches the sweet stench of the slurry hanging in the dark air, as he stands still, listening. No alarm has sounded, there are no flashing lights, and using the towel for protection he gingerly clears the scalene remnants of the window, away from the centre of the panel where the brick struck. He hears no police siren, no barking dog, only the tinkle of more pieces of broken glass as they strike the floor inside, and he takes out his torch, shining it directly into the building.

The inside of the building is dark, save for the red glow of an emergency exit sign, this will be a useful point of reference Flynn thinks, and in the dim beam of torchlight that reaches into the building he can make out the faint appearance of a noticeboard running along the wall and a forlorn and overstuffed rubbish bin in the gloom. He reaches inside for the door handle, turns the catch of the lock and the door swings open easily for him. Taking care not to cut his arm on the shards of glass still left in the window-frame, he walks inside, closing the door behind him. He continues along the passageway, the flakes and splinters of broken glass crackling and crunching under his feet. He stops and listens, and waits for his eyes and nose to become accustomed to the interior, there is still the malodorous chemical smell, but the machines themselves are dormant, and everything inside is as silent as a tomb. There are doors on either side of him which appear to lead to lavatories, but at the end of the corridor, he finds another door that leads into the large floor of the warehouse where the printing machines stand. His torch is inadequate for the job of revealing this room in any detail because the ceiling is much higher than that of the corridor, and there is a line of windows between the walls and the roof. He suddenly thinks it a good thing that the torch beam can hardly reach them, for the appearance of streaks and flashes of light within the building at this hour would certainly alert anybody who happened to notice that a burglary might well be in full swing.

Flynn edges his way forward, with the torch pointed at the floor, and his head feels strangely vulnerable once more under the heaviness of dark space above him, as he moves his way deliberately between the silhouettes and shadows. He hears the tiniest of scratching sounds, perhaps a rat or cockroach or other scavenger, and presently the torch reveals another doorway against the side wall, Flynn reaches for the handle, opens the door and goes through it, finding himself behind the counter and facing where he had stood the previous day. Flynn remembers the gesture of the young man towards the filing cabinet next to the door when asked about address records, and with torch in one hand he tries to pull open the top drawer to look inside. The filing cabinet is locked, and Flynn looks under the counter and across the table along the back wall for a sign of the keys. He sees a small plastic cup of the sort dispensed from vending machines, inside which are staples, rubber bands, pins and sitting proudly on top of this pile are two small keys bound together on a paperclip. Flynn picks up the keys and tries them in the lock of the filing cabinet, and to his enormous satisfaction the key turns and releases the catch with an awkward metallic groan. Flynn opens the top drawer and inside he sees that it is stuffed with hanging-files, which release a powerful coppery odour as he disturbs them. Upon closer inspection, Flynn sees that these folders are arranged in alphabetical order, and trained as he is in the methods of filing, it does not take him long to work out that these dividers contain old invoices and receipts for ink deliveries, paper shipments, machine oil, toner cartridges, office supplies and so forth. Flynn goes through each one in turn to see what there is to be found, and he ascertains that this is the accounts payable drawer. Next, he moves to the drawer below, in which he finds yet more folders, which in this case contain old purchase orders, proofs of delivery, and customer receipts, once more conveniently alphabetised, a-ha, this looks more promising. He goes straight to the folder marked T and pulls it out. Holding the torch between his teeth, he moves methodically through the pile of papers, receipts which relate to orders for Tatchell, Tadlock, Talbot, Teller, Templeton, Thatcher, Thomson, Thompson, Tiffin, Tinkman,

Tittlebaugh, Tonks, Toomath, Toomer, and here we go, Totten. Flynn pauses, and takes this old order slip out of the folder and sees that it is marked with an address, he takes pen and pad from his pocket, and writes it down along with the phone number. He can see that what he has found is the original purchase order and paperwork for the creation of the book, which of course remains reassuringly unnamed on any of the pages; from the dates, we can also see for ourselves that this documentation appears to be just over one year old, and that page one of it has been stamped with all due finality in red, with the words *Paid in Full*. There is a floppy disk bearing the name of the book, and he notes that there are special instructions written at the bottom of the order that the finished article is not to contain any additional markings whatsoever on the cover or any of the pages, and he sees clipped to the order a postcard bearing the image of the Alexandrian Library that was used for the front jacket, on the back the postcard is addressed to Totten himself, and there is the briefest of notes, 'Do not let yourself be haunted, survive by making the world about those whom you haunt. I x.' Flynn places the paperwork back in the folder and the folder back into the drawer, he locks up the filing cabinet, replaces the key, and walks back out into the large printing room. He retraces his steps towards the corridor through which he came, and once again he hears the sound of scratching and scuttling as he crosses the floor, on his tip-toes through the gloom. He reaches the corridor to the back exit, makes his way along it, and once more he can hear the broken glass complaining and capitulating under him as he walks, why is it that the more carefully we tread, the more difficult it seems to be not to announce our presence? He opens the back door with its shattered window and emerges once more into the night.

Flynn now has in his pocket what he is looking for, the address or at least an address, and a new avenue down which he can continue his investigation. He does not recognise the name of the street given on the first line, and the area of the city itself is not one that Flynn has ever had any reason to frequent, as Marrowbone is one of the city's least affluent areas and mostly comprises tower blocks and social housing, homes close to what in Britain are known as sink estates or housing projects as they are known in America, where levels of violent crime and drug-related deaths are really quite high, an area populated by dispossessed and forgotten people caught in cycles of unemployment and misery, and not somewhere you would ever wish to end up if you could possibly help yourself. Flynn makes his way over the waste ground bordering the industrial estate, his heart is heavy that someone such as Barnaby Totten, whom he has decided must in many ways be an extraordinary person, with his literary voice that makes Flynn think of the tormented roars of a caged beast, that anybody should find himself living in such a place; then, he realises he finds it terrible that anybody should be forced to languish in forlorn circumstance, all hope of a dignified and fulfilled way of life receding grimly into the distance of their pasts. Flynn, we can now reveal, long ago relinquished the hope of ever finding the life companion he once longed for, and to whom he might bind himself with a hoop of steel; he has resigned himself to seeing out his days within his own form of solitude, strictly on his own terms and free from harm, but wise is the saying that the grass always seems greener on the other side. Because of this melancholic choice, if a choice it was, he can also be said to have the sort of sensibility which stands in a certain sort of natural relation to what he has just been feeling. This affinity may also be one of the reasons why he has been taking everything up to this point so very seriously, though whether he realises any of this for himself or in such terms we cannot quite say, he certainly has not mentioned it. Pleased with himself for making his exit undetected, he slinks along the edges of the cow-field and clambers up an embankment and over a fence and emerges once more on the main road. He walks along the embankment until he reaches the bus stop, where he stands waiting for the next ten minutes.

Flynn's journey home must once again follow a detour because of the protest march, and he does not arrive back in town until almost ten o'clock because of the oblique and unusual route the bus has to take. He buys his copy of *The Correspondent* and even though he now has a computer and can therefore read all the recent news stories via the internet, he has not relinquished his hardwired habit of buying the print edition, if only to feel that he himself is not contributing to the further decline of the newspaper industry, which looks increasingly as though it will one day disappear entirely. He heads to a small trattoria and orders a heavy meal, along with a half-carafe of Sicilian wine; and as he eats, he tries to think through the evening's proceedings. Bartleby Flynn feels strangely buoyant, the adrenalin has drained away on a river of wine; he feels a warm, fuzzy distance between himself and the other diners, and in this pleasant state finds it impossible to believe that he could have left any evidence behind at the Irvine and Son warehouse save for the broken glass; he smiles to himself, as he imagines the idea of a squad of police cars arriving, the Captain striding across the floor of the restaurant and placing him under arrest.

Nobody could know. Nobody could know, he mutters to himself, with a chuckle (*I am a squadron of one!*), as he recalls how carefully he replaced those files with his gloved hand, and how he carried no identifying documents on him whatsoever, save for his bank card, which he knows is safe because it is sitting right in front of him. Since nothing was stolen or disturbed, thinks Flynn, they will most likely regard the broken window as either an act of vandalism or a case of breaking and entering which had the serendipitous outcome of nothing being stolen, for the reason that the building, in truth, contains little of real value save for the huge printing machines, and how would anybody make off with one of those? As he eats, Flynn is wondering what to do next, should he ring the telephone number he has recovered, should he take a cab to where Totten lives and knock on the door, perhaps under the pretext of returning the book. It will be difficult to explain, however, the tortuous route via which he has come to know where the book belongs, perhaps on the other hand he should simply leave it at that and post the book to the address he has found, but then it immediately occurs to him that Barnaby Totten may have moved in the year or so between having had the book made and today, and that sending the book into the unknown in this fashion is simply a risk not worth taking. Flynn resolves therefore to ring the telephone number first, see if anybody is home, if there is he will ask for Barnaby Totten and hang up immediately once he has gathered whether such a person still lives there; should he get no answer at all or an affirmative one, he will travel to Marrowbone tomorrow to stakeout the address. For now the task at hand for Bartleby Flynn is to crank up his computer once again, the process known as booting, to look for the most recent comments on the web pages of *The Correspondent* from ThomPayne, in order to see what it is that Barnaby Totten has most recently been writing.

Philosophy and Language Part IV: Metaphors

The Correspondent, Friday February 12th

Peter Piper

Comments

BlindBoyGrunt

February 12th 10.29pm

@PeterPiper

> the central importance of figurative language stems from the human need to explain something in terms of something else.

'Real toads in imaginary gardens' – as Marianne Moore wonderfully puts it.

Thank you Peter for saving us from the horrors of the literal.

I have spoken.

Cryptorchid

February 12th 10.45pm

> The metaphor 'Juliet is the sun' tells us what she is like to Romeo, but it is not literally true. 'No man is an island/ entire of itself' is literally true *and* contains metaphorical significance.

Who is interested in taking the meaning literally? Calling Juliet the sun means that she's like the sun in the sense that Romeo's world revolves around her, or that she rises with him, or that life depends on her, or that in some sense she lights up his universe. Achilles is the sun would mean something altogether more dangerous. Obviously, it's trivially the case that no man is a chunk of land.

Context – not just of the words but also how they're received.

Weathereye

February 12th 11.01pm

It doesn't matter whether they are literally true. They're poetically true.

ThomPayne

February 12th 11.08pm

Cryptorchid said:

> Calling Juliet the sun means she's like the sun.

Two things.

Why does every discussion of metaphor have to use this example. *Isn't everybody sick of it?*

Also. I do not think that when you have a metaphor of the form 'X is a Y' that this has anything to do with saying 'X is like a Y.' The whole business of thinking that metaphors can be explained in terms of comparisons or parsed into extended similes is dead in the water. Saying that 'X is like a Y' and 'X is Y' have an entirely different logic.

If I say *Shakespeare is like Marlowe* then I am saying that they're both Elizabethan dramatists, good at metaphors, dead poets etc., whereas if I say *Shakespeare is Marlowe*, I am opening up a whole new can of worms. Why should the same difference not apply to the logic and syntax in figurative language?

It's not quite right to mix up the meaning of words with the meaning of sentences either, especially in the case of metaphors. I would think of it in terms of a difference between the meaning of literal words, and the metaphorical meanings of sentences.

I've been thinking about what Kant was up to in his chapters about aesthetic judgement in the third critique. He has these oracular remarks, which I'm not sure anybody quite understands, where he talks about the 'free play' between the imagination and the understanding.

The idea, I think, is that aesthetic judgement (which he calls 'reflective') appeals to universality in the way that all judgement does (I think he means that when you judge something like a metaphor, as when you judge the weather – the understanding demands a verdict as to whether the judgement is either correct, appropriate, or not).

The fundamental difference between aesthetic and ordinary judgement being that in the case of aesthetic and perhaps in the case of metaphors, the understanding is unable to provide a concept for the thing that is perceived. In the absence of a concept – of beauty, say or also in the absence of a convenient paraphrase in the case of metaphor, in the absence of any absolute semantic meaning or rule of translation – it might be that some kind of 'free play' is what characterises one's experience of those things and is the thing that produces knowledge.

On Kant's terms, imagination satisfies the demands of the understanding for coherence, determinacy etc. by continuing to provide new concepts even though no determinate concept can be found.

What does that mean?

Never been sure, but one suggestion I have, is that this is a way of saying that art-works, metaphors, judgements about beauty are not constrained by any rules. It strikes me that literary metaphor carries much of its potency in this regard – they are little art-works, and there simply isn't a way of paraphrasing, explaining, 'uncompressing' or translating, without some kind of loss to the mode of how you experience them.

LeeValentino

February 12th 11.18pm

Surely the point of metaphors is that they show you things you can't say. A kicking away the ladder kind of thing.

Gaunt

February 12th 11.31pm

@ThomPayne

> Saying that 'X is like a Y' and 'X is Y' have an entirely different logic.

Leave out your X's and Y's and the fake math. I know you like to think that the world is your stage, but I wish you'd make your exit. Pursued by a bear. The point of it is that it's a comparison. You can select the things that are relevant and forget about the rest. It floats between the two. Metaphors are grasped.

Dude, the meaning is not the issue.

PeterPiper

February 12th 11.32pm

@Gaunt

In fairness to ThomPayne, he was getting at something. The world and a stage have literal things in common (extension, mass etc.) but even if it's a simile, the actors and exits are literal features of a stage and non-literal features of the world. That seems significant. The trick is trying to explain what that comparison is.

@LeeValentino
Showing what can't be said. Props to Wittgenstein.

ThomPayne

February 12th 11.37pm

@PeterPiper

> Props to Wittgenstein.

You know Peter I think the jury might still be out as to whether Wittgenstein really thought there were things that can be shown but not said. If he really thought so I would guess that metaphors might be the test-case *huckleberry*. As in: the end of the *Tractatus*, where he's on about 'whereof we cannot speak thereof we must be silent.' Would you take that literally? Because if you do, you're committing yourself to thinking that…the things of which can't be spoken…*can still be spoken about*. Because he just did speak about them by saying they need consigning to silence. That's an argument for another day possibly, but it's the kind of thing to be alert to. When he said somewhere else that *language is a game with exact rules*, he certainly knew exactly what he was doing with that metaphor. Because that's deliberate too. What I would say to you is that what he's doing there is not at all drawing a comparison between rules of games and rules of language. He's saying language *is* a game. A metaphor only works when you understand it in terms of the basic form of the proposition – *that something is the case*. When you say 'X is Y' it has all kinds of figurative implications… but it is not a comparison like those epic similes about wine and oceans that you find in Homer.

W B Yeats says this:

> *An aged man is but a paltry thing/ A tattered coat upon a stick.*

If you change the word 'but' for 'like', the line scans the same, but the impact is different and it strikes me that the impact depends entirely on the semantic difference between saying 'X is Y' and 'X is like Y.' Something very different is conveyed by the literal vehicles. I agree that metaphors are about poetry, there comes a point where you just want to read literature without thinking about it in this way, which is mostly how I feel. Sometimes you feel like putting a different hat on and trying to figure out what's going on. It's like colliding two things together – half the time with metaphors the literal similarities are pretty tenuous. You know, if I say something like *this subject is killing me* – that's metaphorical. Why bother with thinking of comparisons? Where's the simile? Where's the smiley ☺? *Where's the beef?* When you call a film a 'blockbuster' – the word originally referred to a type of enormous bomb that could destroy an American city block. I would guess that's a dead metaphor, but they're embedded all over everyday speech.

Wittgenstein said that the English language is a graveyard of dead metaphors. Clichés, I would say, are the zombie cannibals eating up language, or the vernacular of the living dead.

I would also say from experience that... *love is a losing game.*

And you **Gaunt**, just don't try me. The meaning is not the issue.

And also Gaunt, meaning is not the preferred nomenclature. *Charientism*, please.

Go look that word up.

PeterPiper

👍 21 👎 1

February 10th 12.00am

ThomPayne wrote:

> if I say that this subject is killing me – that's metaphorical. Why bother with a comparison?

I take your point. But what does it mean?

ThomPayne

 9 0

February 10th 1.59am

Peter: when you have a metaphor of form 'X is Y' ('world is a stage') – is it the 'is' of identity or the 'is' of predication? I can't see how it's identity because with metaphors it wouldn't be symmetrical (makes no sense to me if you say 'Y is X' i.e. 'stage is the world'). All right it makes sense, but it's a different figurative expression. If it's predication, then it's false. So what you often get at this point is people using metaphors to define a metaphor. I have heard them described as lenses, and my guess is that they'd be anamorphic in some sense – and I think Max Black explains that in terms of looking at the sentence through a piece of blackened glass. Of course that's pretty clever – because if you assent to it, you have to accept his view of metaphor. Someone else said something like 'a metaphor is a duck/rabbit' – that picture thing in Kuhn – where you can look at the same thing in two ways. It's both a duck and a rabbit, but the two things are not similar. I like that because it shows me what they do and it refers to itself. But if you're asking me what any of it means, you would have to do some serious work to explain the logic of how the one literal string of words translates into another orthogonal sense of meaning. What are the rules of translation? How do you know when you're right? If it's context, then there's encyclopaedic knowledge as much as anything which is presupposed.

Maybe. Maybe what we're doing is just saying something like 'the world, *cough*, is a stage' – where the cough is a sign to the reader that you have to do something different. Maybe it leads you to wondering, if you're dim and humourless, who works in the box office or controls the lights. Which is to say, metaphors are pregnant and prone like all pregnant women to horrible misunderstandings. The thing with metaphors: they're spontaneous and can lead to new metaphors. They make you look at the world in a novel way, so in that sense, the similarity – *if there is one* – is freshly created. Chandler is full of them, and the films do not do it justice. *Dead men are heavier than broken hearts,* as Marlowe says in *The Big Sleep.* Peter, I feel Chandler-esque. I need a drink. I need some life insurance. All I have here at the moment is a coat, a hat and a gun.

BlindBoyGrunt

February 10th 2.07am

Interesting thread and better than last week's.

@ThomPayne – *physician, heal thyself.* What you need is a can of lager, a fishing rod, and some chicken.

Weathereye

February 10th 2.51am

ThomPayne. Maybe there's also a question about paraphrase.

Take the first sonnet my husband ever sent me:

If my dear love were but the child of state,
It might for Fortune's bastard be unfathered,
As subject to Time's love or to Time's hate,
Weeds among weeds, or flowers with flowers gathered.

Lots going on in there. In my mind that means something like:

'if this dear love of mine has only arisen in me because I met him in favourable circumstances, then if those circumstances changed, my love might be shown not to be real.' That's why I love my husband.

But when you suck out the metaphorical content of that it sounds like the most platitudinous and boring thing possible.

PeterPiper

 3 0

February 10th 7.00am

Thom, point taken regarding similarities and novelty.

What's your favourite metaphor?

NathanTheProphet

 11 1

February 10th 7.16am

This thread is nuts.

I'll get my coat.

ConstableGrowler

 20 0

February 10th 8.01am

I'd rather have music. Food of love. Or, maybe just love and food separately...

ThomPayne

 10 1

February 10th 8.17am

Weathereye old girl:

Anthony said to Cleopatra, as he opened a crate of ale*: Finish, good lady, the bright day is done/ And we are for the dark.* I reckon he knew that some girls are bigger than others.

PeterPiper asked:

> What's your favourite metaphor?

There are so many it makes my brain hurt. Can't remember them all anymore. I like Klaus Kinski in the film *Fitzcarraldo* – where he does that crazy eye thing and says *we're gonna drag that steamboat over the mountain!!* I am keen on Shax, some of the time. Take the fabulous extended one from *Timon of Athens* that Nabokov was on about:

> I'll example you with thievery:
> The sun's a thief, and with his great attraction
> Robs the vast sea; the moon's an arrant thief,
> And her pale fire she snatches from the sun;
> The sea's a thief, whose liquid surge resolves
> The moon into salt tears; the earth's a thief,
> That feeds and breeds by a composture stol'n
> From general excrement: each thing's a thief:
> The laws, your curb and whip, in their rough power
> Have unchecked theft.

There's Nabokov himself too:

> *I was the shadow of the waxwing slain*
> *By feigned remoteness in the window pane*

A thing that interests me at the moment thanks to Wikipedia is *Anthimeria* – using a word which is one part of speech as if it were a different one. A noun for a verb or an adjective – a knowing a hawk from a handsaw kind of thing. Thus the Danish play:

> Within the very flame of love, there lives
> A kind of wick or snuff that will put it out,
> And nothing is worse than goodness staying still,
> For goodness, growing to an infectious pleurisy,
> *Dies in his own too much.*

That's brain-blowingly brilliant and sounds so natural, and in spite of the fact that the anthimeria in the last line ought by rights to be dismissed as complete f**king gibberish. To go back to Chandler – *He was eager to help but his legs were rubber* – that always makes me chuckle, and then some. Then there's Ezra Pound: *the apparition of these faces in the crowd/ Petals on a wet black bough.*

One of my favourites of all is from the cartoon *Futurama*, because I like mixed metaphors, especially when they're facetious and fatuously atrocious.

> *If we hit that bull's-eye, the rest of the dominoes will fall like a house of cards. Checkmate!*

Another cheeky one placed in the detective category of the Bulwer-Lytton bad fiction contest:

> *She walked into my office wearing the kind of a body that makes a man write bad cheques*

Aristotle locates metaphor somewhere between the unintelligible and the commonplace. My guess is that they're performances of a sort, performances which illuminate our interior lives. Music does that: think of the *Klagender Gesang* before the fugue in Beethoven's Op. 110. Or think of pretty much any of Dylan's best lines:

> *There's a lone soldier on the cross/ Smoke pouring out of a box-car door*

Compare it to the heartbreaking Billie Holiday in *Fine and Mellow*:

> *Love is like a faucet/ it turns off and on*

I'm not knocking similarities, they just function differently. Neither figurative expression shows what can't be said...because they say it. The perspicuous question hovers way above the battle in these things. Is not the question about what happens when you empathise and think of yourself as someone else? See the world through somebody else's locutions and metaphors? There's the beef, or your Highway 61. The ultimate form of figurative thinking. Anyway I am done waving my prick around on this thread tonight...I am hungry, drunk and tired. Metaphor is the dream-work of language, as a philosopher once said.

Thinking of yourself as someone different is the ultimate strategy when it comes to grasping art and metaphors. There's no smoke without a salmon.

I also have a few fish to fry.

Chuckled the Rascal.

THIS THREAD IS NOW CLOSED

11

POCKETS OF VIOLENCE broke out across the city last night whilst Flynn was making his way back from creeping around the premises of Irvine and Son, how bold he has become since we were first introduced, and although Flynn was not able to see any evidence of these protest marches from his vantage-point above the double-decker bus that carried him back into town, he saw some of the footage on the late news bulletin. The police formed barricades near and around the major government buildings and the President's palace, and the skirmishes began when somebody threw a milk bottle which shattered against the Ministry of the Interior wall, showering glass onto the officers who were gathered below. The offender was arrested, reports say, as were several other protestors who, angry at being strong-armed by the police, saw fit to retaliate with pushes, kicks and punches which saw to it that they spent a night in the cells ahead of arraignment. The leading item of this morning's news is that police have promised a crackdown tonight, should protestors again take to the streets with an escalation of the hostilities. The Deputy Commissioner has been interviewed outside Police Headquarters looking harassed and windswept, surrounded by journalists and photographers, and he has announced that officers of the law will not tolerate the slightest breach of the peace tonight or take any kind of misdemeanour lightly.

The square was quite busy when Flynn stepped down from the bus, there was no rain, just a clammy coldness, and a gibbous moon shone darkly, pale and waxing, in a sapphire sky. Under the crystal of louring heavens, then, Flynn made his way home once more, and he had been staring at the telephone for several minutes, when much to his surprise it started ringing at him.

Hello?

Flynn?

Oh Deputy Chief Librarian. No quite alright, I was wide awake.

I hope this hasn't disturbed you from your busy evening?

Not in the slightest.

Indeed.

What can I do for you? asks Flynn.

Can you possibly come in early and open up tomorrow morning? I have an early appointment.

Yes of course, you can rely on me.

Thank you, I knew I could rely on you.

Really, no trouble.

Then I shall see you later tomorrow morning and say goodnight.

Same here, and the same to you. Sleep tight.

Flynn replaced the receiver, and set his alarm clock for a half-hour earlier than usual. He brushed his teeth, rinsed, opened up his laptop computer and climbed into bed with it, if we could have seen in through his window last night, we would have been able to make out a man in striped pyjamas peering into his computer and concentrating intently, the only light in the room coming from the pale of the screen, casting long shadows onto a white wall behind.

*

Flynn arrives to open the library even earlier than necessary, determined to get a running start on the day, and he is already in the thick of things when the first of his colleagues arrives. The address given for Barnaby Totten, we are now in a position to say, is Flat 2, 15 Myrtle Avenue; and Flynn has ascertained already the whereabouts of this address and decided how he will get there. He has determined that he will take a taxi from work and ask to be dropped in close proximity to this street, from there he will wander around the neighbourhood a while, breathe the air, and try to get a sense of the unknown author's environment, the look of the fast-food joints, the corner-shops, the garages, hair salons, the pharmacies, the height of the kerbs, the drains, and the geometries and dynamics of the infrastructure. He has found that there is a bus which runs to the city every half-hour from this locale, and he has already decided that this will be the chosen method for getting home, after all taxis are expensive, and one can never quite trust a taxi-driver not to take you all round the houses and back again if you are in a foreign city or have no idea where you are; at present Flynn is sitting at a computer in one of the back offices looking at the photographic street-view function retrievable via the website of Internet Maps, trying to get at least a preliminary sense of what the neighbourhood looks like and what there is to expect. 'Hard at work are we, Flynn?' asks the Deputy Chief, who has silently crept up, as he tends to, and already stooping at the shoulder of Flynn's herringbone jacket to peer at the screen. Startled (how is it that this character never fails to be so maddeningly quiet?), Flynn instinctively uses the mouse to minimise the open window of the browser, in order to conceal what he has been looking at, too late of course – the Lurker has already divined what he is up to. Flynn stammers and splutters an apology for slacking on the job; he gets up and grabs the nearest trolley he can find and spends the remainder of the morning in something of a state of hyper-vigilance as he stalks the labyrinth of corridors. Occasionally he catches a glimpse of the Deputy Chief Librarian here or there, craning his head around a shelf or meeting Flynn's callow eyes with a stare as cold as the evening frost, whenever they happen to pass one another on the stairs.

Flynn encounters the Lurker once more whilst eating lunch; this time, he goes so far as issuing a reprimand and reminds Flynn of the library's policy regarding the use and misuse of company computer equipment, after all internet access at work is a privilege which can be easily withdrawn if abused:

Yes, I'm terribly sorry, I had only been using it for a few minutes, I was looking for directions, says Flynn.

Where are you off to?

I'm off to meet a friend, but I've never been to this part of the city.

He taps his finger on the screen, pointing at the map.

You seem awfully busy in the evenings of late. For years you do nothing but work late and now there's no stopping you.

I know, I know.

The Lurker seems to have forgotten that Flynn came in early, for as he leaves he adds:

Don't forget to make up those hours.

Holding a half-eaten chicken-leg in one hand, Flynn, with his legs crossed, opens up today's issue of *The Correspondent* and makes straight for the editorial pages, reads quickly the analyses, and op-ed pieces concerning last night's protest events and the behaviour of the crowds and police. He thinks again of *The Book of the Unknown Author:*

> 'So-called facts are simply opinions dressed in top hats and tails, waving around their degree certificates. Think of all the information in the millions of books in that library, or

even in any library. The history of writing is the history of uncertainty in pursuit of its own illumination. The butterfly of our civilisation is undergoing a sort of reverse evolution. The butterfly is shrinking back into the pupa. Madness and obsessions everywhere. *Deadly writing!*'

A memo is circulated about the forthcoming spending cuts to which the National Library of Books and Publications has now become subject, an internal memo which outlines a plan for how the library might cut some corners and recoup some of the lost funding and some of the ideas they have had for austerity measures; not only will they be laying off a member of staff, they will also try to offset the dent in the finances by increasing the charges to the public for printing out documents, increasing fines and raising the flat fee that is automatically charged to patrons for any book that is lost or damaged.

The memo also details that the notebook which the Deputy Librarian found, and which thence disappeared from his briefcase, is a matter of on-going investigation, and it contains a reminder, which Flynn cannot help but take as directed at him, that excessive personal use of library computers is not acceptable, and since the workforce will soon downsize it is important that everybody gets used to working that little bit harder, because the volume of work is certainly not expected to get any lighter, just because of a loss in revenue. Aside from chatter about these on-going internal issues at the library, there is also talk amongst the workers about last night's protest, and the general state of the nation:

Did you see any of it?

No, did you?

It was on the television.

We could hear some of the chanting from *The Crow*.

Wouldn't like to get caught up in it.

That's for sure.

They say there's a bigger one planned.

I hope they have enough cops.

We don't want any casualties.

Apart from the criminals.

I suppose they matter less.

Well I'd have the bastards shot.

Flynn has noticed that the arrested man from the previous evening's protest, the man who had thrown the milk bottle which served as a sort of unofficial launching ceremony for those minor skirmishes, is listed in the newspaper as being of Manor Road, Marrowbone, and it has not escaped Flynn's attention that this road is in precisely the neighbourhood that he intends to visit later tonight, in order to snoop around, near the house of Barnaby Totten. Flynn quite naturally begins to wonder whether these two men knew each other, a pure piece of speculation of course, after all, it is not true that everybody in a neighbourhood knows everybody else, and in fact it is often very much the opposite. Yet he can't help wondering anyway whether the two of them may have perhaps shared a glass of beer, or simply walked past one another on the street, or crossed each other's paths on the way to the shop to buy a paper, or a bottle of cider, or a loaf of bread, or to go to the bookies; these are the encounters for which chance makes ample provision, and which are certainly not ruled out by any of the information we have at our fingertips.

Whenever he works at a library computer, be it to enter the details of some new arrivals into the electronic catalogue or just to pay an outstanding invoice, or order some new publications, Flynn has taken to keeping a tiny window open on his computer screen in which he is able to see and periodically refresh the web page which displays the commenting history of ThomPayne. Whenever he senses that somebody is near or might be approaching, he quickly holds the ALT and TAB buttons in order to cycle through to the next screen open, in the hope that he is thereby keeping himself concealed, deceiving anybody who might happen to be observing or who had noticed that he does not completely have his mind on the job for which he is paid. It might also be added that if nobody can see what he is up to and he appears to be concentrating intensely, his dedication to his job will undoubtedly seem all the more irrefragable to these observers. Thus, no doubt in fear of their own jobs, they will redouble their own efforts, thereby ensuring that all the work gets done whilst Flynn can keep his eye on things at his leisure. Old Man Time ambles into the afternoon today, in contrast to those days when he dawdles or occasionally strides, the library is quiet save for a smattering of readers who have their heads bowed over manuscripts in the reading rooms, and the library employees shuffle about the place with their sense of intent; they do not want to be caught shirking when they least expect it. The announcement of the staff cut has injected a certain sense of competitiveness between workers, each being keen to be seen to be out-doing the other, and Flynn is no longer the only person who is conspicuous in staying behind after work in order to ensure that everything is ship-shape for the following day. Yet again however, Flynn will not be staying late tonight, because he plans to head to the street of the unknown author as soon as he finishes; he had booked a Yellow Cab as soon as he got up.

And so it is that when the cathedral bell chimes in fives, Flynn is first out of the door, not even taking the trouble to say good-bye to anybody tonight. Dashing into the evening rain, his raincoat half on and trailing, we can see that the taxi is here already, idling just to one side of the main entrance; neat and solitary it stands, as waiting cars sometimes look. Flynn opens the back door and climbs in, there is the creeping smell of stale tobacco, and the brown livery is downy thick and tattered, there are crumbs in the grooves that house the stitching, an alien texture against the corduroy of his trousers that he does not sink into without reservation. Flynn slides himself along the back seat as though feeling his way into a borrowed slipper, taps on the plastic window that divides the back from the front, and confirms his destination, *Let's Go!* The radio, so often a chronic irritation in our lives, sometimes strikes us with a voice of surprising and ironic power; she is capable of providing us with all sorts of thoughts, at the moment when we least expect it; sometimes her voice presents us with the perfect foil or point of reference against which we can scrutinise and question the current dimensions of our interior selves. If you have never had the opportunity to experience the intensely pleasurable melancholy inscribed within us when we savour the quiet of these unexpected moments, then more is the pity, we hope it happens to you at least once in your life, it really is very seductive. We digress momentarily, merely because this is how it presently is for Bartleby Flynn as he is driven across the darkening city in the back of his decrepit taxi, a song from *My Fair Lady* quite naturally, and Nat King Cole singing –

'*I have often walked down this street before/ but the pavement always stayed beneath my feet before*'

– not that Flynn is particularly a fan of Lerner and Loewe numbers or even Broadway theatre in general, nevertheless he feels somehow insubstantial with nervous excitement at the emotions stirred within him by the old song, it provides the perfect soundtrack as the taxi is weaving its way methodically through the warp and weft of the traffic, past the neon of the theatre district with its expensive restaurants. He looks through the rain and sees the shadows and reflections of the people sitting at the tables, a waiter proudly presenting some steaming delicacy. He sees glasses of white wine being brought together, a hand momentarily touching a hand or tossing a lock of hair. Flynn gazes at the people sitting alone, nursing their cocktails; and he thinks how wondrous a thing it is just to be alive at such a moment, as though suspended between the starting-point and the destination, which after all is what all of life is. Even if what he is seeing is at one level quite shallow and representative of the appetitive aspect of what we sometimes call the human soul, as opposed to anything of weightier significance, nevertheless what's wondrous, he thinks, is the simple fact of being able to observe these gilded moments of desire which sometimes haunt us with their transience; and as a logical consequence of this first stage of wonder, there follows within him the dark and blazing realisation of the immense power that he has, in simply being able to observe anything at all.

There are signs that protestors are gathering again, the song finishes and the radio reports that crowds have herded in at least four separate locations, and that they are marching once more and plan to gather outside the Senate Building, but Flynn's taxi has edged its way through the worst of the rush-hour traffic in the city centre, and is moving now towards the city limits, past the giant concrete building from which one of our nation's three main television channels is broadcast, past water and gas towers, past petrol stations and cemeteries, and onto a stretch of dual-carriage freeway that leads north-by-northwest towards Marrowbone.

Flynn pays the driver and steps out onto the pavement in Myrtle Avenue; he feels suddenly as if all eyes are upon him, even though there is hardly anybody to be seen. He walks back along the street towards the main road from which the taxi has turned, and he sees the cabbie has picked up another fare, and is pulling into the inside lane to wait at the traffic lights. It is quiet, and the rain has stopped falling, yet leaving behind the dampness of itself in such a way that Flynn once again feels very cold. He stands now at the crossroads, on the other side of which is a strand of shops, looking as though they have been blinded by the metal shutters which are pulled down; there is a Chinese takeaway and a newsagent that has thick iron bars to protect its windows. Styrofoam food containers are strewn on the greasy pavement beneath the awnings, and above them are what appear to be dingy flats. He notices a naked bulb illuminating one of them, and faded sheets half-heartedly hung in others as perfunctory curtains. He crosses the street and goes into the tiny newsagent, the aisles are narrow and untidily arranged, and the air is oppressively warm from the calor-gas heaters standing near the counter. Not knowing why he has gone in, he buys a packet of chewing gum and a bar of milk chocolate. He stands outside and unwraps it, but the squares are lukewarm and soft, they stain his fingers, he puts them into his mouth and feels the back of his throat stinging, sometimes chocolate is a comfort food yet at others it is as unfriendly as can be. Flynn wipes his hands on his handkerchief, and feeling somewhat nauseous and empty, crosses the street once more and walks along Myrtle Avenue.

The houses on this street as you enter it from the main road run down along the right hand side; on the left there is a school and a large playing-field behind a coarse and galvanised steel fence. Cars line this side of the street, many of which appear to have seen better days, for some are missing hubcaps or appear to have been abandoned. Flynn passes a BMW which is filled from floor to ceiling on all sides with plastic bags full of newspapers, divorced plastic objects, soiled clothing, refuse sacks, a broken umbrella. The houses in this street on the right are semi-detached for the most part and many appear to have been turned into flats, and there are side-streets running parallel to the main road, which appear to lead to more of the same. Flynn still feels as though being watched – as though the people behind those curtains have been waiting for him and must somehow know why he is there and what he is thinking; where do these elements of paranoia spring from when just a half hour ago we were so glad to be alive? There is a vinegar smell hanging in the air and Flynn fancies that it could be from the school canteen; how ridiculous, he immediately thinks, they will not be cooking any meals now, and he is struck by a chain-reaction of memories of the dreary canteen from his own school days, with its powdered potatoes and baked beans, the remainders of which used to end up being scraped from plates into a warm and stinking slop bucket. Many of the houses do not have numbers on them, and he has reached the end of the school playing field which backs directly onto a threadbare and rubbish-strewn public park lined with broken trees. He can see that he has just reached number twenty-seven but does not yet know whether the numbers are going up or going down, he presses on past the park and sees a public house called The Marrowbone and Cleaver, which is marked number twenty-two. Flynn continues to feel ill-at-ease as he stands outside it, realising he is getting closer to number fifteen. It is unmarked, ironically enough, but by counting along, he thinks he has worked out which house it must be, and hazards a guess that one could just about see it through the window of the bar, if one were standing up.

Flynn walks into The Marrowbone and Cleaver, he can immediately smell the ammonia from the cold toilets mingling with stale alcohol; there are men sitting along the bar, and he hears the hollow snap of the pool cue over the pounding of the jukebox. There are round tables surrounded by faux-leather stools, and an area to the right, standing in front of the window, that is raised and lined with tattily-upholstered benches. Nobody pays Flynn much mind, he is a small and unassuming man, and has not dressed himself in such a way as to appear too atypical in such an environment, and thereby averts attracting any unnecessary attention, the crowd loves a victim. He quickly observes that all the men present appear to be drinking from bottles or pitchers of beer and so, rather than order a soft drink or something like a glass of wine, which he senses would be precisely the thing which would draw inquisitude, he orders a bottle of lager for himself and declines the glass. He takes the bottle and walks up onto the platform in front of the long window which overlooks Myrtle Avenue, and sits down in the corner. The ambience of this place is morose, the men at the bar sit with their heads bowed forward like the readers in the library reading rooms, but here they are looking into their glasses and not into books, indeed to produce a book or so-called quality newspaper from one's bag or trouser in such an arena would undoubtedly entice pairs of reptilian eyes to start conspiring with one another. At first, Flynn is panicking because he has nothing to do, but sit. He tries to avoid the appearance of watching anybody although he can't help himself to some extent, for he is wondering whether the unknown author comes into this place, indeed he could be any of the men who are already here.

Bartleby Flynn is keeping his wits about him, and listening to the broken fragments of conversation that he can catch, listening all the time for the name Barney or Barnaby, or indeed any other kind of aural clue which might prove relevant to the course of his investigation. He finds himself studying their faces as they lean over the pool table, or as they emerge from the bathroom, or as they count out the money from the palms of their hands to pay for drinks, and he thinks about the barman. There is nobody present, with the possible exception of Flynn himself, since he neither lives in this area nor frequents

such places, nobody who gives the appearance of being
striking, or in any way out of step with the dreary
surroundings; and Flynn starts wondering whether the
unknown author even bothers to come into a dive like this,
such is the depressing ambience in which he has found
himself. Flynn takes to looking away from the drinkers and
out through the window once more, and watches the stick-
like figures who shuffle along the pavement, battling
against the rain. He sees an old woman pushing a shopping
trolley along the road, onto which bags are strapped, bags
that seem to be full of all her worldly possessions; thin-
faced men emerge from behind the front doors of their
houses and thrust their hands into their jacket pockets and
walk out against the night. He can see through the
windows of some of the flats which make up the houses
opposite, some of them have been boarded over or
covered in polythene sheets because of broken glass. There
appears to be no light at all coming from number fifteen;
Flynn has finished his drink, and gets up, walks across the
patio, and back onto the street; he does not bother to
thank the bartender or say good evening, and staying on
the left-hand side of the street, he approaches where he
thinks he needs to go. Viewed from the other side of the
street, Flynn confirms to himself that there are indeed no
lights switched on and that it appears nobody is home; the
top floor appears to be completely uninhabited and
derelict, but in the evening light he is able to see signs of
habitation through the ground-floor windows, the outline
of a lamp, the back of a television, a coffee cup on the sill.

Flynn continues down the avenue, which he realises appears to be getting steadily darker, because it is lined quite heavily with barren trees at this end of the street, the jagged and outstretched arms of which produce a skeletal canopy over the road itself, and which seems to filter the moonlight. There are no streetlights, and he realises that the street is a cul-de-sac, for there is a dead-end in the form of the concrete wall facing him.

He follows the pavement round, and begins to walk back up the street on the left-hand side. At the main road, he slows his pace and his heartbeat quickens as he approaches number fifteen once more; he is able to see more details of the building's aspect this time, the front door is shabby and the windows do not look as though they have been cleaned in some time. There is a series of doorbells on the one side of the door, he cannot make out what is written on them, there appear to be two flats in the building, both of which are on the ground floor. The house is double-fronted, and what he takes to be the flat to the left has a bay window, but the curtains are drawn shut. The flat to the right has what, on closer inspection, seems to be a picture window, and this is where Flynn is able to see in closer detail the lamp, and the outline of a settee. It appears to be a studio room because he can see the green outline of a digital clock flashing over what appears to be a gas oven. Number fifteen is the right-hand house of a semi-detached pair, and there is a driveway running along the outer wall, that leads to a ramshackle garage with peeling black paint on the doors, which are secured by a thick metal chain.

The skeletal corpse of a bicycle leans against the wall, its front wheel bent inwards. There is an old washing machine in the middle of the drive, and the concrete is erupting with weeds from swollen crevices, nature and our hopeless attempt to impose dominion over it locked in the beginnings of a mortal struggle for supremacy.

Flynn does not stop, does not pause, does not have the nerve to trespass onto the property, but makes his way from this hollow at the centre of his investigations and back towards the main road, the street becoming lighter as he emerges from under the twisted branches of the trees. He sees once more the bar and the school, and quickens his pace towards the main road (what time is it now?), surely the bus must be due any minute. He crosses the main road and walks towards the shop which has now closed, and passes some youths loitering under the flat roof which extends over the pavement in front of the shop. There are dead leaves on the pavement, glutinous from rain; he moves past quickly, continuing down the main road towards a solitary bus shelter, its timetable long unreadable through vandalism, and notices a large group of men holding placards seemingly on the march towards the city centre, walking slightly ahead of him on the opposite side of the street. He senses a certain air of aggression in the purposeful way in which they are moving, he has no inclination to walk further and stays at the bus stop.

It was while he was still standing there that the heavens split apart, and a downpour began.

Riots and Poverty: Open Blog

The Correspondent, Thursday February 11th

<u>Comments</u>

<u>Weathereye</u>

 17   3

February 11th 1.50pm

Not everybody who lives in poverty is from a bad/poverty-stricken area. People might be employed and have so little disposable income at their fingertips that they join in to get a bit, innit.

<u>ThomPayne</u>

 3   7

February 11th 1.55pm

So a few windows have been smashed. Fuck 'em. The odd shop owner or bus company had some property damaged, which they will be compensated for by insurance. I find it hard to feel that bad about it. I had some bad news today. I have bigger problems.

Unemployment is very high, and employers are very choosy who to hire, even for the most menial jobs.

Before the deluge starts on this thread; you do not simply make a choice to work and then find yourself magically getting paid and owning that dream house. First you have to be chosen. In order for that to happen, the employer has to feel comfortable that you'll be the right kind of fit. Being the right kind of fit boils down to how you look – because employers really are that shallow. Employers care about snobbery and racism far more than they do about skills and qualifications. Most office jobs, right up to quite senior managerial roles, require no real abilities or an education. You just need to demonstrate the right 'behaviours.' A willingness to toe the line and knife people in the back when you're told to by a superior. The actual jobs themselves involve doing moronic and virtually pointless clerical work all day or occasionally asking for some new ink for the photocopier. Anybody can do office admin, and I know this because I have done this mindless kind of work. The hardest part of it is staying awake, maybe disguising the book that you're writing and not rocking the boat. Discrimination is rife – over age, being the wrong class, being the wrong sex. Not having the right looks for the job.

Gaunt

 29 15

February 11th 1.59pm

Totally ridiculous, **ThomPayne**. If poverty and discrimination were the cause of the riots, then all poor people would riot, no? Fact is, it was the unemployable. A minority of work-shy criminal thugs. If jobs were so easy, they'd get them, and if there were genuine deterrents, they wouldn't do it. Man the hose and get the rubber bullets out.

A funny episode of *The Simpsons* is where Homer buys a motor-home. Marge chastises him ('you spent our life's savings on a motor-home?'); and Homer says, 'No Marge, I spent our life's savings on the *downpayment* for a motor-home.'

That nails it.

BoiledMouse

9 3

February 11th 2.08pm

Totally ridiculous Gaunt to think that if poverty were the cause of riots then all poor people would join in.

Social unrest is driven by a variety of factors (poverty is a major one). It's a factor that's there to be seen in inner cities. A lot of us have known for ages that there are dispossessed, disconnected layers in this country and we've simply chosen to turn a blind eye to this. Now there has been an uprising – and the powers that be should have expected it to happen. I blame advertising – our society is a consumerist one and a lot of people are motivated by the desire for stuff they can never afford.

Eusebius

 1 0

February 11th 2.10pm

Something else meaningless under the sun ThomPayne?

A chasing after the wind.

My craven superiors have got it in for me, too.

BlindBoyGrunt

 3 0

February 11th 2.20pm

If poverty were a major factor surely the entire upper territory should have been reduced to a smoking crater by this point.

Gaunt

 14 5

February 11th 2.50pm

Most poor folk do not start riots or behave anti-socially. In the case of these riots, idleness and spiritual/ moral bankruptcy is the cause. To fix it: evict them from their social housing, take away their benefits, then throw them in hoosegow to cool their heels. In some cases, I'd also recommend throwing away the key. What we need are harsh deterrents to this kind of thing. It's the only justice they know.

I have spoken.

NathanTheProphet

February 11th 3.16pm

Not sure there's much need for complex analysis. People were simply taking what didn't belong to them, taking pleasure in chaos without a thought for anybody else.

InformationSilo

February 11th 3.30pm

Gaunt, moral and spiritual bankruptcy was what caused people to start stealing goods and burning cars? Examples of the spiritual: catholic priests and children. Bombings in the UK and Spain. Limb amputations and genital mutilation. You think if these people found God they'd fall in line? What a stupid comment.

If we're doing lines from *The Simpsons*, remember the one where Kirk Van Houten gives his advice on what to do with a dead raccoon?*:*

'Throw it over the fence and let Arby's deal with it.'

Conservatism in a nutshell.

ConstableGrowler

February 11th 3.55pm

Read *The Correspondent* if you want your fix of liberal apologetics on feral scum who belong in prison. Middle of the road, centre-ground nonsense from people who are not even affiliated to a party.

BlindBoyGrunt

February 11th 4.15pm

Given you're all from a nation that built its wealth by piracy, genocidal looting and divide-and-rule violence and pillaging, there is a lot of blood to rinse from the flag is there not?

I picture Our Lady of Justice with a stain-devil and washboard, frantically rubbing.

'*Out damned spot!*'

Yet we're continually told that these riots are simply wanton criminality without precedent.

Ah.

Weathereye

February 11th 4.32pm

One problem here is that the right-wing brigade refuse to acknowledge the harm that gross inequality inflicts, and the fact that the decades of policy have caused it. There will never be a solution to social unrest for as long as they do not wake up and smell what they shovel. The hymn of neo-liberalism is about the survival of the fittest. Bankers and politicians loot and steal, and clamber their way over everybody using their 'connections.' Anybody who falls by the wayside is simply expendable spume and flotsam.

My favourite *Simpsons* is where Homer becomes a chiropractor. And because he doesn't have a licence, the chiropractors 'pay him a visit' and trash his stuff.

And Mo or someone says to him afterwards, 'Forget it Homer, it's Chirotown. They make their own rules there.'

JohnnyLegless

February 11th 4.59pm

Interesting how an overwhelming desire for socialism precipitates people looting LED televisions, laptops and shoes. I am watching these feral animals attacking a bus full of innocent people on the television as I type. I'd be perfectly happy to see these people kicked out of their free housing and shot on sight.

NomDeGuerre

February 11th 5.50pm

Whatever the indignation about the burning and looting nobody has been able to hold a single white-collar looter from the city or government to account. What's the difference apart from using a computer and wearing pinstripes instead of a tracksuit? What's the moral difference? They've already had plenty of these looters up before the judge, yet it's been five years since the depression started, thanks to the banksters smashing and grabbing whatever they could get their grubby hands on. Since it's equivalent: why do not we get some of their front doors smashed in, so they can be evicted and locked up for larceny?

Cryptorchid

February 11th 6.56pm

Enough excuses, the events in the capital city are simply organised and expedient thuggery and looting. I feel sorry for the normal people who live cheek by jowl with these animals and the ones who foot the bill.

ThomPayne

 1 0

February 12th 4.35am

I think you are legless, **JohnnyLegless**. But it's OK, I've been drinking too.

@Gaunt: when your life is tough anyway, what use are tough, zero-tolerance deterrents? Not everybody is middle-class, young and full of hope about what their life holds ahead of them. From some of these comments you'd think that the world is everybody's oyster if they'd only sort themselves out. Maybe it is an oyster, come to think of it if you're into WH Auden:

> *The earth is an oyster with nothing inside it*
> *Not to be born is best for man*
> *The end of toil is the bailiff's order*
> *Throw down your mattock, dance while you can!*

Your problem is that do not understand what has been happening. You're like a Venetian count in an enormous ruffled collar who's had his horse and carriage toppled over by a highwayman. You're sitting in the ditch, your wig askew, and you're in a state of shock because the bit of cake you handed out was hurled back in your face. *Why can't we all just…get along?* That's the mentality of people who eat Alpen for breakfast. It could be said. It must be said.

The spending cuts, the banking crisis, have the real trickle-down effect. It trickles down through the system, all the way down to the bikers running meth-labs or the guy hawking cigarette lighters on the street. Everybody is feeling the wind, and even violent criminals know where that wind is blowing from. For the President, it must be like watching a zombie apocalypse. Mindless flesh-eating creatures that he's helped create through bizarre social experiments which can't be reasoned with. They're gathering at the gates of the palace and rattling on the fence. They're coming to get him. I wouldn't be surprised if he wakes up in a terror sweat after a nightmare where zombie hands punch through a wall…where a horde of them have a set-to, rip out his entrails and eat him alive.

My own case is that the company I worked for has just laid off several thousand workers (including me). There's your fucking trickle-down. Lying in a gutter, covered in piss.

The bread bin is empty and the circus animals have fled.

All I have at the moment are clowns.

Isn't it rich? Aren't we a pair?

Eusebius

 0 ⏍ 0

February 12th 5.08am

> *Aren't we a pair?*

Like Dylan sang:

One says to the other, no man sees my face and lives.

Or is it:

If happy little bluebirds fly…beyond the rainbow – why, oh why – can't I (and I)

THIS THREAD IS NOW CLOSED

Lifestyle 2.0: Open Thread

The Correspondent, Wednesday February 10th

Comments

Weathereye

February 10th 1.58pm

> We all know about the big things. But how has the web
> changed the way you do the little things?

Internet dating. Not that I do it very much, but it's how I met my
husband. After a long and lovely literary correspondence to rival
that of Browning and Elizabeth Barrett, we finally met up and
never looked back. We come from different countries, and
there's no way I'd have met him otherwise, and I am happy to
report that in our rapidly encroaching dotage we shall most
certainly be assuaged.

BoiledMouse

February 10th 1.59pm

I use it to buy illegal drugs. Specifically: Ritalin to bring me up
and Vicodin to bring me down. It's a very effective system.

InformationSilo

February 10th 2.30pm

I buy my grocery shopping online, except for the fruit. The fruit is always that slightly suspect-looking kind they sell in corner shops.

MopDog

February 10th 3.00pm

Vicodin and Ritalin doesn't sound so good, **BoiledMouse**?

Narrator

February 10th 2.56pm

It's certainly changed the way one goes about producing books.

BlindBoyGrunt

February 10th 4.15pm

Good to hear of a successful internet dating story Weathereye, these are few and far between.

An American friend of mine tells this story that she agreed to go on a blind date with some guy she found on the internet. He shows up to pick her up with the back of his car entirely full of cases of beer and says, why don't we go to the beach? So they're driving along and he says he needs to stop and get some money for petrol. But instead of stopping off at an ATM or a bank as you'd expect, his idea of 'getting money' is to go and sell some blood plasma at a donor clinic (last I heard you get around

$50 for a sample). So my friend and this guy are lying next to each other with needles in their arms, donating plasma and she's thinking 'how the fuck did I get in this situation' and eventually they're done and they get $100 for themselves. He buys some petrol, fags, magazines etc. and they drive to the beach. He unloads this crate of beer and proceeds to drink his way steadily through it, meanwhile she takes a couple of swigs and suddenly starts feeling dizzy from all the plasma she gave and because she's on a low-carb diet. They both end up being violently sick and she has to call her parents to drive her home. The funny thing is, when she told me that story she was strangely into this guy and was planning on seeing him again.

I have spoken.

JesterJinglyJones
 11   0

February 10th 1.55pm

My brother had this girlfriend he met online who used to steal his possessions, conceal them upon her person and then demand that he 'rape her' in order to recover them. He would then sit beside her afterwards while she smoked a cigarette on the terrace of his house and they would watch the twilight descend. Most unusual! She also was very prone to injuring herself, and after they split up he'd see her from time to time on crutches, and a couple of weeks later the crutches would have gone but she'd have her arm in a sling and then a neck brace the next time. LaJester wonders whether she was just into wearing accident paraphernalia rather than accident prone d:o)

BoiledMouse
 3   0

February 10th 1.59pm

Only if you're a novice at it, MopDog. Plus OxyContin doesn't have the same stigmas attached.

ThomPayne

👍 0 👎 0

February 10th 2.00pm

That's excellent **BlindBoyGrunt.** I went on an internet double blind date with a friend, which ended in my friend and her date and me getting in a stand-up blazing argument. My friend is divorced, but she'd advertised herself as 'single' on the web page because her thinking was that, you know, she's single in the sense that she is not seeing anybody. Fair enough, right? This gimpy looking guy shows up and it comes out in a wholly natural way during the conversation that she's actually divorced, and he suddenly flies into a rage about how she ticked the single and not the divorced box on the profile and was being deliberately dishonest to ensnare unsuspecting innocent men, like she's some kind of gold-digging man-eater (she kind of is a gold-digging man-eater, but that's another story).

So I wade into the argument as a Makepeace, and I point out that there's nothing disingenuous about what my friend said on the profile – that 'single' is the super-class in this instance, and that 'single divorced', 'single widowed' etc. are sub-classes of a larger group – *the group of all single people.* So then he started yelling at both of us, knocked over the drinks and accused me of being a weirdo and so on, so much so that the girl I was with, whom I quite liked and would happily have planted a fuck in, she just fled the whole scene in horror. My friend and I were left sitting glumly in this stinking dark bar, where we proceeded to run up a hefty and enjoyable bar tab. But the moral – is that I am never going on an internet date again. The blood plasma story is just another nail in the coffin.

Phil Spector gets a poor press these days, possibly with some justification but situations like that – whenever I hear The Righteous Brothers and that wall of sound… it takes me half way to the Blue Snowball nebula…

You've lost that loving feeling.

Ah yes. That loving feeling.

Weathereye

February 10th 2.08pm

Good Lord Thom and Grunt, I do not know who's stranger – you or your friends.

BoiledMouse

February 10th 2.09pm

One thing that's very useful are online gift registries for when you have to go to weddings.

ComradeJenny

February 10th 2.00pm

Forum wars and the revolution!

NathanTheProphet

February 10th 2.16pm

Paying bills and transferring money?

JesterJinglyJones – you do realise that only geniuses, gods and lunatics refer to themselves in the third person?

ThomPayne

February 10th 9.18pm

BoiledMouse, the wedding thing is nothing short of a scam. Where you have to look desperately for the cheapest thing on that list and it turns out to be a tiny fruit knife worth three to four times what any sane person would ordinarily pay for one of those things. If the people getting married are doing better than you, which in my experience they always are, it's a no-win situation. People don't invite me to weddings any more thank God. I'm not sure I could take dealing with another fish poaching dish on an aspirational gift list. Then there are these people who get married several times. I don't see why I should be forced to keep up with everybody else's philandering or have to shell out, just because some obnoxious habit they had causes them to have to get divorced.

Not that I have a problem with divorced people, but even now... I am still listening to Phil Spector.

Bring back that loving feeling...

ConstableGrowler

February 10th 9.35pm

I am even worse at online poker than I am at a real poker table. It's the body language.

BlindBoyGrunt

February 10th 9.45pm

The wedding industry is indeed a scandal. Some of the recipes I have used have also ended up in me making food that's completely inedible. Also good for downloading Phil Spector tunes, as buying one of his CDs makes me feel, well, contaminated.

I have spoken.

JesterJinglyJones

 1   0

February 10th 9.55pm

you do realise that only geniuses, gods and lunatics refer to themselves in the third person?

She is all of these combined d:o))

Weathereye

 17   3

February 10th 10.32pm

Any positive stories?

BoiledMouse

 9   3

February 10th 10.39pm

Positive stories: downloading all of *Buffy the Vampire Slayer* for free. Getting virtually any song you want within minutes and spending the money you save on music on other stuff? Grunt, why do you always say 'I have spoken' when you post anything?

ThomPayne

 21   1

February 11th 3.21am

Pleased you mention *Buffy*, BoiledMouse. I love Sarah Michelle Gellar and the silent episode and the one they did with all the songs ♪♪♪♪ *I am going through the motions*........♪♪♪♪♪♪♪ ....as she stabs a vampire in the chest. Great stuff ☺

As for illegal downloads, I'm not so sure. The entire publishing industry as we know it could be wiped out because of illegally downloaded files for Kindle. For authors, who only exist in order to suffer, that will probably have consequences. I was always a fan of Project Gutenberg. If you want to check a reference, very handy and saves you going outside

Gaunt

February 11th 7.10am

ThomPayne: you have morals about things?

FlaubertFlaubert

February 11th 7.15am

How do you do those music symbols?

BlindBoyGrunt

February 11th 7.45am

> why do you always say 'I have spoken' whenever you post anything?

I just like the way it sounds (don't always do it)

Et la!

ThomPayne

February 11th 7.59am

Flaubert – A typographical identity is a private thing. Just look at the credit sequences in Woody Allen films.

How do you do those music symbols?

ɐıןɐɹʇsn∀ uı ǝʌıן noʎ ɟı uʍop ǝpısdn ǝdʎʇ osןɐ uɐɔ noʎ

♪♪♪♪♪

Gaunt, yes I do have morals. I suspect you to be the one lacking thereof.

Another thing I like to do is read relationship advice threads written by women. Someone will come on with a complaint about some minor mishap their man caused or start bickering about a tiny insensitivity, and all these other women come in like a pack of howling banshees and try to diagnose the problem, armed to the teeth with clichéd ideas. You can make things up and see the sparks fly: *my husband keeps referring to a quiche as a flan, I've tried explaining the difference to him but he just doesn't respect my feelings*. Women are from Pluto, Men are from Ur'anus or whatever it is. The thing I've learned in life is that wherever you go, people are made of bullshit, men, women, I don't discriminate. Actually what they should have called that book is… *Men are from Women all are from Made Of Bullshit.*

Relationship threads are funny. It would be exactly like me and my friends giving plumbing advice to people who have sink or bath problems. *What you need there is a 'Johnson Rod'* we'd say – as the charlatan mechanics have it in *Seinfeld*. Whereas what they clearly need to fix the problem is not dubious advice from their so-called friends.

What they really need… is a plumber.

JesterJinglyJones

 1 0

February 11th 8.05am

<sings> *As I went out one morning…to breathe the air around Tom Paine* ♪♪

THIS THREAD IS NOW CLOSED

12

FLYNN IS SOAKED TO the skin by the time the bus arrives, his hair unruly. The bus is already packed with passengers and he stands dripping in the aisle as the rickety vehicle wends and ploughs its course back towards the city. Gone is the feeling of wonder that resonated so strongly on the taxi journey out, and as the bus crawls along, he is finding himself unable to palliate the melancholy in which he has been left after seeing the neighbourhood where the unknown author lives or has lived. He can see mobs of youths gathering on the streets at various junctures and it is clear that shop windows and store-fronts are being broken and vandalised. The bus screeches violently to a halt to avoid hitting a group of them who have run out wildly into the street, whooping and hollering, a sudden emergency stop which nearly catapults Flynn head over heels down the bus and tips over shopping bags with a jolt. The youths howl under the moon and bang the flats of their hands against the windscreen of the bus, eliciting murmurs of panic amongst the passengers, to which the bus driver responds by several long blasts of his horn. There are police wagons lining the streets, the sound of distant sirens, and suddenly a house brick strikes one of the side windows of the bus, not shattering it but leaving instead a large cobweb of cracks that brings home to everybody a sudden and more immediate sense of fragility, a spiderweb of vulnerability, an unmistakeable decrease of proximity between those on board and the madness that is breaking out on the streets.

Flynn peers through the windows and looks down side-streets, he can see lines of police officers protecting themselves with plastic shields from volleys of missiles, bricks, bottles, rocks, planks of wood, the rioters are throwing anything they can lay their hands on, and these groups appear to have mobilised in tandem with one another in order to start a running battle. The police radios crackle and hum as the officers on the front line call for back-up: '*Man Down!*' They are woefully underprepared for the scale of what is unfolding and appear to be struggling to protect themselves, let alone to restore order. The bus forces its way through this churning, thrumming throng; the detour it takes eventually lets Flynn off some half a mile from the square, and he makes his way down side roads and back streets in order to avoid as much of the confrontation on the main streets as he can; and as he makes his way through the labyrinth, he is caught in dead ends and blind alleys, with their skips filled with stinking rubbish, giant metal fire escapes snaking up the sides of office buildings, and all around him is the sound of breaking glass and shouting. Emerging onto a shopping street, right in between the retreating police and an angry mob, Flynn is struck by a missile which grazes the side of his head, and he can feel warm blood trickling down his face, gathering itself at his ear. He holds a hand up to the wound and is startled at the crimson stain on his fingertips; he sees police officers gesticulating for him to get out of the way, and all of a sudden he realises that he is in the middle of a crowd of bystanders, all of whom are running through the open streets as fast as their legs will carry them. It is during this adrenal rush that he becomes suddenly aware of the acrid smell of melting plastic and burning timber on the night breeze, somebody has thrown a flaming milk bottle full of petrol through a shop window, the first of the fires has broken out.

There is very little traffic on the streets save for the emergency vehicles and night buses, and Flynn is through the worst of it by the time he reaches the square. There are small groups of hooded youths making their way across it in the direction of the centre of the city, with a look that seems to resemble intent, and even malice aforethought, but they are not for the moment breaking into any buildings or trying to torch any of the parked cars that line Flynn's street. He slows to a walking pace and strides diagonally past the National Library, whose penumbral darkness and silence are somehow deafening in the midst of all this, by the mute way that the building itself seems to be simply bearing witness to what is happening, the books after all have seen it all before. Flynn reaches the front door of his building, turns the key and closes it behind him with a bang. He is sweating and stands for a few moments, trying to catch his breath; a door opens on the first floor and a sliver of yellow light seeps out and onto the faded carpet, he can make out the shadow of his neighbour, the one from the smoking incident, who is in his dressing-gown and peering hesitantly into the dark stairwell. Flynn moves, and the motion-sensitive switch in the passageway clicks, bathing the walls in white light. With a mixture of relief and resentment:

Oh, so it's you.

Flynn can barely recover his breath, and at first he is only able to cough a response and greeting, as he makes his way up the stairs towards the first landing.

Are you alright?

I fought my way through.

Your forehead is bleeding.

I had to dodge missiles.

It's all kicking off.

Like an army of zombies.

Our cat has just died.

I'm sorry, that's awful.

Keeled over at breakfast.

At least, was it peaceful?

Sixteen years old.

A great innings for cats.

I just feel so anxious.

Try taking up smoking.

My God, dreadful advice.

It was just a suggestion.

You should look at your forehead.

You could get a new cat.

It feels a bit early.

I can see why.

It's still in the kitchen.

Don't leave it too long.

Well, there we have it.

Try and sleep well then.

I will do that, *Good Night.*

The neighbour retreats into his flat, and Flynn hears a mortise lock spring into place. He climbs a further flight, stopping on the landing below his own, and peers out of the mezzanine window, out from the back of the building and across the other side of the city. The window ledge here is lined with long-neglected plants, and he runs his fingers over fragile, dry leaves which look as though they have been sprinkled upon the sill, and which crumble into dust. The staircase light switches off automatically with another click, and he stands a little longer, here in the dark, looking first at his own faint reflection in the glass, and then further, out towards the darkness of the river, coiling its way slyly through the glows and glitter. Finally, he stirs himself to move; the light clicks on once again, and the view from the window vanishes; he begins to climb the final flight of steps.

Flynn does immediately as advised once he is home, he picks up the little chain and fastens it over the door, which is something he has never bothered to do before. He takes off his coat, puts on the television and walks to the window, and peers down at the familiar shape of the library. Everything looks calm below, and he can see faded orange tendrils of sunset dissipating into the night, yet he can hear the wailing of the sirens and see the blue lights of a police car flashing, as it speeds along the road which runs parallel to his terrace on the far side of the square.

He turns and sees rolling news footage on the television, fires have been started and a furniture warehouse on the wharf, some three miles from here, has been set ablaze with petrol bombs. Great amber flames roar wildly from the roof of the building, licking at the surface of the darkness pressing down on it as if trying to set the night itself aflame. Television footage is being beamed from a helicopter and Flynn can see that the windows of the warehouse have shattered in the bellowing heat of the firestorm, and he makes out a few tiny figures on the opposite side of the road shielding themselves from the inferno. A solitary fire-engine stands next to a hydrant, the firemen are aiming what looks like a parabolic rope of water into the incandescent pyre that is dwarfing them, and which seems to be having no effect whatsoever at controlling the conflagration. The television cuts, and Flynn watches a live report from the centre of the street, the reporter is being urged back by the police; he holds his earpiece to his head, and is announcing that looting and rioting have broken out in five areas of the city, and that the police have lost the battle for the streets tonight; they are unable to restore order. There is a panel discussion from the studio, they debate whether martial law should be declared, and whether a city-wide curfew should be established tomorrow, and whether it could be realistically enforced. There are further reports that more rioting has broken out in other cities tonight, albeit on a lesser scale; the President, who is abroad on a State Visit, has announced that he will be returning first thing tomorrow in order to deal with the crisis, the panel discuss whether the riots are politically motivated, and whilst it is agreed that these people do not have a unified political ideology as such, nevertheless, says a bearded commentator, it must be recognised that there is a serious question as to why it is that these riots are happening, and that if one asks that question seriously, he says, one is compelled to admit that any mass outbreak of violence or widespread public display of dissent is a fundamentally political occurrence. Pish posh, says the Interior Minister, this is criminality and savagery of the most mindless kind, these people are just copying one another, no decent human being could behave in such a fashion, ah yes replies the bearded commentator, but you remember the monster in *Frankenstein*, it was not just a mindless brute. Like Mary Shelley's creature, this mob now stands up and asks itself, Who am I? Why am I here? What am I for? It has begun to see itself as a distinct and powerful entity, separate from the ruling classes, who according to the bearded commentator, have looted and pillaged the tax-payer, now it is flexing its muscles and exacting its vengeance on its creators, or on what it perceives to be the cause of its disaffection, and all hell is following on.

Reminded of his head-wound by a drop of sweat that suddenly stings the cut in a series of prickles, Flynn switches off the television and showers; he stands for a long time under the pins of water, and allows them to prickle his face and shoulders, he washes away the blood from his temple, and emerges from his bathroom as he did in Chapter Three, red and in a cloud of steam. He dresses the wound with a salve, applies a plaster and closes the curtains. He pulls on his pyjamas and once again gets into the little bed with his laptop, whilst the city, not far from where he is lying, billows and burns. The internet is alive with stories of these riots, Flynn glances at them, and once again we leave him peering into his laptop, late into the night.

*

Flynn sleeps but little, and once again takes himself across the square for his morning coffee, there has been no more rain, and the morning sun reminds him of an egg-yolk in a white of cloud, in a cold cobalt sky. He has become inured to the dull ache in his head, caused by the missile, and the girl with the big eyes greets him warmly as he walks in, and he notices her eyes flicker across to the side of his head where there is now a dark bruise and cut from where the missile had struck him. For one horrifying moment, it occurs to Flynn that perhaps she thinks he was one of the rioters, until she asks him all of a sudden:

Are you alright, how did you get hurt?

Flynn explains how he was struck by a missile on his way home and was caught in the middle of a running battle.

My goodness, are you sure you're okay?

Yes I think so.

Have you seen a doctor?

No, I'm sure it's alright.

Concussion is nasty.

So they tell me.

He holds her eyes for a moment longer than he would usually have the courage to do, partly because of the ingenuousness of her concern, and partly because he cannot quite think of all the things he would really like to say.

I almost got caught in it too, she continues.

You should be careful. Do you live far?

My sister and I live near the river. It's not so bad, as long as you can make it safely through the centre.

Brought together a little by shared experience, by cultivated intimacy, the conversation suddenly opens into a new landscape of friendliness.

Do you work around here? she asks. I see you here by yourself all the time.

I work in the library across the way, and I live over there.

I don't mean to be nosy, she then says, hesitating. But do you mind me asking whether everything is alright?

Not at all. What I mean is that I don't mind you asking. What I mean is that I'm fine. Why do you ask?

She turns back to the coffee machine, hits a button, and begins to put together Flynn's *Americano*.

It strikes me that you never seem very happy.

I've had things on my mind.

Don't we all.

I suppose so.

She places a steaming mug of coffee on the counter before him.

My name is Flynn, he says, gesturing at the library employee pass clipped to his jacket as if to prove it to himself, a bold gesture on his part compared with the previous standards he has set for himself, at least with respect to interactions of this sort; she points at her own name badge, eyes dancing with amusement.

And I am Sophia. Nice to speak to you properly. And they glow before one another for a little moment, each feeling less deceived than before, each with a sense of relief perhaps, or of a thing being settled.

The café door opens and two businessmen walk in, the moment has been lost, and Sophia turns back to her espresso machine, Flynn slips away from the counter and sits down at a table, and watches her as she makes their coffee, admiring her speed and proficiency, and of course he finds himself once more thinking of the words of the unknown author:

'Memory is by far the lesser of two evils. Our ineptitudes in the present are by far the more corrosive sorrow. Given enough time, the burning part of the living moment fades and it becomes possible to savour the distance, with a wistful sense of melancholy that disturbs us not a bit. I expect this is what some people call nostalgia; or that untranslatable Galician word *saudade*. The memory is an illusion, even though the history of the world is at bottom a history of different memories. You also have to admit the illusory aspects to the present, in all its relations, divisions and appearances. The practical, the most mathematically important question becomes this: of these two illus- ions, past or present moments, which is the one which is bearable with the least pain? The trick has to be to somehow work out how to make the unbearable...bearable!'

Flynn has left the café, thinking once more of '*the unspeakable shame of the present*', and is walking decisively across the square towards the library, leaving his coffee un- drunk and still steaming on the table.

'The infection of our minds with stupidity,'

says ThomPayne on a thread,

> 'is as difficult to rid from our brain as it is to rid our homes of vermin and parasites, following an unpleasant infestation.'
>
> (👍1 👎1)

and also,

> 'Even at the end of Camus' *The Plague,* the rats are never far from the surface of that white city. Even after the plague has gone and the rats are back underground, there's a sense they'll come back – that the return of hygiene is merely a temporary relief.'
>
> (👍20 👎0)

Flynn is trying to block this from his mind, and trying to block out the olive skin of Sophia and the perfect crescents of white teeth which flash when she smiles. He strides into the library, removes his coat and sits down immediately at a computer, he has not bothered to stamp his time card or to see whether anything needs to be done in the post room. Flynn has not even said hello to anybody, rather he is looking for the unknown author once more by searching for Barnaby Totten's *Friendspoke* profile, he finds a new comment,

> 'Am I alone in thinking that our glorious leaders have *little cloven hooves* – clippety-clopping beneath those minis-terial benches?'

And,

> 'Is it wrong to hope, in all seriousness, for these govern-ment cheese-people to be rounded up, exterminated, and their bodies steamrollered?'

Or possibly:

'bulldozed into a lime-pit?'

Meanwhile, (and we are now finding ourselves hop-scotching between texts like real scholars,) on the web pages of *The Correspondent*, ThomPayne says this:

'I could count on one hand the number of competent people I have ever worked for (and I've got one finger missing).'

By mid-morning Flynn is already so tired from lack of sleep and nervous tension that he can hardly keep his mind on anything, and as we so often do at moments like this when we feel as though we might explode or are in danger of shutting down, he makes his way to the men's toilets, locks himself in one of the cubicles and sits down. He puts his head in his hands, and he can feel cold sweat running down his arms and soaking his shirt, and when he feels his forehead, the skin is cold and clammy. He has not been in the room for very long, and he has been alone, suddenly he hears the door to the toilets open and the echo of footsteps as somebody walks in. Flynn pays this little mind and continues to sit, putting his hands over his ears, dreading the cacophony of flatulence and bodily expectorations that one encounters in such toilet facilities, an assault on the senses of anybody who is prone to lock themselves away for a few minutes each day in a stall to recover their wits only to be ambushed and assailed by the banging doors, the rattle of toilet roll dispensers, the roar of the hand drier that echoes so loudly because of the hard floors and all that porcelain, the ghastly sound of crapping men, and so Flynn is a little surprised when he hears nothing. He sees under the gap of the cubicle that the feet belonging to the person who has entered have stopped in front of where Flynn is sitting, a pair of nondescript men's black shoes, plain black loafers with unremarkable laces, and he can tell that someone is standing not two feet away from him, who it could be, of course, we cannot say.

Bartleby Flynn remains silent where he is sitting, and the feet in front of the cubicle door still do not move. All of a sudden Flynn is aware of a hand reaching under the door, a hand that is slipping a folded piece of paper towards Flynn's feet, before the owner of the shoes turns on his heels and walks back out of the toilets again, closing the door behind him. Flynn is petrified, by day most shoes are black, and he stares at the folded piece of paper on the tiled floor which has been thrust under the door, and which is now lying expectantly at his feet. He bends down to pick it up and opens it to see whether it contains anything, all that is inside is the word *Eusebius!* in letters that have been cut out from the pages of a newspaper. Flynn stares at the word in disbelief, his own secret name passed under the door like that, and he immediately stands up, flushes the lavatory and scrumples the piece of paper up and tosses it into the waste paper basket as though it were infected or contagious or covered in filth. 'I prefer to be stabbed in the heart than in the back,' recalls Flynn from the threads, he washes his hands, rinses the forehead, and for a second feels cold air moving over his wet skin that blows in from the open window, and he catches the smell of disinfectants and urine. He dries his hands under the inadequate and ancient hand drier, the noise of which has always seemed to him to be in an inversely proportional relationship with its effectiveness, and he goes back outside into the corridor feeling timorous, shaken. Library workers are coming and going, nobody is there waiting for him, everybody is going about their business. The stackers are wheeling trolleys from the Post Room, the clerks are carrying books from the Classification Room, and everything seems to be proceeding as normal when he walks again onto the floor of the central rotunda. In fact everything is proceeding quite as one would expect. As to the note that was passed under the toilet door, Flynn is wondering about possible culprits, perhaps the Socialist, who takes care of the library computer system and who, if he wanted to, would no doubt be able to monitor the web traffic and internet patterns that run through the library's machines. The question now, thinks Flynn, is whether this person bears me any malice or whether this is simply a strange coincidence, the evidence against me is only circumstantial. After all, even if someone knows that the intruder from the other night reads the same web pages of *The Correspondent* as Eusebius does, this constitutes no direct proof against me as the culprit behind the unauthorised entry. Flynn walks back from the toilet and slumps down once again in front of the computer, as he has been doing all day.

The Lurker, whose obeisance to the Chief Librarian has been steadily growing ever since the announcement of the job-cuts, spots Flynn at the computer once more and strides over in full view of everybody else in the office and gives Flynn a little piece of his mind. The words *totally unacceptable*, and *inappropriate* and *unbecoming* and *meretricious* trip from the Chief Librarian's tongue, and who does Flynn think he is doing nothing all day, *has the cat got his tongue*, it's been going on for quite a while. As things stand, continues the Lurker, Flynn has managed to get himself to the top of the list of people being considered for the sack, and unless he disinters his work ethic, he will undoubtedly soon find himself put out of a job. Flynn pleads mitigation, pointing to the cut and bruise on the side of his face.

I have a headache, I was struck during the riot.

The Deputy Chief Librarian responds merely by pointing out that only an idiot would have gone out last night, everybody was expecting trouble on the streets and had been talking about it all day, what was he even thinking? Everybody is staring at Flynn, there are dark bags under his eyes and his cheeks are sunken and white, save for the yellow bruising starting to gather around the gash on his temple. He asks whether he may go home to rest his throbbing head, promising to make the necessary changes once he is feeling better.

Yes. Get out of here, says the Lurker. Don't come back tomorrow unless you've pulled yourself together.

Flynn rises and walks out into the central rotunda, the Chief Librarian is wandering about looking preoccupied, but noticing again the dishevelled Flynn, shoots him a stern look and gives a disparaging shake of the head before wandering back towards the staircase, he is planning to go back to sit in his office. Bartleby Flynn passes the Socialist in the square, who stares at him and shoots him a smirk. Flynn suddenly decides that it must have been the Socialist who passed the note under the door of the cubicle, and precipitated the showdown with the Lurker, after all he is the one with access to computer records and probably the only one who can make sense of them; and as the Socialist passes him, Flynn begins to feel unleashed within himself a burning, raging fury, rage at the world, his predicament, his future, his solitary existence, and instead of walking home he goes in the opposite direction, and across to where the bus shelters are.

He hails a taxi and asks once more to be taken to Myrtle Avenue. On the journey, he is able to see up close the consequences of some of the havoc that was wrought upon the city by the looters and rioters last night. Tradesmen are boarding up broken store-fronts, some of them with blackened brickwork from the fires that were started inside; the pavements and roads are strewn with debris and broken glass, and there are cordons of police tape suspended across thresholds, which flap in the morning breeze. The burned-out shell of a bus sits at a jaunty angle in the middle of one of the roads, we can see the blackened upholstery and twisted metal within, and Flynn listens to the radio news report and to the eyewitness accounts. There is a news story that yet more disturbances are to be expected tonight, the rioters appear to be systematically co-ordinating themselves if internet chatter is anything to go by. Flynn pays the taxi driver and gets out of the car, beside the drab strip of shops at the end of

Myrtle Avenue. He crosses the main road, and walks briskly along the right hand pavement towards number fifteen, and directly up the driveway. He approaches the front door and inspects the rusty series of doorbells, there appears to be an old-fashioned intercom system, but there are wires protruding and Flynn thinks it unlikely that this is in working order. The buttons are not numbered and he inspects the embossed name tags under each of the doorbells; he sees the name Totten under one of them, presses the button and hears a tinny sound coming from within. The curtains are closed, and no further sound comes from within, no sense of footsteps, no sense of somebody perhaps cautiously peering out to see who their visitor might be, Flynn bangs on the front door with his fist and rings the bell again but there is no response.

He runs his finger along the line of buttons and presses the one next-door, the sound of this bell is much closer than the other, as though it is right next to the bay window on Flynn's left; he listens closely and there is the faint sound of a television or radio coming from within. He looks at the letterbox, and sees that leaflets of various kinds are strewn amongst the leaves on the doorstep; he can see that the brickwork of this entrance way had actually once been rather grand but has sunk into disrepair and decrepitude, who knows where these processes of decline begin? He hears the sound of footsteps and a woman's face appears briefly at the bay window, she glances out and looks Flynn up and down, and all of a sudden he hears her unfastening the chain on the front door and turning the lock. Slowly, the door opens and she peeps out looking suspicious, as she is not expecting a visitor,

Hello?

Flynn does not introduce himself by name, he simply tells her that he is looking for Mr Totten whom he has reason to believe lives in the next door flat.

I thought the police had finished here, she says.

Oh I didn't mean to give the impression that I'm with the police.

Well you look like a detective in that trench-coat, and Flynn notices her unkempt hair and piebald complexion.

I was hoping to speak with Mr Totten. I have something of his which I wish to return.

You'll have a hard time doing that, says the woman, somewhat callously. *They took the body away early this morning.*

*

Flynn begins to feel a little dizzy; he leans his hand against the wall, and the woman seems to notice that all the colour has drained from his face.

Were you a friend?

No.

(and then)

Why, yes!

Well, no.

I don't really know, he splutters.

Well you can come in for a minute if you would like, she says. The whole thing has been quite a shock.

She opens the door fully for Flynn to enter the building and shows him into her living room, the room is unkempt and shabby, there is paint peeling from the walls, and a large discoloured patch on one corner of the ceiling that Flynn thinks looks like mildew; the entire flat has a sharp musty smell, like old food in a warm fridge. She gestures towards a tatty, threadbare settee, and Flynn sinks into it, without removing his coat. The springs have long since lost their strength and straightness, and the cushions feel lumpy under his weight. He notices an ashtray on the table, volcanic with dog-ends, and next to the fireplace, which runs along the far wall, there is a neat row of empty gin bottles.

Would you like a drink of something? she asks as he lights a cigarette, and Flynn suddenly realises he has no idea how old this woman is; she retains a youthful figure and what appears to be a head of naturally blonde hair tied into a ponytail. Yet her face is wizened and pinched, she has a raspberry complexion with the texture of a battered leather jacket, and he catches a glimpse of dental wreckage when she speaks, teeth like the eroded tombstones of an old churchyard. Flynn nods at the offer of refreshment as he lights a cigarette of his own.

I can make you tea, or you can have something stronger, she continues. I normally have a little livener myself about now.

Yes please.

Well which? Tea or gin?

Flynn tries to regain his composure, and wishes now that he had brought her a bottle.

The livener. Gin would be fine.

She nods and walks to the kitchen, and Flynn allows his thoughts to collect in a blue plume of his own smoke.

I have tonic water but you'll have to make do with no ice.

Gin would be fine.

The freezer's fucked, she rasps back cheerfully. *That's why there's no ice.*

Have you spoken to the landlord?

Don't get me started on that thieving bastard.

Moments later, she returns with two full tumblers. She puts them on the coffee table and Flynn reaches for one of them, raises it to his lips with trembling fingers, and takes a sip. She has mixed me up a stiff one here, he thinks; the drink is room-temperature, warm even, and he can smell the vapours of alcohol and juniper which have gathered like a swarm of flies above the mixture, he can almost see them hovering above the dirty rim of his glass, as if the liquid were a naked bulb in a dingy room. He takes another sip, replaces the glass on the table, and looks up at the woman.

My name is Bartleby Flynn. What happened here?

Johnny Piper's Review
The Correspondent, Saturday February 12th

Comments

InformationSilo

February 12th 2.30pm

> A new blog for young people in which gap-year student Johnny Piper reviews the latest in entertainment news for *The Correspondent*.

Jesus Christ that was one of the most witless, embarrassing articles I've ever read. Why did the Corry commission you?

You're about as funny as a mouth cancer.

FlaubertFlaubert

February 12th 2.31pm

> *This comment has been removed. Click here for FAQs regarding moderation*

Mook

February 12th 2.32pm

> *This comment has been removed. Click here for FAQs regarding moderation*

BoiledMouse

 24 1

February 12th 2.35pm

> I realise I'm very lucky to be able to spend my gap-year broadening my horizons with a media internship.

Yes you are. Why don't you just gloat about it a little more.

For your information: the indy-music and films you know nothing about are fucking village too.

@Mook
> bedwetting shits like this.

Keep up the good work, don't think they'll let that one stand IMHO

SilasTComberbache

 19 1

February 12th 2.37pm

> *This comment has been removed. Click here for FAQs regarding moderation*

BlindBoyGrunt

 27 1

February 12th 2.38pm

> if ever there was an appropriate time to say OP is a faggot, this would be it

That's insulting to gay people, @Flaubert.

What did we do to you?

ThomPayne

 13 0

February 12th 2.38pm

This comment has been removed. Click here for FAQs regarding moderation

ThomPayne

 19 1

February 12th 2.39pm

This comment has been removed. Click here for FAQs regarding moderation

Peacewarrior

  1 23

February 12th 2.39pm

I hope he slits his own throat

I can't believe some of the vitriol being directed at the author on this thread. You should all be ashamed. I thought the piece was very witty. Keep up the good work Johnny ☺ Some folk are simply jealous.

BerlinGirl

 50 2

February 12th 2.40pm

You wouldn't be related to Peter Piper, would you Johnny? Far be it from me to suggest that nepotism is well and alive on the media merry-go-round.

Frontwheel

February 12th 2.42pm

and not a single fuck was given that day

ROFL

I would like to smash this kid repeatedly in the face

FlaubertFlaubert

February 12th 2.42pm

Apologies @Grunt. Don't take it personally.

How'sYourFather

February 12th 2.43pm

Oh shit, @BerlinGirl – just looked up Peter Piper on Wikipedia and you're right.

http://en.wikipedia.org/wiki/Peter_Piper

His eldest son is called Jonathan.

What a pile of pickled peppers this fuckwit picked.

@ThomPayne – just so you know, those are the most disgusting comments I've ever seen. Are you ill?

FarmersBreakfast

 20   2

February 12th 2.46pm

@BerlinGirl – *doing a johnnypiper* could be fruitfully thought of as a whole new word for nepotism.

FriendOfDorothy

 2   43

February 12th 2.48pm

Give the kid a break, he's obviously got a bit of talent. Lots of mean spirits and jealousy on here. Why don't you show yourselves instead of hiding behind sockpuppets?

I thought not.

Weathereye

 21   2

February 12th 2.51pm

Shameful.

Spongle

 10   3

February 12th 2.52pm

The poor little poppet – did they do this to him deliberately? The quims at the Corry should be ashamed on several levels.

TrouserChuff

 7   3

February 12th 2.54pm

This has to be a joke of some kind?

MarisPiper

February 12th 2.54pm

Hi Johnny, this is your mother speaking ☺

Come down here immediately.

@Peacewarrior, @FriendofDorothy

Wouldn't be, cough, *a friend of JohnnyPiper,* would you?

EnglishBatsman

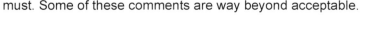

February 12th 2.55pm

Best thread ever.

PeterPiper

STAFF

February 12th 2.58pm

Come on people, leave Johnny out of this. Blame me if you must. Some of these comments are way beyond acceptable.

Clamjouster

February 12th 2.59pm

Johnny, what's your opinion of the Pompidou Centre?

Have you ever seen a grown man naked?

Ever been in a Turkish prison?

Lemonparty

February 12th 3.00pm

@PeterPiper

> blame me if you must

OK, Peter we will.

Peter, it's all your fault.

Your progeny is a dingo and your family is a Class A exhibit of social parasitism. With gender issues.

I seriously hope you all die.

Frontwheel

February 12th 3.01pm

> *This comment has been removed. Click here for FAQs regarding moderation*

Babydinner

February 12th 3.03pm

PeterPiper – not only do we have to put up with your pointless articles, now we have to put up with more of the same from your family.

Of course it's not the kid's fault. But this is a wonderful example of how up your own arse and incestuous the trendy set is.

Lemonparty – (affects Meryl Streep voice) *a dingo stole his baby*

FriendofJohnnyPiper – superb cacophemism.

ThomPayne

February 12th 3.04pm

– are you ill?

That was uncalled for on my part. I shoot first, ask questions later. I've been drinking (as I imagine a lot of others are – some threads you go on, all there is, is drinking). Actually, in a moment of clarity, I feel a little sorry for this guy.

But I don't know whether to weep with tears of laughter or sorrow.

It's like Nicholson says in *The Shining* where he's axeing down the bedroom door:

'Heeeeeeeere's *Johnny!*'

CommunityEditor

February 12th 3.05pm
STAFF

Comments on this article will shortly close.

InformationSilo

February 12th 3.06pm

Fucking fascists

THIS THREAD IS NOW CLOSED

What Is Music?

The Correspondent, Saturday February 12th

Peter Piper

Comments

ThomPayne

👍 2   👎 0

February 12th 11.23pm

@PeterPiper

Sorry about what's happening on the other thread Peter…but as they say, there's no smoke without a salmon. With respect to the matter at hand:

'Instrumental music is strictly meaningless yet expressively significant'

I met an Indian guy once in a bar and we got to talking about this. He drew me a picture which I still have to this day. It consisted of a circle and from clockwise round the circle, if you can picture that, he listed the main art forms, and in the following order. The formatting is not quite right.

Music   Architecture

Narrative poetry/ fiction   Sculpture

Landscape painting   Portraiture

Then he did something which made my imagination sparkle. Over the right hand side he wrote '*Space*' and over the left hand side he wrote '*Time.*'

Like so:

TIME   **SPACE**

Music   Architecture

  Narrative poetry/ fiction   Sculpture

    Landscape painting   Portraiture

Formatting that took me fucking ages. Anyway, I am not a fan of this kind of thing usually, but it seemed at the time to work rather well and I still like it. Architecture is an exploration of, or takes place in, pure space. A sculpture is the refinement of space, a landscape painting is a depiction of space etc., but as you sweep your way round the circle you get to art-forms that are more concerned with time or how it passes for a subject of awareness. At the crudest level, it takes an hour to sit through the Goldberg Variations, and when that theme is repeated at the end, you always find that it sounds a little different following all those transformations and canons.

We both agreed on a definition of music that didn't include songs, or music that is imitative of things like birdsong or the sound of buzzing flies in that Bartok concerto. It doesn't work in all cases, but what you often get in typical cases of musical expression are these changes of light, or the sense of movement from an expression of one attitude to another (it's no coincidence that the sections of classical works are called 'movements' either. Because they move through time, in whatever figurative sense you care to take that). So I do not know about this business of saying it's 'meaningless.' There are grammatical rules, as it were, for music that seem roughly analogous to the semantic rules for translating sentences. It could be that there are apt and less apt ways of understanding music's expressive potential:

If I said that the Appassionata is Beethoven's happiest piano sonata I would be saying something absurd.

What's wrong with using the word meaning there – to say that anybody who doesn't have a tin ear and is suitably acculturated into the musical way of life can make apt or less apt statements about the music? And that the apt ones correspond roughly to a meaning.

Weathereye

 1 2

February 12th 11.40pm

I would have thought that music can mean anything you want it to mean, or that it depends on the context in which you hear it? How's Johnny feeling?

PeterPiper

 0 0

February 12th 11.50pm

Agree on the Appassionata example Thom, I wonder if all cases are so cut and dried. What about, say, Op. 109?

ThomPayne

 2 0

February 13th 5.23am

Well Peter I never said I had all the answers, it's just an interesting one to reason through. I was thinking about the metaphor piece last week and where I was going on about the similarities. I think the trick with metaphors might be that the similarity is *created* with the creation of the metaphorical speech act. The world looks a little different from the way it looked before your imagination was fired. I got to thinking about what happens in those cases. And what happens, I now think, is that the metaphor is something I come to inhabit, a pair of glasses through which I see the world. Quite clearly, what is required of me is an empathic gesture of some kind in the direction of whoever it was who came up with the metaphor. I see the world, for a moment or two, as they do. Cohen actually says this in his book on the subject. He also points out that when I make an appeal to someone – of the form 'you must hear this', 'you must see that' – what I am doing is crying out for someone else to inhabit my point of view. To see the world as I do and why that thing is significant.

Music is strikingly similar there: to figure out what it's about, you have to come to inhabit a point of view that's separate from your own. To be able to hear, in some sense, what a movement from one emotional state to another sounds like. When you do it well, it opens up a new vista of inner experience for you – not so much feeling sorry for yourself and slashing your wrists to some indie band or The Beatles. What you get is a deepening of a capability for emotional experience. There's this oracular remark of Nietzsche's in *Beyond Good and Evil* where he says something like 'we do not hear well music that is foreign to our ear.' This business of hearing well, hearing what's inside or behind the notes, is something that takes practice, maybe freedom from prejudice and the right background in making these kinds of judgements, precisely in Hume's sense of those criteria that you can read in his theory of taste.

And to anybody who says that the Hume thing is a circular argument – *it's not.*

PeterPiper

February 13th 9.32am

OK Thom, all is forgiven – but how does that get us closer to meaning?

ThomPayne

 0 0

February 13th 11.55pm

@Peter – Because it presupposes a minimally normative standard of what is appropriate to say and not to say. Where if we wanted to, we could look at the relationship between, say B minor and B flat major in the *Hammerklavier*, and say that the B minor functions as a leaden weight which disrupts the B flat major idiom. And that as a consequence when that relationship is exposed – say before the fugue in the first movement or at the end of the second with all those octaves – you have a sense of movement between darkness and light.

But Peter I can't be bothered saying more. I can hear the tumbleweed blowing along this thread and the sound of chirping crickets. My contention though is that if you look into those things sufficiently, you will come to see things as I do. Which is what we all want, is it not? To be able to go home of an evening from our useless jobs and be able to say, in a rich and fundamental sense, *I was heard and understood.*

If egghead linguistic theorists do not like calling that a meaning because it doesn't tango with whatever supposedly comprehensive system they've set out, then that's fine with me. I'll just call it a *'cough cough, nudge nudge, wink wink, know what I mean'* type of meaning, especially to appease their profound unmusicality and scepticism.

Stanley Cavell says the following thing about the cabaret routines of a certain species of sceptic in *The Claim of Reason:*

> Scepticism and solutions to scepticism...make their way in the world mostly as lessons in hypocrisy: providing solutions one does not believe to problems one has not felt.

Good article though Peter, what music is all about is undoubtedly one of those problems that people come to feel. Music, like love, can make you feel as though you're walking on air. In my own case, I am trudging through cement. Goodbye.

THIS THREAD IS NOW CLOSED

13

BARTLEBY FLYNN HAS JUST HEARD about the end of the unknown author from the next-door neighbour; she has not given Flynn her name, and he did not think to ask. She had not known Barnaby Totten well, she says, they would say a quick hello to one another on the occasions that they passed in the street or met at the front door, he had never bothered her in the slightest, and she had never seen reason to bother him. He was a small man, says the neighbour, rather unremarkable in appearance and the only slightly unusual thing about his existence seemed to be the large number of packages which he would have delivered. He was living in the building already when she moved in, three years ago, but she had never been inside his flat. He once told her that other families formerly lived in the flats above, until the dry rot made them uninhabitable. He appeared to work sporadically, she would see him leaving the house at regular times for several months at a stretch, sometimes in the morning and other times at night, yet months could go by without her hearing so much as a peep during the day time, although she could often see that his light remained on late into the night; on the odd occasion she had herself arrived back in the early hours of the morning, she was often aware of his light, the sound of music, or other signs of activity. He rarely knocked on her door and she rarely knocked on his, the only circumstances where this ever occurred being when one of them had received a package for the other and held onto it for safe-keeping, a neighbourly gesture to be sure, and during such encounters he had always been quietly spoken and well-mannered, not much given to small-talk, simply a polite and self-contained person who seemed to like keeping to himself.

He never received visitors, she said, nor was there really any evidence of human relationships of any kind, as she had never once heard the ring of a telephone. Of late, she said, he had become noticeably thinner and more dishevelled looking, still friendly but 'hunted', according to the neighbour, 'I didn't like to ask.' Nobody can ever quite know what is going on with another person, she believes, at the heart of everything there is either a question mark or a void. Flynn is not much interested in her philosophising and asks her to continue the account of recent events. She was awoken at around five in the morning by a loud thud, she says, a thud that was accompanied by the sound of breaking glass, splintering furniture and things falling onto the ground. At first, she had assumed it was to do with the riots, but upon looking outside it was immediately clear that the street was deserted, and that the thud had come from inside the building; further, that it must have come from next door, because these are the only two inhabited flats these days. She had knocked on Totten's door in an effort to see what it was that had happened, as she told the police earlier on, but upon receiving no reply, she had gone outside and tried to peer in through the windows, but was unable to see a thing because the curtains were drawn, as they invariably were. Both our flats have letterboxes, she explains, and she describes how she had lifted the flap on Totten's front door, and tried to look inside. All she had been able to make out was what seemed to be an outstretched hand lying still on the floor next to what seemed to be hair, followed by the unmistakeable shape of a human ear. She phoned the police immediately, she says, and they arrived within minutes with an ambulance, and battered down the door to find that Barnaby Totten had hanged himself from the ceiling without leaving so much as a note, the crash must have been from his body falling, when the electrical wire snapped under his weight; how long he had been hanging there, nobody knows. Pretty straightforward case, the detectives had said, no sign of forcible entry or any suggestion of foul play – 'they looked as though they had seen it all before', she said, as another instance, perhaps, of somebody in a crummy neigh-bourhood deciding they could not go on any longer for some reason best known to himself, a case of somebody simply relinquishing ownership of conscious existence and handing himself back to the universe. Flynn asks whether there is any family he might contact, or whether the woman knows of any funeral arrangements that might have been made; she shrugs uninterestedly, and says that she does not have any idea. Flynn thanks her for the drink and rises to his feet.

'No, I won't stay for another, I really must be going.'

She places her own glass down on the table and follows him to the door. They say goodbye, both of them have the sense that they are unlikely to see one another again and are therefore suddenly keen to disengage. She closes her door behind him, and standing for a moment in the hallway Flynn notices that the front door of Totten's flat has indeed been battered in, there are fragments of wood all over the faded welcome mat, the landlord has not yet secured the entrance way and the door itself is slightly ajar. He stands for a further moment in the hallway, listening to the rattle of the chain as the neighbour locks her door behind him, and the sound of her footsteps and the chink of the gin bottle as she re-fills her glass.

All of a sudden Flynn thinks to himself that it's now or never, he pushes open the broken door, ducks his way under the police cordon that has been stretched over the threshold, and walks inside, shutting the door behind him as quietly as he can. The interior of the flat is quite dark because the curtains are closed, and Flynn stands for a moment on the threshold, his eyes opening to the gloom, and he carefully looks around. The flat is actually deceptively spacious and not the studio that Flynn had initially assumed from his reconnaissance mission. There is a door at the back which leads to a separate bedroom, whilst the front room appears to function as a kitchen and sitting room combined. The near wall is lined with bookshelves from floor to ceiling, housing an impressive-looking collection of texts on all varieties of different subjects, lateral thinking, personality disorders, philosophy, popular science, art, and there is a table in the bay window upon which there are piles of yet more books, apparently unsorted, commercial releases of cinema films on video cassette and DVD, and a laptop computer inside a battered-looking case. There is an old leather settee in the centre of the room which is covered in cushions, and a coffee table with yet more books and what appear to be volumes of sheet music, a magnifying glass, an old typewriter, a bust of Socrates, and along the far wall is a large flat screen television which provides an incongruous contrast to some of the other artefacts which Flynn sees strewn around.

He walks quietly across the room towards the kitchen area, there are newly-washed dishes and coffee cups standing neatly on a gleaming draining board, the entire place in fact is very clean, and Flynn looks inside the kitchen units to find yet more books, and neatly organised stacks of papers. There is very little food in the fridge, and Flynn looks into the bedroom, where he sees a double bed which has been neatly made and a little night-stand with a clockwork alarm on it, a smaller TV stands on a table facing the bed, and Flynn looks inside the wardrobe to find a line of freshly ironed shirts and several suits hanging on the rail. There are several small bookshelves along the wall, each filled with yet more books, and little hand-carved statues. The air is as still as a tomb, and there is a smell of fresh linen and incense quite at odds with the flat next door and the musty hallway. Flynn returns to the living room, just beyond the settee is a white outline on the rug which appears to show the outline of a human body, and a vase of flowers which appears to have been standing on the coffee table has shattered on the floor, leaving petals and stems strewn across where the body had lain. There are shoe prints on the coffee table, and Flynn looks up at the ceiling and sees that a length of electrical cord has been fastened around a beam which is just about visible through a hole which has been punched into the ceiling. The cord has evidently snapped, there is no sign of the rest of it, and Flynn goes over to the television, which is mounted on the wall above a fireplace and looks at some of the photographs which have been framed and put on display beneath the enormous screen.

The photos are all of people, who they are of course, we cannot say, but one face stands out from several of them. It is the face of a man, who appears to be somewhat short and slender, and who is usually standing next to the others in the photographs. The man has short hair and a pair of dark eyes that strike Flynn all of a sudden with such poignancy that he realises he is beginning to weep; tears fill his eyes and he can taste the salt in them at the back of his throat. Down his face they pour, splashing onto the earthen surround of the fireplace, he cannot make them stop. A picture larger than the rest shows the same person, evidently in happier times, sitting diffidently next to a beautiful girl who is smiling at the camera, the man's eyes are lowered and do not look directly into the gaze of the camera, they seem to be looking far off into the horizon at something, and there is the slightest hint, Flynn thinks, the slightest flicker of an ironic smile on his face in this picture which, he infers, must have been taken several years ago, for in the photograph the man appears to have a lower hairline at the forehead and his face looks fuller, and somehow more youthful than the gaunt and haunted figure that appears in some of the other pictures. In several of the photos it is clear that this man is missing a finger on his right hand and that one side of his face is marked with a number of scars which lend it a rugged and strangely vulnerable quality. Flynn goes to the settee and wearily lowers himself down onto it, once more he feels the prickle of tears and a flush rise to his cheeks. He kneels and gently touches the ground with the palms of his hands within the white line that the police have left and where the unknown author's body must have landed and lain.

Flynn gets up from the settee, and sinks to the floor, trying as best he can to lie within the outline of the body; he arranges his arms and legs to fit the pattern, and softly closes his eyes. Looking at nothing but the blackness of the inside of his eyelids, he begins to imagine how the life of this stranger might have unfolded in such a dwelling, his final resting place, and he begins to wonder how the unknown author ended up here; then, he pictures him hunched over his laptop at the table in the window, and furiously writing, scribbling down the book perhaps, and almost certainly writing furiously on the web pages of *The Correspondent* each night and setting down in a kind of beautiful and desultory form the written documentation of his inner states, beliefs and private feelings. Flynn thinks of all the questions he should like to have asked, thinks of how he wishes that he could have had the courage to pick up the phone, or knock on the door, to return the book, how such a gesture might easily have been the tipping-point in the life of this lonely individual and persuade him that in fact, the earth does not need to be too solitary a place, even when it feels like it, even for people in whom all hope has for whatever reason been extinguished or abandoned. Flynn arrived here a day too late, and he holds his fingers to the bridge of his nose and slowly shakes his head, he has got to his feet and is now looking around the sad little room, a room which nevertheless betrays little signs here and there of the character who used to dwell within it and which therefore bestows on the atmosphere within, an unmistakeable dignity upon the things it contains, despite the evident material poverty which was so apparent in the writing that he found.

There are empty wine bottles in a row to the right of the microwave on the tiny kitchen surface at the back of the room, evidently placed there to be taken out to the glass recycling bin at some point. There is a half-empty bottle on one of the bookshelves, and Flynn pours small amounts of it into two glasses. He holds up one glass towards the photographs in a silent toast, we do not know yet whether there will be a family funeral or whether the unknown author will simply be buried, dissolved or cremated without witness; the second glass, Flynn holds high and he pours the contents of it over the fallen petals that came from the spilled flowers and over the terrible white outline of the body that has been left on the floor, our shadows are not the only things we sometimes leave behind. He pours the wine on the ground slowly, as if he were consecrating it, and as it soaks into the faded rug it leaves a crimson stain that darkens and spreads. Holding the wine glass by the stem, he then shakes out the remaining droplets as if it were an aspergillum, sprinkling them until the glass is completely empty. When this is done he rinses the glasses at the sink, dries them on a dishcloth, and places them neatly back in the cupboard. There is a back door, and Flynn can see through the window that it opens onto a veranda overlooking a garden in a so-called natural state, the grass has not been cut for a long time and there is a rusting barbecue grill overgrown with weeds. He hears a scratching sound at the door and looks down to see the head of a grey kitten poking its head through a cat-flap; it walks into the flat and rubs its body along Flynn's ankles, purring loudly. He picks up the little creature, now it is softly purring in his hands, as it pushes its head into his, tickling his face with its whiskers.

He puts the cat down on the floor, it immediately leaps onto the settee and curls up, suddenly there is a flat, electronic sound from the computer at the table and Flynn notices a series of green lights which tell him that the machine is still running. He walks over to it and drags a finger across the mouse-pad, and the screen immediately lights up, revealing the familiar banner and typeface of *The Correspondent*. Flynn can see at a glance that the sound was a warning that the machine will shortly run out of battery power, and he can see that the profile ThomPayne is still logged into the website. Flynn sits down, and clicks the link that will enable him to look at the user's profile information, and he pauses for a moment wondering what to do next. There is very little juice left in the machine, it may shut down at any minute, and Flynn suddenly has the idea of changing ThomPayne's password. He locates the little icon that shows him this option; and Flynn immediately changes it to *nightcat* which is also the password he has been using for his own account, and therefore something he will remember. He closes the browser window to find that there is also an email client open, and he begins to arrow down through the unknown author's personal messages, there are receipts for books that he has ordered – 'internet bookshops – where all writers meet, for a penny plus postage,' as Flynn recalls ThomPayne saying on the threads. There is a fair quantity of junk messages, some newsletters, and a large number of emails from somebody called Isabella Armande, an alluring name that strikes Bartleby Flynn immediately as somehow reeking of hopeless pheromonal madness, but before he is able to open one of the messages and read the contents, the computer gives up the ghost and shuts off entirely. Flynn sees a wire leading to the mains and draped across the floor, he connects it to the laptop and re-boots the machine, but he is taken to a password screen and is unable to guess, for understandable reasons, what this password might be. He writes down the name of this unknown woman, this *l'Arlésienne* as the French say, perhaps or perhaps not, this is the person in the photograph. Flynn considers whether or not to zip up the laptop in its battered case and simply walk out with it with a view to trying to get the Socialist to recover the information. He decides against this with the thought that some turns in a labyrinth are simply best not followed; whatever has been left said or unsaid is a private matter for these people, the mystery must remain, we are not entitled to seize such information uninvited. He closes the laptop once more and looks again at the little cat sitting contentedly on the settee. Without hesitating, he picks it up, and realising that there is nothing more to do here, he opens the door to the flat, steps into the hallway with the animal in his arms and slips quietly out of the front door of the building, into a spinning sleet.

10 Symptoms of the Modern Age

The Correspondent, Sunday February 14th

Comments

NathanTheProphet

February 14th 12.16pm

Is it just me or is the eleventh symptom of the modern age grouping things into ten?

Weathereye

February 14th 1.58pm

So there's austerity and greed. Is it just me or should we also be struck by the similarity of the anger against the bankers... and the olde olde story of Jesus running amok and going haywire in the temple by overturning the money tables?

BlindBoyGrunt

February 14th 2.00pm

NathanTheProphet: are you one of those people who think that there are two kinds of people in the world...those who believe there are two kinds of people in this world and those who do not? When I see all that stuff burning on TV, I am thinking it's a tentative 'yes' to 'The Huger Nation'... or whatever that ludicrous phrase is.

ThomPayne

 9 3

February 14th 2.05pm

@Weathereye

> or should we also be struck by the similarity of the
> anger against the bankers... and the olde olde story of
> Jesus running amok

Indeed we are all very struck. Not to turn this into a New Atheism
thread, God help us, but I am actually far more struck by the
apocryphal account of Jesus shouting:

> *'I have cast fire upon the world, and look! I'm guarding it 'til it
> blazes.' (Thomas, 10)*

I can't say enough about my enthusiasm for the Gnostic codices.
I almost prefer them to the book of Ecclesiastes:

> *The words of the Teacher, son of David, king in
> Jerusalem:*
>
> *'Meaningless! Meaningless!'*
> *says the Teacher.*
> *'Utterly meaningless!*
> *Everything is meaningless.'*
>
> *What do people gain from all their labours*
> *at which they toil under the sun?*

As for society itself – neo-Feudalism is the political landscape
zeitgeist.

> *What is crooked cannot be straightened;*
> *what is lacking cannot be counted*
> *For with much wisdom comes much sorrow;*
> *the more knowledge, the more grief.*

Save yourself, Weathereye old girl.

That too is a chasing after the wind!

I am a big fan of King David, the story where he fucks Bathsheba and gets her husband killed notwithstanding. According to Robert Pinksy, David had the soul of an artist as well as the soul of a warrior. He mastered the harp as well as the sword: *'a poet as well as a warrior killer, but as a poet he is far above any other hero, and as a killer no one among poets can touch him.'*

There's a moment in the book of Samuel, where Nathan attempts to show David the awfulness of what he did to Bathsheba's husband. He accomplishes it elliptically, with a story, by telling David the parable of the poor shepherd. This, of course, is a technique that not only tells us something of the power of stories; it also appeals to the poetic side of David's sensibility. David demands to know who the rich farmer was that stole the poor man's lamb. And in a moment of genuine literary power, Nathan turns to him and says:

"Thou art the man."

That never fails to make my imagination sparkle.

Eusebius

 0 0

February 14th 2.10pm

@ThomPayne That's marvellous; I'm facing the possibility of redundancy in my own job at the minute. Things aren't going so well for me; I used to cope with myself so much better than I now do.

ThomPayne

 5 0

February 14th 2.24pm

Eusebius, don't let it grind you down. You could always play Sancho Panza to my Don Quixote. I suspect you simply lack perspective or haven't seen beyond the veil. Precariousness and uncertainty are not restricted simply to whatever it is that you happen to do yourself.

If you look at these modern times of ours: social institutions no longer have the time to solidify or function as points of reference for long-term life plans. Bauman says that individuals simply have to find different ways to order their lives. So you could say that a well-adapted human being is one who can thread and weave a continual series of short term projects and activities that do not add up to anything like the old-fashioned concept of a career.

I have known long-term civil servants, who joined the bureaucracy and simply vanished for forty years pushing bits of paper around. Some of them were kept on the payroll, even when there was no work for them to do. They re-emerge and retire, blinking in the sunlight, unable to comprehend why everybody's lives are not similar to theirs. Most likely they are very dull people.

We live in the time of fragmented lives. You can do a degree, go to graduate school, end up working in a call centre and then being sacked. You might end up selling shoes or working in financial services after that. You might get a lucky break writing your first book. What modernity requires are flexible individuals – adaptable individuals who are constantly ready and willing to change their strategy at the drop of a hat. *And if anybody wants to start a war with me, I am on a constant war footing.* All the fucking time.

You have to be prepared to abandon your commitments and loyalties without regret and to pursue such opportunities as happen to be available. Nowadays: individuals must be able to act, plan their attack and calculate any gains/ losses of acting/ failing to act under conditions of endemic and systemic uncertainty.

BlindBoyGrunt

February 14th 2.45pm

ThomPayne you're a man after my own heart. Let's bang it into some semblance of shape on an anvil. With hammer and tongs. My biggest gripe with modern times: that societies and nations have been turned into security operations for corporate interests, who have purchased all the political capital. How do we get to the promised land?

ThomPayne

February 14th 2.04pm

BlindBoyGrunt – well you've gone and said it. I do not know the way to Arcadia, for me or for anybody who doesn't smell right. It's like that old Irish joke. There's a lost tourist and he bumps into a little Irish chappy who is trotting his way through the peat bogs. And the stranger asks, 'how do I get to Dublin?' And the Irish chappy says, *'Well, if I wanted to get to Dublin, I wouldn't start from here.'*

But you know, there are strangers everywhere. People who do not fit. We've tried to control nature and ourselves with bureaucracy, laws, taxonomy, categorisation – the purpose of which is to remove uncertainty and chaos in our lives. A classification system can make the chaotic things in the world have some semblance of order in them. Here's the rub – when you organise the world into recognisable and controllable systems – there are always groups or individuals who cannot be controlled in this fashion. It could be individuals excluded from social groups because they have a bit of an edge, or it could be something as simple as an animal or book that defies categorisation. It's the way of thinking of the flâneur – the urban wanderer who is detached from, yet part of, the phenomena he is perceiving (in between coffee shops).

Sometimes you meet someone you like and you think you might have a rapport with them; that you might even be capable, between the two of you, to take care of one another somehow. First it starts as an ache, then it becomes a sound, then it turns itself into a deafening roar that drowns out everything else. Of course you're not fit for purpose, find yourself fucking rejected, and end up feeling even more alone than before.

These people – sometimes they just make you sick.

Gaunt

 14 5

February 14th 2.50pm

Freedom and safety are the modern age's gifts. Freedom to be who you want to be, freedom from oppression, and an unprecedented range of choices; typically there will always be the ungrateful types on this thread who think the grass is greener. We're better off than we have ever been, and we'd spread it around the world if it weren't for the whingers.

Weathereye

 3 0

February 14th 3.58pm

Gaunt, don't forget the bad television and pointless sequels.

ThomPayne

 5 0

February 14th 11.04pm

For Christ's sake Gaunt. Answer me this: what's so free about a market when it's totally controlled by the people with all the money. When the state prints out hundreds of billions in bank notes via quantitative easing…and gives it over to the banks so they can pay their gambling junkies outrageous bonuses – that sounds a lot like 'socialism' to me – socialism for the wealthy. Meanwhile there are mass redundancies and there is not even much left of a state for people to fall back on.

The central tenet of the ideology is that wealth ought to be extracted from the general population and handed over to the 'right people.' Supposedly these people can more 'efficiently' apply that wealth as capital and generate wealth for everybody else, through their natural aptitude and excellent education. It's actually rather similar to what the Soviet state was up to – except that in our case, it's a social class nicking the property instead of the state infrastructure. Before you say it – yes, all this austerity business that is immiserising everybody and driving them onto the streets in protest is a perfect example of this kind of confiscation, with some hocus-pocus to make everybody think it's inevitable or can't be avoided. All the while, what the capital holders really do is apply the capital to buying for themselves nice big houses, stupid cars or maybe the odd gated compounds patrolled by guards with machine guns. Or if you're Russian, it's a yacht with anti-aircraft batteries on the side. Or perhaps they'll do a little property flipping with their second homes and keep you in your outrageously priced rented garret – in a state of permanent serfdom.

Maybe you're doing alright Gaunt. But the rest of us have been conned into a system that just makes us poorer and increasingly disenfranchised. A return to feudalism – that's your modernity.

Eusebius

 1 0

February 15th 12.00am

ThomPayne, is it really so bad? Don't do anything rash, and I mean that; my gripe with modernity – if I have one – is that it exacerbates my sense of isolation. Maybe I would have been isolated in whatever age I happened to be born in. Omar Khayyam has it like this:

Myself when young did eagerly frequent
☐ Doctor and Saint, and heard great Argument
About it and about: but evermore
☐ Came out of the same Door as in I went.

With them the Seed of Wisdom did I sow,
☐ And with my own hand labour'd it to grow:
And this was all the Harvest that I reap'd—
☐ 'I came like Water, and like Wind I go.'

Into this Universe, and why not knowing,
☐ Nor whence, like Water willy-nilly flowing:
And out of it, as Wind along the Waste,
☐ I know not whither, willy-nilly blowing.

Gaunt

 14 5

February 15th 12.12am

@ThomPayne

These people – sometimes they just make you sick.

Time and again, when you share your prejudices, you simply show yourself up as a leftist misanthrope with pretensions. You've been off your game of late too; why don't you go out and do something useful?

ThomPayne

 3 0

February 15th 2.04am

Alritey then Gaunt, if you don't want to have a light sabre duel with me on the internet, I really don't mind…I wouldn't want to throw up on you – which is undoubtedly what would happen.

Speaking of strangers, **Eusebius**, there's a funny thing they do on 4chan/b/. For anybody who doesn't know it already the 'OP' of this is 4Chan argot for 'original poster'... the dude who started the thread. I have been obsessed with this during the lonely nights.

You have a lot to drink, procure some amphetamines – maybe bang a few lines of toot off the dinner service

You go on the chat thing at **www.spongle.com**

You find somebody
You write, 'What is OP?'
If they say 'a candy-ass', or such, they are not infected
If they're a little confused, they are a survivor
If they ask 'a/s/l' (age, sex location) they're a zombie and you blast them BLAM! BLAM!
You get six shotgun shells
You meet with survivors to reload

The good part: *you copy and paste your conversation on a thread.*

I'll start.

You're now chatting with a random stranger. Say hi!

You: What is OP?
Stranger: a candy-ass
You: FLAWLESS VICTORY
You: Four zombies in a row, I was down to 2 shells
Stranger: Saved by the stranger
You: /b/est of luck out there soldier, give 'em hell
Stranger: give that bitch some ammo
You: Nothing says I love you as a buckshot to the face
Stranger: We are legion
You: We are one!
Stranger: We do not forgive!
You: We do not forget!
You: Sail safe stranger, do not get bitten.

You have disconnected

ThomPayne

 3 0

February 14th 3.27am

I also just found these ones from last night. If modernity is anything, it's wasting my time on this.

> **You're now chatting with a random stranger. Say hi!**
>
> You: What is OP?
>
> Stranger: *'We are the music makers,*
> *And we are the dreamers of dreams;*
> *Wandering by lone sea-breakers,*
> *And sitting by desolate streams; -*
> *World-losers and world-forsakers,*
> *On whom the pale moon gleams;*
> *Yet we are the movers and shakers*
> *Of the world for ever, it seems.'*
>
> You: Michael Jackson?
> Stranger: I don't know. I found it on tumblr
> You: *BLAM* *BLAM* *BLAM* *BLAM* *BLAM* *BLAM* DIE ZOMBIE!
> Stranger: Still alive
> You: Cancer never dies
>
> Your conversational partner has disconnected
>
> **You're now chatting with a random stranger. Say hi!**
>
> Stranger: Hermione?
> You: What is OP
> Stranger: OP?
> You: Indeed
> Stranger: an operatical performer

Stranger: Opium
You: Try again
Stranger: orange peels
You: close enough, hello Civilian
Stranger: lol hey what's up?
You: zombies attacking, do you need help?
You: you look distressed
You: we must get you to safety…follow me
Stranger: alright then
Stranger: but can I ask you something?
You: Make it quick, Civilian
Stranger: OP is operation?
You: It doesn't matter. Zombies everywhere. Here, take this gun
Stranger: Thanks, did we just become friends?

You have disconnected

You're now chatting with a random stranger. Say hi!

Stranger: Hi! horny 20m here, looking for women with cam to chat with and Skype

You: What is OP?
You: Fuck!!!!!!
You: I count this as a/s/l. *BLAM* *BLAM* *BLAM* DIE ZOMBIE DIE
Stranger: *sigh*
Stranger: stop ruining the internet
You: BLAM BLAM BLAM. Goodbye

☺☺☺☺☺☺☺☺☺

Eusebius, I am not as I was. As Velda says in the immortal *Kiss Me Deadly*:

First you find a little *thread. Little thread leads to you a string. String leads you to a* rope. *And from the* rope, *you hang by the neck.*

Pray for me.

BlindBoyGrunt

February 15th 9.45am

Thom that is about the most pointless thing I have ever read. Do you not have better things to be doing?

JesterJinglyJones

February 15th 9.49am

laJester dislikes zombies, even though they are an accurate (though somewhat stylised) portrayal of consumers in capitalist societies.

But the interesting question is that since zombies do not eat each other, preferring to eat only non-zombies, can they truly be said to be cannibals?

:-s

THIS THREAD IS NOW CLOSED

14

W E FIND FLYNN WALKING dejectedly back along Myrtle Avenue to the main road. The cat fidgets and strains in his arms, and he hails a taxi, he is in no frame of mind for another bus journey, especially with an animal, so he asks to be taken straight back to the square. It is mid-afternoon, there are no signs of further protests yet because the sun still hangs in the cobalt sky, and Flynn watches the faces of the unknown people in the city as they go about their business, pedestrians, shoppers, slipping in and out of the high street stores, couriers, delivery men, chuggers, and those decrepit-looking lost souls at the fountain drinking containers of alcohol masked by brown paper bags, people in headphone bubbles; he sees men in suits and smartly dressed women stalking through the revolving doors of office buildings with mobile telephones pressed to their ears. There is a universe of difference between seeing, looking, and observing, these words connote qualitative and quantifiably different modes of experience, and so we are being careful when we say that he observes this unknowable globe from the window of his taxi, it looks to him a fishbowl, and Flynn's thoughts turn once more to Barnaby Totten; he is unable to shake off the haunting feeling, plain in a factual sense, that a light has been snuffed out, a light which, if it did not burn particularly long, nevertheless has left him with a lingering sense of depletion and lack. A light that seemed to burn peculiarly brightly for a time, although nobody was there to notice it, this light, or so it seems to Flynn, has simply been removed from the world, snuffed and extinguished, almost as if it had never been there at all. The cat is curled up and purring on his lap throughout the journey, and Flynn strokes it gently. He pays the driver, takes the cat upstairs, and goes out to buy cat-food and litter from his local shop. He then returns home to feed the animal. Next, he goes to the café opposite the library and orders himself some coffee from Sophia, the girl with the big eyes; she can see that his face is flushed and that his bright blue eyes are swollen at the edges, marked with thin encroachments of red veins, like the minor roads on maps. She does not charge him for his coffee, the café is empty and she sits with him for a moment.

A friend of mine died today, he says, without thinking whether this is the right way to be putting it, she expresses her condolences and gently places her hand on his shoulder.

Flynn's head is bowed, he is unaccustomed to such gestures and he feels an unmistakeable shiver of electricity pass upwards through his spine in a trail of sparks, he feels transparent as he raises his left hand to place it gently on the top of hers and as she turns it around he feels her squeeze his fingers; he has never done this before and finds for himself a strange sense of release in this tiniest of moments, he closes his eyes and wishes with all his heart that it would never have to end. She is telling him that he can stop by and talk at any time if he feels like it, and so on, and he hears himself thanking her and saying that he will, of course, thank you for your concern, all at sea as he is from this most unexpected and fragile moment of intimacy. He finishes his coffee and stands up, he takes a deep breath and his lungs feel heavy, this time he is sure to say goodbye to her before he leaves, and if we linger in the café for a moment we can watch him walking slowly across the square and back towards the building in which he lives. The girl with the big eyes watches him for a moment as he disappears, before turning back to her enormous espresso machine. She turns one of the switches, and a hot jet of steam loudly blasts out of one of the nozzles with a serpentine hiss. She picks up her plastic bottle of disinfectant, and continues spraying and wiping down the surfaces.

Back in his flat Flynn picks up the telephone and calls the police station in Marrowbone; after several rings, he is put through to the duty officer.

There was a suicide on Myrtle Avenue this morning, the gentleman was a friend of mine, would you be able to let me know of the funeral arrangements once these have been made?

The officer tells him that she cannot give him any details as yet but if he would leave his telephone number she will do what she can, situations like this are always upsetting, but there is the matter of the autopsy and coroner's report before anything else can be done. She asks Flynn whether he knows of any relations to the deceased, the police have been unable to track anybody down. Flynn replies that he is unable to help in that regard, but says that he remembers the name he saw briefly amidst the unknown author's emails: Isabella Armande, and he spells it out for the police officer.

Yes, he says. And then, *No, it's spelled with an 'e'.*

An unusual name. Do you know what the connection is or where we could get hold of her?

I don't know her personally, I just have the idea that she needs to be informed.

Why do you think that?

I can't quite say.

What kind of an answer is that?

I just have a feeling.

I suppose we can't always explain a feeling.

How right you are about that.

Sober and serious, Flynn goes downstairs, walks across the square and up the seventeen steps to the library. Everything there is very much as he left it earlier; the Lurker is creeping about in the central rotunda, and the Chief Librarian is standing at the window of his office and surveying everything that is going on below as he peels and eats a banana. It is reaching the end of the working day, the reading rooms have been gradually emptying, and Flynn surprises the Lurker by walking up to him from behind, tapping him on the shoulder, and looking him straight in the eye.

I feel I must apologise for my poor conduct of late, he says. A friend of mine has been ill and he died this morning. My mind has been on other things.

A new look of compassion and concern illuminates the bone-pale features of the Deputy Chief Librarian like a rising sun, and he immediately looks serious and attentive to what Flynn has to say.

I'm sorry to hear that, I didn't know. Perhaps it is I who should apologise to you then Flynn, *if there's anything we can do…* (etc.*)*

Flynn smiles. It's alright, he replies, I should just like to be able to return to my work and try to get myself out of the bad books. If you would like me to, I could work late tonight.

If that's what you would like, please go ahead, but really there is no need.

And with that, the Lurker slaps Flynn on the back heartily, extends him the glad hand, before turning on his heel and walking off across the central rotunda once again. Flynn looks away for a second, and when he turns, the Lurker seems to have vanished and vaporised from view, quite to be expected of course; perhaps he is somewhere behind a shelf.

Later, Flynn remains in the library alone and working late once again; after the neurotic strain of his exertions and escapades, it is a welcome relief to be wheeling his trolley once more, along the long corridors, collecting books which careless readers have left on the tables of the reading rooms, and taking them back to their proper locations, in order to lovingly replace them in the numerical order in which the system dictates they must be kept, picking up the occasional piece of litter as he goes. Flynn thinks again of *The Book of the Unknown Author* which is still lying in a dark drawer in one of the offices, and he walks back through the central rotunda and retrieves it from its resting place. It is now a little dog-eared, and dirty from its adventures; Flynn attempts to flatten the pages, and wipes the cover carefully with a paper napkin. He takes it to the Classification Room and switches on the computer; he navigates to the page where the details of new arrivals are entered, and slowly and deliberately types the name of the book and *Author Unknown* in the appropriate fields, recording the existence of the book for the first time in the library catalogue. He prints out a barcode and the small violet sticker bearing the book's new Dewey number, and carefully attaches them to the spine. Next, he takes a blank index card, and in brown ink inscribes it in his best hand with the same details he has keyed into the computer system. He takes the card and the newly categorised book and walks to the units of wooden drawers at the back of the central rotunda and files the card carefully away. He has decided that the book will be classified as belonging with the collection on the theology balcony, owing to the fact that this is where he found it, although to anybody else this designation might appear somewhat arbitrary; and so he makes his way to the old chapel at the back of the library, and ascends once more the stairway to heaven. He has not been up here since he disposed of his own notebook several days ago, and he wheels the ladder along the wall of books until it reaches the shelf where classification protocols dictate that the book must be inserted. He ascends the wooden rungs until he is high enough, gently moves some of the books aside, and makes a new place for the volume, and all of a sudden it is sitting snugly on the shelf just as if it had always lived there, and had only ever been borrowed. As he climbs down the ladder, he glances upward, he is no longer able to pick out its spine from the sea of titles that are its new companions; it is as if the book and the words it contains have suddenly faded into the very fabric of the library itself, a tiny footnote or clarification within the longest of conceivable chapters. He walks down the stairway to heaven, and his heart is still heavy and aching as he pushes his empty trolley back towards the central rotunda. The library is shrouded in darkness, just as it was on the first night that we encountered him here, the books will continue to keep their silent vigil, and the cathedral bell is chiming seven. We can just about still see the shape of Bartleby Flynn as he disappears once more into the shadows.

*

There is a message from the police on Flynn's answering machine when he arrives home, the body will be taken to a funeral home in the suburbs tomorrow, and they are grateful to him for putting them in touch with this Isabella Armande, and he learns that she will be seeing to the particulars of the funeral arrangements, given the deceased man's apparent lack of friends or family. They leave a contact telephone number, should he wish to contact her in order to find out further details, information which he writes down and inserts into his wallet. Flynn spends a little time at his laptop as he waits for his eyes to grow heavy. Presently, he clambers into bed, switching off his lamp and lying still for a while and hearing, staring into dark beneath the ceiling, listening as always to the traffic; he is relieved that tonight it appears there are no riots, a turn of events he feels is strangely apposite given the circumstances, and it is with these thoughts in mind that he finally sinks into sleep.

Four days later, Bartleby Flynn makes his way to the funeral home where the body lies displayed, before it is finally taken away by the gravediggers or the crematorium, to be reclaimed by the winds of the world. He intends to leave a wreath or some flowers, perhaps to spend a little time in quiet contemplation, we all do that before funerals, and perhaps he will ask for details of any service that might be held, and which he might be permitted to attend. He wakes early and decides to walk to the funeral home at leisure, despite the snow that has been falling, and as he arrives Flynn notices his reflection in the large mirror which is in the hallway; the frost gathered on his head has made his dark, dyed hair look a hoary shade of winter. He runs his hand through the slush atop his cold cranium, and when he arrives at the chapel of rest, he sees that there is an open casket, and looks for the first time upon the flesh of Barnaby Totten. It is surprising how there is always very little to see when it comes to the dead, we can only imagine how those features might have looked before sensibility was snatched suddenly away, when they were animated from within, perhaps in conversation, or laughter, rumination, anger, or desire. The face of the unknown author is simply blank and without expression, peaceful but for the mauve and green traces of bruising around the neck and throat which betray the questionable quietude, markings that the funeral directors have attempted to conceal with an application of pancake make-up. It appears to Flynn at first that any evidence of strength and inner life has simply deserted the form and frame that remains; and he pictures, as he should, the idea of particles returning to the void. If in the unimaginable future we could see these tumbling particles, he thinks, or if we possessed eyeglasses of sufficient magnification that large objects lost their shape and solidity and all we saw were their atomic structures, would we one day encounter the material constituents of a recollection, a fragmented accumulation of sensory data perhaps, or would we even encounter a cluster of dreams themselves? And now it hits him with the cold precision of a diamond bullet splitting his forehead, that it is in the faces of the dead that we see what the truth is, a pessimistic and gloomy thought admittedly, although hardly our fault at this stage that this is the reaction he is currently having. Flynn suddenly remembers his childhood home, how following the death of his parents years ago, he had returned to the old house some weeks after it had been cleared, the occasion where he noticed how dirty the carpets suddenly seemed, how all that remained in the rooms were stiff and helical protrusions of wire where a television had once been connected, empty shelves, dust, wardrobes with empty coat-hangers, the dark outline of the oven etched against the kitchen wall; what is it that lingers in these walls, Flynn had wondered at the time, what is it that remains in the rings where jam-jars stood, or in the matter that collects in the corners of cupboards. He had thought of the creeping shadows and panes of yellow light which glide silently over our bedroom walls in the night, they pass over us like spirits as we lie sleepless, they watch over us in all of their flight and bliss; and then he wonders of the sense in which silhouettes and stains, reflections, memories and encrustations of dark filth, might be profitably thought of as permanent markings somewhere in the dark hole of one's head, indelible gatherings and engravings upon a fragile film of feeling.

The clouds shift, and the shadow of a sycamore tree outside the chapel window spreads placidly aslant the dead man's face; and Flynn also fancies, perhaps in the twist of the lips or in the fall of the brow, that the expression now appears slightly whimsical; and it occurs to him that perhaps he has glimpsed a revenant, now that the light is right, a faint reminder of the glow that used to flicker vibrantly with all the signs of the inhabitation and domesticity that the warmth of life brings. The clouds change once more, and the expression is gone. You can take everything away from a person, thinks Flynn, up to and including life itself, but loneliness is not a commodity that can be removed like the furniture, even though, and as the self-help books keep telling us, it may be something that can be simplified, communicated and written down, in order to share the load perhaps, or simply to be noted as a striking phenomenon by morose types who have nothing better to do. When all is said and done, thinks Flynn, his thoughts gathering pace, it is loneliness, secrets and private hopes that are the only possessions we are permitted to keep for ourselves once the thin membrane of life is punctured; and we will be thinking of *exactly that*, thinks Flynn, when we suddenly feel ourselves frantically deflating, flitting chaotically across the room like the wrinkling shrivel of a party balloon, or gasping for air in a shrieking vacuum, or in that final moment as our flesh is flayed, and we find ourselves stripped to the bone.

There is nobody else in the room, and Flynn lays a small wreath at the side of the coffin, next to a single garland of flowers which has been left there by somebody else. Flynn has asked Irvine and Son, the printers of *The Book of the Unknown Author*, to run off another copy for him, an express, so-called *print-on-demand* job, and one for which he therefore had to pay considerably more than would be normal, when he went to pick it up yesterday. He takes the pristine new copy of the book and places it inside the dead man's jacket, directly over the heart. As Flynn leaves, he thinks he recognises the face of the girl from the photograph by the exquisite flatness at the bridge of her nose, whom he assumes must be none other than Isabella Armande. She is dressed in dark clothing and her face is pallid, she conducts an intense conversation with a man in a dark suit at the back of the room. She glances at Flynn briefly as he walks by, and he finds himself feeling fleetingly floodlit, suspended in a lamp-like gaze,

'*Stars, stars, and all eyes else dead coals!*' as the unknown author himself had quoted from *The Winter's Tale*. She has eyes of the most brilliant kind, thinks Flynn, those irises the colour of clear honey; these are the eyes that leave their impression scorched into you long after she has left the building on Nymphalidae wings, long after the spellbinding little moment in which they briefly projected starlight and gave you the fleeting glimpse of another universe. She appears to be about to say something to him, but he immediately looks down at his feet; what can I possibly say, he thinks, how can I explain myself to anyone when there is nothing left to be said? The funeral itself will be later this afternoon, and he intends to be present, despite the awful weather predictions, and for all we know they will be the only two people who will be there, apart from the priest and the gravediggers, the only people watching as the coffin is being lowered slowly into the ground on canvas straps, in the fog and the driving rain. They will each sprinkle a handful of dirt into the grave perhaps, and watch as it mingles with the raindrops threading their way down the shining varnish of the casket; and it occurs to Flynn, as he is walking back towards the city, that perhaps he will have the chance to speak to her then.

Riots: Rubdown

The Correspondent, Thursday February 27th 6.15pm

Comments

JohnnyLegless

 17   2

February 27th 8.59pm

> Claims that the tardiness of the police response was deliberate need to be investigated.

Well they're obviously bruised from the kicking they took over the Tribune's computer hacking thing last year. I wouldn't put that level of cynicism past them.

Weathereye

 17   3

February 27th 9.08pm

> Questions also need to be answered as to why the President and Minister of the Interior delayed returning from holiday, and the impact that this had on the government handling of the crisis.

There needs to be a public enquiry, that's for sure. They should take a long hard look at themselves for staying comfortably in the sunshine whilst cities burned.

BlindBoyGrunt

February 27th 9.15pm

I took the view that it's probably better that they stayed away, **Weathereye.** They are not really the calibre of people you want handling a crisis are they? Having said that, I would really like to have been a fly on the wall of the plane, and seen their faces as they circled the airport. Looking down in horror at a city suffused in an incandescent orange glow.

Weathereye

February 27th 9.58pm

Point taken, Grunt. Haven't seen ThomPayne for a couple of days. He usually takes great delight whenever there's hypocrisy and carnage abroad

BoiledMouse

February 27th 9.59pm

Weathereye, yes it's odd that Thom isn't around – he hasn't missed more than a day's hard work on here for a good while.

Gaunt

February 27th 10.10pm

Boiledmouse

odd that Thom isn't around

You say that like it's a bad thing. Hopefully he's realising it isn't worth it and finally thrown in the towel.

ComradeJenny

February 27th 10.24pm

Thom is probably lurking. They banned him for a while, but he came back like the clap.

BifidusRegularis

February 27th 10.27pm

There needs to be an investigation into how the riots escalated and weren't properly controlled. It's been said exhaustively on previous threads, but what we also need is to take a long hard look at why this happened. People do not start burning things en masse, all out of the blue.

Gaunt

February 27th 10.40pm

What we need **Bif**, is harsh sentencing. No excuses. These witless savages were copying each other, there's no more to be said. Bunch of twunts.

ThomPayne

February 27th 11.10pm

Hello Gaunt and thank you for the good wishes.

I haven't been killed by today's riot. As they say at the Playboy mansion…

Gentlemen gentlemen, be of good cheer.

For they are out there and we are in here!

Think of me as Petrouchka's ghost flitting over the chimneytops, a metaphor here to terrify the Charlatan, somewhere from beyond the grave.

BlindBoyGrunt

 0 0

February 27th 11.45pm

ThomPayne – how goes the witching hour? How about a tune?

NathanTheProphet

 11 1

February 27th 11.55pm

There will be the usual socio-economic arguments on this thread. FWIW, everybody will just be echoing one another or their usual cabaret routines, and eventually it'll end up with Hitler. These threads are getting tiresome.

Gaunt

 1 3

February 28th 12.10am

I haven't been killed by today's riot

It's that most poignant of comeback scenarios: farce replayed as tragedy.

Narrator

 978 0

February 28th 12.11am

These threads are getting tiresome.

As you can probably tell, especially if you're reading the hard copy, we don't have far to go.

JesterJinglyJones

February 28th 12.12am

laJester knows the dark side of Gaunt. He is heavily into S&M, indeed he is addicted to it and is frequently chased by the police for pursuing this practice in public. He has a fixation with attractive female jesters whom he chases obsessively from location to location across the internets. And he is a flasher – *laJester has seen him!* He also growls and roars ferociously during intercourse..... *she has heard him!*

ThomPayne

February 28th 12.10am

BlindBoyGrunt, The witching hour goes well thank you. In der Nacht sind alle Katzen grau. I've been busy actually, I think I may have found myself.

Mook

February 28th 12.58am

I'm getting a little tired of the excuse that poverty justifies criminality. I hope to heaven that we do not get some softly softly outcome once they've boarded up the shop fronts and cleaned up the blood. Five deaths is no joke.

ConstableGrowler

 9 0

February 28th 12.59am

Mook, there's a distinction between explaining these riots and justifying them. You may not agree with the explanation, but that's another question. Nobody seriously thinks it's justifiable aside from the odd anarchist. Surely we want to understand why it's happening if you take my meaning.

BlindBoyGrunt

 2 0

February 28th 1.02am

Amen Growler. Even the swap meets around here are getting pretty corrupt (*crazy Dylan line, no?*)

AM Gatward

 1 665

February 28th 1.15am

> *This comment has been removed. Click here for FAQs regarding moderation*

Cryptorchid

 2 0

February 28th 1.56am

> With fresh disturbances on the cards for tonight, there will be further serious questions to be asked if the police once again lose control of the streets

I'd send in the military as opposed to those clowns.

JesterJinglyJones

February 28th 3.21am

I'd send in the military as opposed to those clowns.

Do you not listen to a word I say? Enough coulrophobia!

Ich lehre euch den Überscherz. Der Mensch ist Etwas, das überwunden werden soll. Was habt ihr gethan, ihn zu überwinden?

Where is the lightning to lick you with its tongue? Where is the frenzy with which ye should be inoculated?

Lo, I teach you the superjester! She is that lightning! That frenzy!

Or if you prefer – Brunnhilde's immolation from *Götterdämmerung*:

Fliegt heim, ihr Raben!	Fly home ye ravens!
Raunt es eurem Herren,	Tell your lord the tidings,
was hier am Rhein ihr gehört!	ye have learned here on the Rhine!
An Brünnhildes Felsen	To Brunnhilde's rock
fahrt vorbei.	first wing your flight!
Der dort noch lodert	There burneth Loge:
weiset Loge nach Walhall!	straightway bid him to Valhalla!
Denn der Güter Ende	For the end of godhood
dämmert nun auf	draweth now near.
So - wer' ich den Brand	So cast I the brand
im Walhalls prangende Burg.	on Valhalla's glittering walls.

ThomPayne

February 28th 3.33am

Mook – six deaths, not five, always the possibility of a 7th.

BlindBoyGrunt — I don't really know what I'm writing. I never know what I am doing, or whether my words are even my own any longer.

There is more to the life of a low-level worker than tedium, limerent spheres of feeling, especially if, for whatever reason, you aren't the kind of person who quite smells wholesome to the others. I'm something of a lost cause and I do not do well with people. In certain other respects, my amps are turned up way past eleven. The book I'm doing, if it's about anything at all, is about asymmetry in a certain sense. You see versions of it everywhere, in metaphors, as in life — alongside questions of fit. My writing is simply a patchwork quilt, an enormous stew of all the words that have ever gone in, have you ever found yourself disappearing into a river of text? There's a certain pleasure in acknowledging Mistress Melancholy and writing about her, the logical consequence of which is that eventually you get to see the world from something of, shall we say, an *unencumbered* point of view.

I daresay I will never have children to worry about, and none of that mer-mer fucking moral high-ground bullshit that people seem to put up with in relationships. So I like to think that the grass is not always greener, even if you're living as I do, on scorched earth. I have also got access to a lot of books, vast numbers of them, all at my fingertips and whenever I want. There are beasts down in the labyrinth, although you will not fully grasp what I mean by that. To continue with a clumsy allusion however, there were only ever a few stories, the threads of the rest are weaved together from other things.

I approve of the Nietzschean sentiments above, but I prefer something a little gentler…and more succinct.

As Schumann had it in one of his songs ♪♪♪♪ (the words are by Heinrich Heine):

Aus alten Märchen winkt es.

Or,

From old tales, someone waves.

♫♫♫♫♫♫

♪

THIS THREAD IS NOW CLOSED

Also available from Jellicle

The Tea Elf

& Other Stories

A M GATWARD

"There is considerably more to the life of an infantryman or foot-soldier than getting up at the crack of dawn, rigging up explosive devices, jumping out of aircraft, being shot at by strangers, and blowing off heads."

32 ingenious and darkly humorous short stories from the author of *Thread*, ranging from the sprightly opening fable, to imaginative tales of absurdity, madness, and folly.

Amidst decapitations, murderous mountaineers, suicides, and lost souls we are introduced to Bloomberg the French-speaking cat, a so-called Wire-lender, and a girl who disappears into the sky.

Included in the collection is *The Barnstormer at Goofy's Wiseacre Farm*, previously published by Sentinel.